A Timeless Life
~ *Maddie's Story*

A Novel

By

Ruth Lee

Lee Way
PUBLISHING

LeeWay Publishing
Naples, Florida USA
www.LeeWayPublishing.com
ISBN: 978-0-9970529-6-1
Library of Congress Control Number: 2018955980
Printed in the United States of America
First Printing 2018
Cover design by Sarah Barrie of Cyanotype.ca

Other Books by Ruth Lee

Novels

Angel of The Maya
Writing in Spirit ~ *Jeanne's Story*
Within the Veil: *An Adventure in Time*

The Books of Wisdom From
The Teachers of the Higher Planes

We Are Here
The Work Begins
The Art of Life ~ *Living Together in Harmony*
Now is The Time
The World of Tomorrow
Bliss is It!

Other Works

The Word of The Maya
The Making of a Scribe ~
How to Achieve a Life You Can Write About
Can You Pray? ~
We Are All Here to Seek the Way
Writing in Spirit Workbook
Writing in Spirit Notebook

A Timeless Life
~ *Maddie's Story*

A Novel

By

Ruth Lee

Table of Contents

Dedicated to women of previous generations who strived to improve the lives and careers of women in the future.

Why do people hate winners?

Winning the BIG prize was supposed to change my life—and it did, but not as I had hoped. So I won? So what! I never begrudged anyone winning—regardless of prize money or prestige. I was happy for them, assuming that one day I would win and everyone would be happy for me, too. I thought my peers especially would recognize how hard I worked to be recognized, but it didn't happen that way. You can keep the prize!

When you win, professionals aren't supposed to behave like they did when I won The Pulitzer, so I'm not going to continue to submit my reporting for ridicule and nasty reviews. I could write a nasty, snarky essay, article, or blog and invite former colleagues to call me out, but instead I'm going to ignore the trends and what others think is best. I'm going 'Where the Girls Are' and write about them!

Just wait and see what comes of that...

☯Chapter One

Who wants to run our country? You? Are *you* into doing it? Most women sit back and wonder what they would do if President, but feel no responsibility to do anything about it. I know, because I'm not doing much to get my party to work harder either, but I'm beginning to realize it's because I resent them. Not actual resentment, but a lack of contentment with how they represent what I want done. Not easy to say, even harder to write, so how to make a difference and get something done for once?

For starters: I'll go out and about interviewing women who have a bit of clout—having earned a good living or inherited a pedigree. See if any will run the country now that we are recovering from 9/11 and have gained a bit of perspective about it. It isn't going to be easy to convince busy women that the time to act is NOW—that they are needed immediately and must start running for public office NOW, if things are to ever change in the 21st Century, but I'll give it a try.

Having made up my mind that this world will change today, I'm going to change, too! I'm going to start by choosing more ambitious friends. Women who will invest in the future of this country along with me.

My first try was less than stellar. I was met with the usual rebuff you get from a certain kind of woman. "Next time you're in town, let's do lunch." She had to have practiced saying it ever so crisply and firmly, as if biting off each word—intentionally conveying that we won't be meeting again, if she can help it. It was so obvious she wanted to be rid of me that I chose to ignore her polished pose and lackluster prose, deciding instead to intrude upon her mind a while longer—just for fun.

"Yes, I'll look you up next time I'm in Seattle." Meanwhile, I didn't bother writing down her number or pretend she was worthy enough to be included in my PPR (PalmPilotRecorder), as I love to describe it to officious friends—*because it really gets them every time.*

Probably just to aggravate her, I said, "You play the most charming drums. They speak of Latin rhythms— and I really dig that beat! Are you Latin?" I said it with a straight-face, because I knew she hated being called '*Latin*'. Who knows why? She claims to be Cuban, but when someone recently raved about Gloria Estafan's latest album, she attacked Gloria full frontal!

I do find this kind of reporting tedious and boring, yet can't resist trying to find something remotely interesting to write about or say to huge egos. After all, they're making the big bucks—not me.

Stifling a yawn, I said, "I'm returning to New York tomorrow to meet with publishers about my upcoming book. It's about women in politics. I wish I could include you, but doubt you're interested in running the country, since you have your own corporation to run, but then again, you do have dual citizenship in the US and Cuba."

The words barely cleared my lips before she attacked. "What are you talking about? I am not Cuban—never really was. I came to this country as a tiny baby and was christened an American citizen then."

A baby when they came here? How convenient, but now I have a way to get more out of her than before, and I may yet regret not putting her number in my PPR.

With one hand raised, apparently waiting for me, she said, "You are not serious when you say you are writing about women of power who can run this country—Are you?" I nodded.

"I see! You are not as foolish as so many reporters. They come and knock on my door—very offensive! They ask me how I got money. Who gave me a start? Who do I owe gratitude? This is very offensive to one who has done everything alone—without any help. Include that in my interview! I want it all written down."

What? She must have stripped her gears. I was kicked out the door—never to see her again, and now she expects me to interview her at length. So, I nodded, hummed, inserted a nod or smile whenever she stopped talking, and occasionally said some trite gem of hers will make good copy.

I was lost in thought, having given up trying to end this miserable would-be interview, when she surprised me. "You seem to be thinking. Do you do that often?"

You know, she really is funny in a weird way. It might be me—not her who hears nothing worthwhile as she grinds on and on about what she calls fascinating conversations all about her. This so-called interview is obviously going nowhere, but it won't end easily unless I agree to include her in my book. So, what to say?

"Yes, I'm always thinking, and now I'm running through what I have to do when I finish talking to you."

"That is so rude! You should be totally devoted to whoever you are talking to—not drifting off as you do. You can't be a real writer, or you would never do that to *me*. I'm not at all sure I want to be in your book!"

Stepping on my own toe to suppress a smile, I tried to sound contrite. "That's okay, no problem. I sometimes drift, wondering what will be most interesting to readers when they evaluate someone like you. So, if you want to be considered as a woman who can run the country, let me know, but I really have to go!"

As I pulled away, she started teetering on her five-inch spikes—almost falling into me. Heavily made-up, but still a gorgeous brunette who obviously wanted me to stay—probably because I wasn't impressed. There are a lot of women like that—and none of them should run any country, so I said, "I really gotta' go, Connie! Take care of yourself."

At that moment I couldn't remember where she came from, but knew my brisk dismissal registered. She no longer looked nearly as confident as when I first asked to interview her. I couldn't help wondering why she fell apart so easily.

Having no more time to wonder, I said, "I'll call when I get back to my office, but since I'm on the road, you can expect to hear from my secretary about setting up a time when we can talk for an hour or two."

Her brilliant smile and unwrinkled brow paid tribute to the scalpel of the best plastic surgeons women can afford. So sad that she believed she needed such help. Her face was great the way God created it—a lot better than what surgeons had done to it. Unfortunately, it was her fractured, ugly mind that needed psycho-surgery.

Trying to smile through lips stretched taut over expensive and expansive cosmetic dentistry, the woman many cast aside as *'just another prima donna'* spoke with precise diction. "I will not bother you now. You have that look of a gifted artist who is not able to remember her name. I will call. Please take down my number again."

This time I did enter her number into my PPR, awarding her a point for noticing I hadn't done it before. She was a lot sharper than anyone gave her credit for but remained a bore. I don't want to be bothered by her any longer, but probably should do an interview just to be sure. After all, I did regret not writing down her phone number the first time.

To err on the safe side, I said, "Thank you, Ms. Angeles. You are the pride of the Cuban-American community and may be the woman to lead them." My gorge rose as I spoke, but I couldn't stop myself. Really! What comes over me?

The Latin beauty stopped, appearing to be in deep thought, then smiled and whispered as if to a best friend, "You know you really need to do something about your skin. It's a bit dehydrated—not very pretty, but you could be beautiful if you really tried. I mean it!"

As if thrilled and flattered by her inventory of my flaws, I smiled, because I felt she was just being herself. She is, after all, the biggest purveyor in America of cosmetics sold in Latin American countries. That should be enough to keep her on top of any poll related to women who could run for public office, if it wasn't for her personality.

As I turned away, she grabbed my sleeve, almost pulling me off my feet. Breathing into my ear, she said, "You know I was born in Cuba—right? Does that exclude me from being President?"

Nodding I said just as softly, "Arnold in California is trying to get that all changed. He wants to run, so you may not have to worry about it."

She looked worried, but insisted she was an American citizen, which must not be the case. However, being born a liar translates into a great campaigner if the electorate continues to exist in an extreme state of denial.

Eyes on the ground, wimple in place, a nun quickly passed by. I noticed her earlier checking out the would-be Latin-American candidate and thought nothing of it then—but now? Why would a nun wear a habit? Aren't they liberated and able to dress or do whatever they want—within limits? I thought some even have some kind of Papal dispensation. I should check it out.

Someone somewhere once said our would-be Latin candidate had considered becoming a nun when young. If it's true—and if I decide to include her in the book, I think it could be a brilliant way to set up her story and what she can do for mankind.

There I go again! Off and running an interview with a candidate I would never want to see run any country. How simple we are when we too quickly write nice things about people without examining their lives. This prima donna would never agree to anything that isn't as flattering as her signature violet eye shadow. How could I submit to that?

"Are you a magician?"

Startled, I looked directly into the dark eyes of the nun who was now standing up-close and personal, watching me as I wrote on my PPR. I wasn't feeling witty, so she repeated, "Are you a magician?"

Stuttering through my confusion, I said, "No, I've never been able to pull rabbits out of hats. Why do you ask?"

The nun looked at me as if trying to overlook an ugly face, so I stared back until she laughed. It was forced—but it was a laugh, and passersby looked at us twice.

"I'm really not surprised that a famous New York reporter wants to interview such a woman as Constance Angelina Perez, but I had hoped I was merely having a vision. That it wasn't really happening."

Constance Angelina Perez sounded just a tad catty—and coming from a nun! She obviously knows more about *"the woman who would be queen"* than the tabloids. What might she add to such an interview, if I do go through with it?

"Are you referring to Ms. Angeles—the woman I was just talking to?" I tried to look innocent, but instantly knew she could easily read me.

When she nodded, I said, "I guess she is very famous—and people do look twice when they see her talking to someone—even a nobody like me."

Tossing her head while snorting, the nun said, "You're not without talent, Ms. Worthington, and I've long been a fan of your insightful interviews with people from all walks of life, even though you never interview nuns—at least to my knowledge."

In spite of my determination to not share my emotions—especially with a nun in wimple and black veil, I couldn't stop smiling as I said, "You're right! I don't think I ever interviewed a nun. I guess I better correct that oversight sometime soon. Do you know of any nun or *Bride of The Church* who would want to be interviewed for an upcoming book about how women can change The World?"

I had not meant to sound sarcastic, but the crack about *Bride of The Church* slipped out too easily. Why do I say such things? Maybe I want to alienate people, so I don't have to write about them?

Glancing at me, her words resounded like boot heels clicking to attention. "What do you mean? You are determined not to listen to me. You do not want me to know what that woman is up to—and I need to know—now!"

Shot from the hip, as only a nun could do it, I recoiled, but said nothing.

"I'm asking you to identify why that woman was talking to you. Why she was sharing confidences with you, because she is no good!"

Startled, I said, "Now that's enough!" I barely got it out when she took a half-step back. I guess no one talks to nuns like they talk to kids, but she made me mad.

In a more conciliatory tone I added, "I'm not responsible for what you experienced in your life, or what you think about women who are highly-placed in society, but I am responsible to any and all readers to act responsibly, and interview only those I think will produce interesting news and views. So, can you do an interview—soon?"

What just happened? I was stunned! How could I ask a nun—especially one who yelled at me in public, to talk about running for public office? I must be losing my mind.

Smiling benignly, she extended her hand as if we were friends meeting after a long separation. I numbly shook her limp hand as though she were a vibrant lady of the world, which she accepted as if she were. At that moment—and only then, I remembered how she had accosted me. I had to know what she meant. "Before you agree, I need to know what you meant when you asked if I was a magician."

The nun's face reddened a bit as she said, "Oh, that! I was just mad because Constance always gets so much attention from The Press, and all she has done is augment her breasts and Botox her lips and collagen whatever, yet *never* has enough money to give to *The Church*. She used us—now acts like we abused her!"

I get it, but what does this have to do with calling me a magician? I paused a fraction of a second too long before saying, "I thought you were blaming me for something evil when you called me a magician. Sort of like saying I'm a witch. What were you really saying?"

She obviously wanted to drop the subject, maybe the entire conversation, and walk away, but did not. Maybe she remembered I didn't have any way to set up an interview with her. Anyway, I acted as if I didn't notice her shift in mood as she said, "I wasn't feeling good when I arrived in town, then I saw Constance talking to you and wanted to throw up. My teeth were on edge when I recognized you as a famous reporter. I knew you were doing business with her."

What? Nuns talk like that, too?

"I thought she had you wrapped around her little finger—and you were interviewing her about her new work."

"What new work would that be?" Nothing like an enemy to blab what you need to know to make an interview grow.

"She has some kind of new fragrance she says is made in the jungles of Mayaland. She also claims she wants to make it there and give back the profits to heathens who aren't really Christians."

"Wow! That is interesting, but what does it have to do with me being a magician?"

"Nothing! I don't even know why I said it! Sometimes I get excited and say whatever pops into my mind—instead of thinking it through. As I age it seems to be getting worse. It must be the after-effects of menopause."

Will wonders ever cease? Nuns talk about menopause! I have to talk with her a little longer. "Are you free for lunch? We could sit and talk about your mission and what you want to do once you can't work as hard as you do now."

Transformed, she no longer scowled or stomped her feet to emphasize what she said. Smiling, she acted like my new best friend. Maybe that is why she called me a magician?

What is happening here anyway? First a famous woman industrialist of the cosmetic persuasion pursues me for an interview—and now a nun! Both act as if they love me. Is it me or my PPR?

With the look of a zealot, the nun tried to smile as she said, "I have to go now. I was supposed to run to the post office and return home immediately, but when I saw you talking to Connie, well. Are you available tomorrow?"

Her smile appeared in danger of becoming extinct, so I extended my hand again and said, "Tomorrow at noon will be just fine. We can eat anywhere you like. It's on my expense account."

The nun was like a new woman. Smiling radiantly, with lightning speed she named the most expensive restaurant nearby. The motherhouse must be close—or is it the mothership?

"Until tomorrow, have a nice day and take care of yourself—and the other nuns. I want to hear all about your convent and order, and who you all would nominate for public office now."

Stroking my hand, she said, "If only everything was this easy…"

I freed my hand since her touch made me feel a bit creepy. Her smile cemented in place, I could tell she walked away without another thought about me.

The life of a social reporter, or feature writers in general, is to cover private lives and public affairs and isn't conducive to being loved for oneself. Many seek us out as if we are gifts from heaven, and just as quickly trade us in for someone else. They don't care who we are— really! Publicity seekers just want someone to build up their careers and weird egos and will never forget anything written about them that they perceive to be negative. Most want to be portrayed as larger than life, with careers they will never achieve.

Every conversational interview appears to end when they wilt and begin talking about friends and family they left behind. They all leave people behind—and the bigger they are, the more they ignore their folks. Only those who still do their own work seem to know who helped them become successful. Everyone else keeps on looking for others to take advantage of next.

Hmm, there it goes again! The inner cynic rises— trying to take over and prevent me from writing about ego-driven women. So, which of the two I talked to today intrigues me enough to spend months writing her life story?

☯Chapter Two

*Madeline Worthington, ace reporter currently working in Washington...*The very idea produced a smile as Maddie closely examined the altar cloth being displayed by an old woman sitting opposite. How had she come to interview a group of devout women who offered to help her produce a view of life as it exists in a modern nunnery—not a convent?

Nunnery was the term they preferred to use to describe their lives in this huge overgrown mansion. How to best describe this life, comparing how it once was to what it is now and what it promises to remain until the last nun disappears? With no idea what they had planned for the present or the end of their idyllic dream, Maddie hesitated to begin an interview that normally would be fairly routine.

What held her back was trying to figure out who was in charge. Apparently, it was neither the nun she originally met on the street, nor the one who suggested she investigate this strange and wondrous new lifestyle for women of a certain age. Women who seek communal housing and companionship, as well as a vocation they can handle alone and with a group.

As usually happens, Maddie's worry proved to be unfounded. The oldest nun present started talking without any prompting. "When the work of one nun is done, several others pick it up and do it over and over again. That is because we are not irreplaceable, merely instruments of God. We don't expect to stand out as individuals. We seek anonymity, instead of fame and fortune. Some women here have had fame…and when they came on board, all brought with them a fortune of some size. This is indeed a brave new world and our women are seldom bored—not like millions of women locked into or out of '*the real world*', the world these women managed to escape."

While fumbling to tape the nun's words on her old, battered recorder, this otherwise needless operation gave Maddie time to organize her thoughts and take command of the situation—or so she hoped. Glancing around the room at large, she said, "I'm the one who came to you. I'm the one who proposed you all can help today's women go far—further than they are now. I also need to know if any of you can run for public office. Is that even allowed?"

Turning off the tape, Maddie noticed the other women were quietly ignoring her. Showing no interest—obviously no answers forthcoming, so she tried a different approach. "If you all can live your life as you see fit, and you believe it's better by far to live together as you do here, what would you advise the government do to emulate your lifestyle? You know, help others enjoy this lifestyle without taking orders?"

When no one spoke, she added, "I know you're all private people who established a life designed so you can live without being annoyed or ridiculed by those living beyond these gates, but why not let everyone know what they're missing, and could possibly do—even late in life? Why not help other women realize they can move into a nunnery like this and live peacefully with others of like mind?"

A voice rose from behind a screen at the side of the room. "We do not subscribe to women leaving their everyday lives to join us or The Church. We believe you are *'called'*, otherwise it is a fraud. You are not invited to join this life, but not prevented from exploring it. We are not here to spend our lives seeking investments and such from women who are bored and want more of whatever."

Since her old recorder was obviously struggling— and not knowing who was speaking, Maddie wrote "Nun #9" plus a few key words on her pad. 'Why bother to ask names when they won't consent to my using them later?' Since it was likely they would deny having said anything, it was her plan to create a composite of all interviewees, as if one did all the talking.

Hoping to change the tone of the interview, Maddie said, "How about a look around? Can you tell me how many acres you have and how you pay taxes—or not? What will you do for cash if you run out of converts or whatever you call new nuns?"

When the oldest nun gave no indication if it was proper to ask questions, she tried another tack. "Are you aligned and organized like other convents or nunneries? I mean, do you have a Mother Superior everyone follows. I mean…Well, you know what I mean. Don't you?"

A lovely nun who had remained silent until now smiled and said, "I am anointed Mother Superior, and my name is Mother Mary Michael. All questions relative to this house are to be referred to me, but you can talk

25

to anyone privately, as long as you do not bother those unwilling to talk."

Stunned at the double-talk, yet readily able to understand its intent, she wondered how such a woman came to be Mother Superior. She seemed so *'un-nun-like'*.

Maddie decided to start asking questions to see if an open-door policy was truly in effect. "Mother Mary Michael, could you demonstrate how freely the others are allowed to talk to me—or not, about serious subjects?"

The Mother Superior's smile disappeared as she nodded, as if granting permission to others to speak.

"May I say, you seem too young and vibrant to be a Mother Superior? I mean, I expected someone older. Someone who talked softly and bowed her head after every sentence." I had to stop. Everyone was giggling, even the eldest nun.

Softly, Mother Mary Michael said, "I have been in *The World*, as you say, most of my life. I came here to the sheltering arms of God because I was tired of life as lived now in the United States. I wanted a change—and I got it. Now I am bridging my two lives, managing the nunnery like a business, while learning all I can about Mother Nature. Freely ask whatever questions, but why not begin by asking what we all do and why we are here?"

Just a hint of crispness in her voice indicated I better not stretch the point, so I won't. "Thank you, Mother Superior, for all you've done to help this project get started. When I drove onto the grounds I found the beauty and solitude of the convent and its grounds breathtaking. I never thought it would be a business.

I mean, it never occurred to me you weren't the usual convent. I mean—"

The younger nuns smiled, and one hid her mouth as though laughing, but the older nuns refused to humor me. Obviously, I better retract what I said and begin again. "What I'm trying to say is, like readers from all over the world, we don't know what to expect when talking to and about nuns. For instance, I didn't know there were nunneries. I thought this was a convent. What's the difference?"

From behind the screen, the same voice as before said, "A nunnery is a very old concept not often used today, due to confusion about what women do when they sequester themselves away from the worries and cares of The World. We are not here to take orders and live lives totally dedicated to Christ, as a convent must, but we are close enough to that concept to be considered nuns by others. We create our own individual ways of working with The Holy Spirit and God. We are daughters of Christ—not brides."

Thoroughly confused, I hoped another would better describe the order later. "Are you saying you aren't in Holy Orders—as Roman Catholic nuns would be?"

"We are not nuns in the same sense people today see such women who dedicate their lives to God. Most here have been in orders, but some have not. We work together as a team to unite and free up time so we all can spend time daily in contemplation and prayer. It's not easy to provide such time. We had to come up with a plan that worked for us. It's not the same thing as a nunnery in the Middle Ages, but it's similar."

She was no longer the only nun talking, but her words were all I could hear clearly. I could now focus on one voice and clearly understood only one message—none of the others—then switch to another and another. It's a gift any reporter or writer would love to have. How does it happen, and why is it happening to me now? All is a mystery!

The Mother Superior raised her hand slightly, pointing in the direction of the clock. She appeared to frown, but all the nuns turned and walked away from me. I hadn't realized they observed time as any other work group would, so I apologized for taking too much of it from their daily routine and prepared to leave.

When the last nun left the room, Mother Mary Michael said, "You don't have to leave. I'm here to show you the grounds and help you understand the way we live. You will be able to see things, but please don't write about it until *after* you've completed all of your interviews. I want to be able to speak freely, knowing you aren't writing or taping every word. It isn't often that we have visitors, but we expect to have many coming around very soon—within the month of June."

Although I wondered what she was talking about, I have found it's best to look like you're thinking, and not say much when you want others to talk a lot. I nodded acceptance of her conditions as we entered another room, where I looked around.

"This room is where reporters will sit and talk while waiting for someone to greet them. You are the first reporter granted the privilege of interviewing our order— and we aren't sure why, but we are prepared to follow through and do whatever is required."

Perplexed, I said, "What you're saying is interesting—and wonderful, but what do you mean you've never done this before? Are you opening up to me because *you have to?* You don't ever *have* to talk to me or any reporter. I would love to capture the essence of your life here, including your individual stories, but I'm writing a book that won't be published until I combine many other stories—which may take years."

"That is why we are willing to talk to you. We don't want advance publicity but need someone who won a Pulitzer Prize in Journalism to open the eyes of those who despise our way of life. We want you while here to show the world what goes on inside our lives; how we exist— and why. That will close the loop and permit others to follow our life plan, too. We want women to follow God and work in love—not worry about what The World will do if they work hard and dedicate their lives to God. I hope you understand."

Funny, but I clearly saw how the book would look when done. It wasn't what we had talked about over the phone, yet exactly what my publisher really wants. I could make it a lot easier for myself if I set up the book and all interviews hereafter based on our talk today. I need to get it together and deliver the package—and it begins here and now.

Speaking in reverential tones, Mother Mary Michael said, "I can see you're imagining how you will produce a coherent book that includes many different theories and ideas about how to live better while here and now." With that she escorted me to the front door. All I could do was follow.

Once outside, she pointed out a building I hadn't noticed when driving by the front of the mansion. "We have a lot to do every fall—and a bit each spring, but most of the time we don't have to do that much. The orchard provides us with apples and pears we preserve. This is our way of saving money. We don't sell anything now, thus saving money, while feeding our family well."

Picking up the pace, Mother Mary Michael said, "We don't want to take in anyone else right now, but we might like to provide shelter later for women unable to live successful lives without our help. Not all are here to get well or recover from a bad spell, but some lives have been improved by therapy, so they want to practice it here. Recognized as a church, we have non-profit status and pay no taxes—and we alone decide what to do with our time. It's perfect for our lives now."

Obviously pleased with all she surveyed, I could see little out there where she was staring intently. Having been raised in New York City, trees never catch my attention, but these are nice—not Central Park, but nice.

"You look unimpressed, Ms. Worthington. You don't see the beauty or the bounty, but once inside the house you'll see much that will astound you. I promise." Turning abruptly, she walked toward the end of the manor's grounds—or so I thought.

"This is where the wall ends and the fence begins. We have cows who live with us. We keep them, and they keep us, so you can see we live together, but not to be described that way to your readers. You obviously know how many have no sense of humor."

Her abrupt laughter amused me, so I laughed, too. It was fun to watch her pick up her skirt and run across the field toward a distant barn. Pausing so I could catch up, Mother Mary Michael said, "The barn is way over there, so we don't smell the cows, thus we have to walk a long way to get milk. We're forced to realize how much work these ladies do to provide milk for our use. We make butter, cheese, and such, but not that much. Only one here is devoted to churning and such, and she wants to do everything her way, so we seldom do anything without clearing it with her first. It works for us."

Churning butter? Are they actually working like dairymaids from days of yore?

"We use modern conveniences, because we were raised that way. Each of us brought dowries large enough to repair the manor and maintain the farm, as well as whatever work needs done now." Without pause, she added, "Have you ever trusted anyone?"

Stunned, I immediately denied that I didn't trust others, and that my family constantly condemns me for trusting others too much. I added that my friends constantly warn me not to trust those I help or want to help.

"You see, you never truly trust anyone until you throw in your lot with them and work together. When you live under one roof for the rest of your life—that is when you learn to trust others— nothing less."

"Oh, I see. You have a communal life style."

"Yes, in a way, but more God-centered than hippies ever dreamed of creating. They wanted life to go away and never take responsibility for themselves. We aren't that way. We want to find a better way to live together here and now—a way that doesn't waste land or abuse people who use it. We first need to live such a life in order to prove it can work for others, too."

It is never wise to show you are impressed too soon, so I said, "In a way, you're trying to create a utopian village lifestyle?"

"No, nothing utopian about this. We are nuns with no interest in making love to others or being loved by anyone. Having tried that path, we have no regrets, and no desire to go back and become such women again. We want to use our minds! We want to devote our time to work that glorifies life on this side. We want to make a difference without forcing others to applaud and say we're doing a great job. I believe we are wise and mature, living within our spiritual lives—not wandering about wondering what our inner lives might be."

What an extraordinary idea! I'm beginning to think my life is surreal and theirs is real. How did this happen so fast?

Having nothing to say has happened only a few times in my life, but all I could do now was look toward a nearby field and say, "What's happening? I think I see ostriches running around?"

"Oh, you spotted the emus! That is a flight of fancy of one who brought a huge dowry to our House. For whatever reason she wants to raise them. Since she can pay for them—and take care of them, why not?"

Why not indeed? Apparently, dowries provide the ability to buy what you want to do here. Are these women crazy or is it me?

"You look amazed, Ms. Worthington. I can easily say this is not a fairytale. It's about women doing their thing and living their lives within the protection of a world dedicated to peace and non-violence. Our order is built on a firm belief system, which in turn is built on trust and faith—and the belief that the human race isn't going to last if it continues as is at the present pace. We want to do something to stop the ruination of Earth now! Aware there is little time left, we want to turn back the clock and create a better life for all, recognizing what has been lost so far—to help us stop the destruction!"

The interview had taken such amazing twists that all I could honestly think was I had lost my way, but opted instead to say, "I think that is commendable, but why a farm?"

"Why not? I assume you eat every day, but never cook, yet you don't look as if you have too little to eat. So, what do you do for food?"

I had noticed all the nuns were in great shape, able to hold their own in any race, but enough about me being out-of-shape—I'm not, but how did they stop eating as much as average American women?

"You're thinking about eating, aren't you? I'm sure you know that food you buy at stores isn't pure, and you must realize buying food others cooked is likely contaminated by their lack of hygiene. Most purveyors of food don't care if you enjoy it or not—which isn't good for you."

"Hmm, Hindus believe something like that. One guru said that if a Brahman home wasn't clean, or the family argued while preparing food or serving it, they must throw it away. It's contaminated by ill will. Is that what you mean?"

"In a way. We obviously see things differently than yogis, and we don't follow the work of those who have gone before us. Instead, we prefer to be free of dogma and treatises about what humans can achieve. We want to be free to worship God, and use the teachings of The Holy Spirit as directed by our inner being or soul."

"That sounds like Catholicism. Doesn't it"

"Not at all a Catholic thought, but a good way for The Church to start over. It's not a good idea to continue following a path constantly narrowing, thus unable to develop larger flocks. They have lost so much! Some women in our House refuse to admit they practice Catholicism religiously, and we never ask why. Some may want to talk about it but are generally silenced by others." Her straight-forwardness surprised me.

"So, there is dissension among the women living here when it comes to practicing their religions?"

Staring at me for the first time, she said, "Don't go there! You're now looking like a typical, starving reporter—not a nice sight to see, so cover your mouth and ask forgiveness."

She walked away more quickly than before. I wondered what had just happened. I'm obviously out-of-shape, but feeling lighter, happier, and now more interested in writing than at any time since my youth.

Stopping to point, Mother Mary Michael said, "This is the lane that leads to the lumber mill. We are going into production soon, but first we want to hire someone who can produce good lumber from old wood not being used that stands in the way of younger trees needing to grow taller."

What to say? I knew I would gain little, but said, "Sounds like you're not environmentalists."

She smiled and said, "No, we're conservationists. We don't waste anything—including time, nor do we expect Mother Nature to do everything and we not help her thrive." Appearing to enjoy herself, she added after a slight pause, "I think you need more material about why we are here. Right?"

Trying not to heave and sigh, as a result of being totally out of breath, I stopped walking and nodded, embarrassed that she was obviously older and, just as obvious, in much better shape.

"Let's sit and talk now. I've worked you long and hard to see if you have what it takes to do a really good job—if we should decide to begin talking to the world through your pen now. Let's sit outside the grape arbor for a spell."

I wanted to sit and rest but was caught off-guard. All I could say was: "This is such a beautiful spot. Why not sit under the arbor out of the sun?"

"You've never lived in the country. Have you?" I readily agreed, so she added. "You'd best not sit under an arbor when bees, birds, and other critters are harvesting their share of the bounty. Bird droppings can be fearsome!" Not bothering to conceal a chuckle, she led me to a bench closer to the fence where Concord grapes grew.

"Why don't you sit here and enjoy the view, while I head back to continue my tasks. This is a nice place to meditate and get centered, so you can hold your own when you begin questioning the others."

Grateful for the opportunity to do just that, I couldn't help but wonder how these seemingly sequestered women beat me at what I do best. I doubted they had, but couldn't help wondering why she brought it up instead of me. Nodding, I said I would rest for a while and then begin interviewing everyone.

It was three hours before I sensed discomfort from sitting on the wooden bench. How could that be? What had become of the day and all my plans? Obviously, much had happened during that time, but I felt it was all I could say when I finally started interviewing the nuns.

Did anyone wonder why I was sitting still that long without writing? I know I would have wondered if something was wrong—or if I had died. How could I idle for hours under a hot sun and not feel it?

Lost in thought as I approached the rear of the mansion, I barely noticed that the door had been left open for me. Once inside I found myself surrounded by women eating and talking loudly as if a big family. Apparently, I looked confused, because a nun seated at the end of the table said, "Are you all right, Ms. Worthington?"

Unable to identify who said it, I spoke to the crowd. "Please call me Maddie, all my friends do."

Immediately, everyone said, "Welcome, Maddie!"

It was like dropping in on an AA meeting, but this one was filled with wonderful aromas and lots of friendly faces, although no one stood out from the crowd. Since I didn't want to stand out, either, I quickly took the first empty seat. Having put on a few extra pounds recently, it wasn't an easy fit, but I managed to squeeze in without grunting—aware once again that everyone else was much thinner than me.

The food was delicious! In fact, it tasted divine, like manna from heaven. I was suddenly eager to read what I wrote earlier but would have to wait until I returned to my hotel to make sense of today.

A clear soprano voice rang out: "Maddie, you are welcome to stay here with us while doing your interviews. We have rooms set up for visitors but haven't worked out what to do after that. If you don't mind what you eat every day, you would be our hospitality service guinea pig."

I wanted to shout 'yes' but did not. When I get back no one will believe my description of this place, but what if the nuns are just looking for publicity?

Smiling, the Mother Superior stood and said, "The first step toward trusting others is the most difficult. Obviously, you don't have to stay here. You are welcome to leave and return every day."

Why did that reassure me? I don't know, but I was surprised to hear myself gush, "Oh, no, I would love to stay, but tonight I have to go back and get gear I stowed at the hotel—and pack my bags. I can start working tomorrow and stay over then."

The nuns looked at me as if I was crazy. What did I say that was stupid or dense?

"We thought you were working today. We saw you writing a lot on what looked like a small computer of some kind, maybe one of those Palm Pilot things."

The nuns continued looking at me as if I was an enigma, but I have no memory of writing anything, so I smiled and said, "What I mean is, you all will have to start working!"

They didn't respond in kind, so I said, "I've been gathering insights into life here. What it must be like to give away everything you own and start over with others you don't really know. Stuff like that, but not about what I saw today."

They all relaxed, some laughed. Mother Mary Michael said, "Seems we need to believe more firmly in what we preach. I suspect there was a bit of mistrust among some of us, too."

Her smile melted my heart and I felt like I had to run or be swept into their fun. I would never want to be a nun! Would I?

Somehow, I got out of there without enlisting in their order. I asked if they had a good spot with a sturdy chair where I could write and work all day and night, if Spirit chose to move me to do so. Apparently, they were as shocked as I was that Spirit was an active part of my life. All eagerly proclaimed that anything I wanted would be provided, which I doubt is possible, but they seemed to believe it. We will see.

❧Chapter Three

My ballet slippers wore thin as the week wore down, but I never felt better. I can't imagine doing anything more worthwhile or more amusing. I now feel like writing a book about my new friends' Order, and how they live and what we did, but it's not to be. They have no wish to run the government, or even run for local office—not a single one of them. I planted the seed, but so far nothing has come of it.

What did I say to encourage them to run for public office? I told them the freedom to live their lives as they wished will not always exist—governments change, if people of faith don't permit everyone to worship in their own way. I also mentioned that deists formed the United States and still run the government—which is fortunate since Christians aren't nearly as tolerant and can be very demanding. What if future leaders change the Constitution to suit themselves, and you have to worship as they choose? No use! The nuns don't think it could happen— End of Discussion!

My dilemma today is that I have another story in hand and wonder if I should start it or write about the fascinating lives the nuns provide each other now. Should I wait to see if their future turns out as they plan, or work hard to include them in my stories about women who have the power to change the world? I think the publisher wants me to follow that line rather than the first chapter I submitted, but I could be wrong.

While working on the book, I continue to wonder about what I jotted down that first day while sitting in the convent's orchard. I still can't imagine why I wrote as I did and wasn't able to access it until after I left. It's always on my mind and threatens to change *me* into a different person—or so I think.

When you study what you write, checking it for flaws, you obviously can do it more easily when you alone choose the words; but what to do when your book, chapter, or page appears to be written by someone else? Do you change it or just edit enough so readers can better understand it? I'm not sure. For now, I intend to print it and see if it makes sense to others I respect.

Maybe I should start a dialogue about power—and women who can change the world now. Yes, that will work best!

If you receive a package from Fed Ex or UPS that has been opened, you tell the messenger it's not as it should be. The messenger then makes standard apologies and reports back to headquarters, or wherever, that someone tampered with your package. To me they are angels! Uniform in behavior, delivering messages of importance to the world, and why I hesitate to change what was given to me that day under the trees.

I can't seem to throw any of it away, continually wondering why I got this message: *We are all here and want you to serve God. We can help you serve God better than ever. We want you to reach out and use your many lives in this time to help others trapped and otherwise ensnared in today's vices, unable to think out loud or pray.*

You are to write. You are to create a novel that talks about a life or two that helped develop your nation. You will talk as if that woman is necessary to develop the next day or two—or not, but she must make up her mind to act now. You will not meet anyone already doing what they can, only those who wonder if they can now complete the next few steps.

You will talk to these women at length, then repeat their best words so they are admired by your readers. If that works, you are an empire builder. If it does not, you have done no harm.

Today is a beautiful day and many support you from afar. You can ask for money to do this work and be paid before you deliver it. That is a measure of faith you must now accept in order to dedicate what you will do for this nation. You will stop the infamy and produce a destiny others will desire, pray for, and produce. You will not do much to induce change today, but you will lead others to women who may.

Here is the letter you will prepare and adapt before sending it to each woman who comes to mind and can climb. We do not decide who will receive this letter. You are given the list and expected to cover each one—no exceptions!

You came to this nunnery as a result of your new way of working with YOU. We want you to work here and now quietly. In their own way, the nuns' solitude and prayers for the world will produce a work of art.

You will do this work in half the time other writers could produce such a book, even if asked to do it. Calm your mind before writing our letter...

Dear Ms.

Thank you for living your life to the fullest and for all you have given the world so far! You are one of only a few women who can put your life on hold in order to help others 'do their thing' and win now. I wish to interview you and write about how you arrived at this stage in life without making enemies yet creating enough of an estate that others are envious of you. I would also like to talk about your work. Why you began this work, and how you create it. Can such an interview be arranged now?

My curiosity is far from unique, but my reasons may be. You see, I have been asked by our nation's largest publisher of probing, intellectual works to seek out women who could run the country—and you are one of them. How was this decided? You know! You have worked diligently for many years as if driven to seek a better way every day. I want to talk to you about running for public office and how you might be able to change future lives without undue trouble now.

My office is staffed round the clock with answering machine and fax, so call or send a reply. Do whatever suits you best. The quickest way to respond is via email, but some do not trust it now. I can understand that, so choose a time that is good for you and I will shape my life to comply—if at all possible. You will enjoy our time working together!

This may sound too breezy but signing each letter will inspire them to relax and not get uptight and tense. If they don't wish to be interviewed at length, I think I can create a story based on their public bios—I hope.

That will not happen! You cannot imagine now how many women would run for office, if asked. You are going to be overrun with responses, and many others will want to be interviewed, too, once they hear about it from friends.

Do not alter this list or falter! You have your assignment—now do it!

As a writer, my life has been fairly predictable, but suddenly I'm not a writer, but a scribe. A scribe who gets messages from other spheres! Am I losing my mind or what? Can anyone write like this and continue to write in their usual way?

The message that came through while I was sitting in the nunnery's orchard makes total sense—in a way, but I don't remember writing it. How can you access what you weren't really into? To me it was more like being in a coma or deep trance. Can someone go in and look around, then report back to me while I think about all this?

Nothing popped into my mind that I want to check out when I return to the nunnery next month. It's my intention to see if it happens again; and if it does, keep my mind open far enough to see what is going on then.

☯Chapter Four

A diva invited me to join her for lunch last week, but when I arrived I could see the table was set for only one. Thinking: *This is not good*—and wondering where the grand dame was, I took a seat facing huge windows,

While surveying the opulence of the living area, I continued to wonder why the maid placed me where I could easily see the table was set for only one, then noticed a long, paneled wall dedicated to souvenirs and such gathered over a long and illustrious career. Interesting that I never thought of her as being that old. Apparently, she gets her looks via a surgeon's deft fingers.

Can flimsy pieces of paper portray a well-lived life? Hopefully, there is more to this woman of the world than what I see here. Restless, I walked around trying to find a good spot to conduct the interview away from the eyes of the ever-present maid and out of the sun, so she would not have to squint, nor I whisper.

When I spotted a little wooden box with a faded ballerina painted on the lid, it reminded me of my childhood. Without thinking, I reached for it—only to have the maid sweep in and move it out of sight. I couldn't help wondering: *What is in that little box?*

Obviously, it's a mystery I'm not to inquire about. Can anyone reveal its secrets to me? Having almost said this aloud, I meekly (for me) sat beside a huge-screened television. It held a far more prominent position than fans of her fabled glamour would have thought possible. But then again, what is real life vs. *reel life* to a soap opera star?

Maddie's musings ended when the woman of great beauty and fame swept into the room, swirling her skirt as though she, too, watched the old Loretta Young Show. With an exaggerated Marilyn Monroe-like whisper, she said, "I want to thank you for coming so quickly. I have a lot of work coming up this week and have to always be available to my agent. Today is an island or oasis in time where I can forget my career and my business affairs for a short while, so I thank you for being prompt. You probably heard that if a reporter isn't on time, I won't grant an interview."

Maddie nodded as she quickly calculated how best to respond. How do you begin asking personal questions about the future of a woman who has no real-life past anyone knows about? How do you talk seriously about governing the nation with a woman who seems totally self-absorbed—most likely politically naïve? When nothing useful came to mind, she fell back to using an old opener capable of ending any conversation before it began. She asked the diva what she loved to do when not working.

Perhaps taken aback that Maddie ignored her gushy act or the fact that she had not read a suitable script in over four years, the aging star bit too quickly. "I guess I love to act more than anything else. I have acted all my life, and so far, I've acted my way into and out of love so many times I can't remember what it feels like to really love another."

Assessing Maddie's non-reaction, she became aware she was not impressing her audience of one enough to write down her well-rehearsed speech, so she added, "I guess I love acting so much, because it gives me a way to interact with others I would never have the nerve to meet or talk to in real life."

When she paused, Maddie smiled and nodded as if to imply the older woman was doing great.

Perhaps it was because she was out-of-practice, but it was a heady experience to be interviewed by such a well-known journalist, thus she spoke too fast to maintain her cool. "I think I can pretend to be so many different kinds of women, because I'm very complex. When it comes to business, I think like a machine, and I have no regrets about my investments and ability to work with anyone equally as serious about their work as I am. I seldom feel the material provided now is real—capable of changing anyone over time, and I truly regret having lent my energies to such trivial and frivolous work in the past. I always wanted to make a difference—or do nothing at all."

Seldom shocked, Maddie now realized she had tagged this woman to be poorly educated and flaky— as well as totally self-involved, hardly worth the time it took to stop by for lunch. She had to atone for being too judgmental, thus coming into the interview totally unprepared. How to begin again? How to mold the material she had gathered and intended to use to define this woman as one who whines and whines before abruptly ending interviews?

With fresh interest Maddie analyzed the woman who was all mystery to the public. She now recognized someone she had never expected to meet here—a woman of great intelligence who did whatever it took to amass enough personal security to live on her own terms alone, doing whatever she wanted. What a wonderful present she had been gifted by those guiding her through this amazing book about women and life today!

Lifting her pen to point at the sun, Maddie indicated she was willing to sit elsewhere, just as the maid rushed in and added another plate to the table. She could only wonder what that was all about.

Smiling graciously, her host said, "Thank you, Francine, for adding another plate. I forgot to tell you Ms. Worthington would be staying for lunch."

Trying to follow a rehearsed script no longer in play, the maid appeared unsure as to why her mistress now insisted the reporter should stay for lunch—rather than be ordered to leave as practiced earlier.

"How nice of you. I intended to treat you to lunch at your favorite restaurant, because the pleasure is all mine." It was dumb—not refined, because Maddie was innately incapable of flattering her subjects while working with them. In this rare instance she sensed someone who was down-to-earth and could handle honesty.

"It was I who asked you to lunch. I seldom go out during the day, except to a favorite spot I will not betray by taking you there today. I want it to be *my place*—a place where they know who I am and never let on. We act our parts, and they keep outsiders at bay. It's nice to be remembered, but not to be jostled and talked about by people who don't know you."

As the elegant star spoke, she glided toward the Georgian sofa with its myriad of embroidered silk pillows. Before the other could sit, Maddie said, "If we could sit at the table—assuming that is okay with your maid, I would like to write and talk about whatever you care to share. A table makes a wonderful prop."

"Why Ms. Worthington, you do sound like you were bitten by the acting bug at one time. Were you?"

Stunned to find herself the one being interviewed, Maddie mumbled that she had acted in small companies in the long ago past, but nothing ever came of it.

Smiling, the actress said, "You are too modest, I'm sure."

Unable to not smile, Maddie admitted that she indeed was not being modest about her lack of success in the acting business.

"No, I mean you are too modest in the traditional sense. You feel awkward standing out and demanding attention from others—flaunting your body and doing things you would never do in real life—that kind of modesty. To become a star, you have to give it up early—which wrecks your ability to take yourself seriously ever again. You become much like all these insecure women who ask men to take them out, when anyone knows you are giving away your power then. Where did women get such an idea? Do you know?"

Nodding, Maddie said, "They got it from watching you! You trained today's women—probably in greater numbers than anyone else—to dominate men. To weary women, you appeared as Cleopatra must have appeared to her court. You reigned over the airwaves—and what you said is repeated and copied to this day. Men are expected to react similar to the way men reacted to you on screen—and that's when it gets crazy." She was laughing, but not so her new-found friend.

Looking off into middle-space, the other woman said, "I think you may be right. How terrible to create a life that leads others into evil—to doing themselves in. What a waste I made of my life, if I ruined women whose lives could have been better than mine. I'm humiliated by the idea, yet it fits. I think you're telling me a great truth, and I need to hear everything—right now. What else have you observed?"

Stunned at being the one to answer all the hard questions, Maddie sat mute. As the moment stretched too long, her host said, "I guess I'm being too confrontational—like a soap opera queen. Right?"

Smiling, Maddie said she couldn't identify why it was weird for her to be interviewed, but that was the case. She didn't want to talk about her work, because she was there to discover if this aging TV star would consider running for public office, so she reorganized her thoughts—again.

Sitting quietly, the idol of millions of women was apparently musing about something she hesitated to discuss. Indeed, the veteran actress was shocked at the nature of this interview, too. She never expected any worthwhile writer would consider including her in a book about prominent women, because she never thought of herself as a leader, yet here sat an impressive journalist asking her to consider running for public office.

"I guess it's a bit much to ask a movie/television idol to consider stepping down into the world of dirty politics to help other women get on with their lives, but I think you're perfect for the part." Maddie had no intention of being funny, nor did she expect her audience to cry—yet that was what happened, and not at all what she wanted or needed now.

Sobbing, Jennifer Gibson waved away her maid who was trying to give her a glass of water. She needed tissues, not a drink. When that message got across, she gently wiped each eye so as not to dislodge the recently applied double-layer lashes. Unsuccessful in saving a lash on one eye, she ripped off the other while managing to say, "I think maybe we should sit for a moment and not talk." Having said this without looking at her visitor, she missed the misty-eyed look Maddie tried to hide.

Right then the maid reentered and abruptly placed a salad in front of each woman. It was passable, but looked like an afterthought, not what Madeline would have imagined the actress would serve, but perhaps it was originally one salad now made to serve two? Upon closer examination, she decided that was the case.

"I guess we didn't think you would stay long, once you found out I wasn't going to accept the play."

Maddie nodded and said, "You know, I'm not Charlie Rose. I don't interview people when they have a new picture out or books to tout, and I'm not exactly a journalist right now. I'm writing a book to please me and reflect my ideas about what the world needs today. You see, I want to make changes, and do it with others of like-mind. When someone suggested I interview you, I was surprised, and amazed when you agreed to meet me immediately. On my own, I never would have thought to call you."

Shocked at Maddie's bluntness, yet aware it was her way, according to close friends, Jennifer nodded and said she was not prone to discuss business with friends, nor inclined to deliver sermons or lessons of any kind. That was why she became an actress! Acting allowed her to repeat what someone else thought and everyone believed was her idea. In real life she seldom agreed privately with what she said publicly. It was tough enough staying employed without aggravating producers and writers who could write you out of any script if they chose to do so.

Surprised that the most famous television star of her day was unwilling to admit she bought what she taught on stage, Maddie abruptly stopped talking. What more could she say? Sometimes it was wiser to stay quiet.

"I think you now need to meet my maid, Shelly. She is a Harvard MBA candidate—not formally accepted yet, because she doubts she will enjoy the Executive Management courses they offer. She thinks it has little to do with '*the real world*'."

Noticing Maddie's bewilderment, she winked and said, "Shelly is a woman of the world who chooses to stay hidden away all day with me in this cave. She has a limited time to earn her way, so she chose working with me and doing whatever it takes—so today she transformed into a maid."

As Jennifer laughed, Shelly popped back into the room, apparently having been waiting off-stage for her cue. By now Maddie was laughing and stopped only long enough to say, "This reminds me of a movie I saw years ago—or was it a dream?"

"No, Madeline, no movie was ever made about women who slave for others, giving up their youthful promise to protect families and others, who then go on to be huge successes once they pass menopause. It's never been done!"

Nodding solemnly, Maddie said, "You know that is pretty much the premise of my book. This is what I'm trying to uncover and explore, and I wasn't able to figure out where you would fit into it, but now I wonder who you really are—and what you will become."

Leaning in close, Jennifer said, "You're an explorer, Madeline, and want to see who is around the next bend, but remember—egos are so much more difficult to handle than climbing the Himalayas. You are very wise to select only a few women to talk to about politics, or what they want to do to change the world, and I'm much aware I never said aloud anything like that to anyone but Shell—until now."

Imagine that—this woman really does want to run for public office! How could this be? Where would she fit in, and what could she *really* contribute?

As the sun slipped behind a cloud of haze and disappeared, the room dimmed as a bright silvery wave of pigeons flew by the windows. The fading rays dappled the soaring birds' beautiful iridescent wings as they basked in the thrill of flight. Just then Shelly walked in and said she was going to remove the salad plates and serve their entrée before it got cold.

Both women picked at the food while talking about trivial matters, meanwhile Shelly paced the hallway. She obviously wanted to talk about whatever they usually talked about at this time of day, every day. She was not about to lose a posh job by barging in now, so she waited until she heard the magic words…

"Yes, I could work in government—and would like to, but no one would take me seriously enough to appoint me to anything other than a cameo role in an embassy or someplace where no one likes Americans anymore."

Laughing, Maddie said, "That would be any embassy in the world now. We could use a better view portrayed of life in the US today. The one we have now is no longer positive, because too many of our men are disliked all around the world. Women, on the other hand, may be able to change the way we are portrayed—and get back to where we were—working hard to help everyone live the good life—not just the pushy, greedy liars."

Jennifer's mood turned serious. "You look like someone who has enjoyed the good life, Madeline, and been given a lot. Why do you think other women don't like you?"

Stunned at the direction the interview was once again taking, Maddie blurted, "I didn't realize women don't like me. Where did you hear that?"

"Oh, I'm very much aware of everything that goes on around me. I watch *all* the news programs, including Charlie Rose, and all the shows pretending to interview hard-working people—who are actually actors delivering lines about work they have little knowledge of."

"You sound bitter, Jennifer. I wonder if you would feel that way if you were starring on Broadway now." She hadn't intended to be so blunt. Why had she attacked—especially now that she really wanted to interview her?

"Now you can see why women don't like you, Madeline. Can't you? You speak freely and quickly— when most can't think that fast. You return volleys faster than anyone on television and could be the one everyone wants to interview or hear, if you could be controlled—but you can't be tamed. You're a tornado who bowls over phonies without knowing it—so no talk shows for you—and no-go on shows that want women to look pretty, but stupid. I know all about it. I watch all the shows!"

Nodding in recognition of the actress's assessment of her ambitions and lack of ability to acquire same caused Maddie to pause—unable to frame another question until she thought this out and knew what direction to take next.

As they sat in silence, Shelly walked in and took over. She framed her employer's chapter in the upcoming book exactly as it needed to be, in order to make everyone aware Jennifer Gibson was a huge success, because she knew what people were thinking. She was gifted with insights into life now and knew what to do with her own life, thus had amassed a tidy estate that could fund a run for public office—if asked. That was the tough part, according to Shelly. How to get readers en masse to enlist Jennifer to run for Congress?

The three women sat at the table with food half-eaten while they talked about politics, economics, and whatever it takes to make the country better for everyone than it is now. They bandied about all sorts of ideas and found most were in alignment or could easily be aligned. They talked as if this was a long-running conversation they had had many times in the past and were finally able to make happen.

To end the interview, Maddie stood and straightened her back to ease a crimp that bothered her whenever she didn't move much for hours. Looking at her watch, she gasped, "My gosh, look at the time! I allotted three hours tops to stop by and chat—and I'm sure you didn't allow even that much time, and here we are five hours later—and far from done. I have to come back!"

Obviously having enjoyed her company, Jennifer laughed heartily and said all was arranged to meet again. She would be home any day Madeline could make it, so they decided to meet the next day, and set up a third meeting for later in the week.

Each knew it was going to be a wonderful week, with all happy to meet again. They unanimously decided they must have been a family of distinction in another time and place—meeting again now to pick up where they left off long ago or maybe even on another plane of today.

☯Chapter Five

This is definitely the beginning of a new era! In times before the Modern Age began with the Greeks, women led and were better-educated than men. They taught Aristotle and others a bit of what they knew, but certainly not everything. What happened then to shock women into remission—then submission? Women hung back and let men erase what they thought, even stole credit for what they taught them.

The Goddess who ruled for centuries was suddenly silenced—until now. 5,000 years later women once again study and work together, determined to take back the power they gave away so long ago. The pendulum swings both ways, but this time women know what will happen if they don't step up and work hard to create a new and better world for all—especially children. Women cannot afford to continue living as they did in the past. It is time to rise again!

Today is not just a time, era, century, or whatever, it's the end of a huge epicenter of energy that began way back before humans were ushered into this world or given this planet to understand. We were never aware of when it all started, but we know now what will happen when it ends. We know, because it's imprinted on our souls.

The idea that Christ could die, then rise and walk the Earth again wasn't doubted, because he wasn't the first. In these pagan times, we do not appreciate what we find in books and artifacts left behind for our use. We too often blindly accept that whatever is written in Bibles is right. We even ask others to advise us if something is wrong, based on what they believe to be right—which is wrong!

The work of a few women can unhinge a lot of men. That is why this book will have to be read under cover and in bed—not on the bus or in the office—at least not among those you can't trust.

I fear for women who have no ability to steer clear of men who lack humility. They will bear the brunt of the discontentment that will flood men when the time arrives where they can no longer run the country and others. By the way, that time is fast approaching—and much feared by those in power here and now. Why would anyone who has been sitting around, acting like he was enacting laws while producing only mental farts want to give up and go back to where he lives and do whatever with his kids, while women work hard and change whatever they think will make our world run and operate like it can and should?

Now that I have power, due to many heads coming together to create a message about what women want, I can and do run on and on…I think I see the future better than some, because I was raised in the old ways. I was given this opportunity to bridge the nations and times as they changed so I could help women and men let go of what once was and do what they know.

Men want to do what they love to do—hunt, fish, and roam the globe—not have to come home every night to see the wife. That is what men really like, but women trained them to stay close by or they might take off with another guy. Thus, men competed to be known as good providers. They mysteriously became excited about making money— too suddenly.

Why? Women wanted to prove to other women they had not married *down,* rather moved up in status. They made men work and do whatever it took to compete in the world arena, rather than look like a mistake anyone could make.

As that day ends and few men want to work like that ever again, many are floating around now and forgetting college. Women are not! They are cheered on by fathers— more than mothers. Urged to do their own thing, because men know what this world needs more than women of their age.

You may be surprised that I could be a grandmother now, but not about to spend this life being one. I can't look at those I bred and lie about their performance and minds. I can, however, without malice see inside a whole generation as to what they need. Grandmothers need to do that—or their tribe cannot survive as well as they might.

When you travel about the country talking to women of a certain age, you can sense they want to do something new, but are confused about what they can do. I say all the time: *"Why not start now? Do whatever you can for your political party!"* Most of the women I talked to this last month-and-a-half laughed at the idea, but some are gaining interest in it now.

What can a woman plan and execute without the help of many others? She can start small and spread her influence over the next few years, which won't take her far if she is over 50. If you are to work in the political arena now, you need to be launched and able to really flaunt your life experience by the time you are 45, but things could change. We could all decide women who worked and can now rest on their laurels make better leaders than men— Right Now!

That really caught you off-guard. Didn't it?

If you headed a political party, what would you do to get a woman of means to enter into and rescue your favorite scheme? What would you do to get her to work for you in ways others refuse to work now?

Such questions flow like torrents in a wild, summer storm, but only The Divine can figure out why, as well as how much time it will take to make a better country from one that has been run into the ground. This country needs people to come to the forefront immediately—before it falls apart, but only a few are willing to contemplate doing something so foolhardy as to run for public office now.

Men have been hard on themselves and their need to be with women, so now they can disqualify each other, based on things they did to wrong them. Women are not called out or noticed as doing anything wrong— so far—by members of the opposite sex. They need only be pronounced as singularly in love with men, even if not actually committed to any one man, to be deemed 'electable' or 'promotable' or whatever allows women to run for office now.

If you listen to the media, the wave of women in power will not crest for a few more decades, but it isn't going down that way today. Women are getting law degrees and reading history as they haven't done in eons— and they are beginning to scream and demand that men be men. That does not bode well for the way this country was raised to use women every day.

The time has come when women will do whatever they want done—not send in men to do whatever, then critically analyze what they did wrong and when. You will notice more and more doctors and lawyers are women, while more and more men are bored with whatever chores they once performed in businesses all over the world. Women are not noticed as being that involved now, because men don't consider them a threat yet in any competition. Wake up everybody—that life is dead!

This is a world where too many women are bored, yet able to do things they never thought about before. They know how to rule and dominate others without seeming to do so. They can spread their wings over crowds now, not just cowing sons who are never sure what their mother wants. Women can dominate men!

Having said that, how do we all get started?

There is a building in Athens that stands above all others. It is the domain of Athena, Queen of Wisdom, who reigned supreme, but not seen that way today. Can you name anyone who truly believes women are queens who can gain political power now without losing their femininity?

The work of this world is not to help a few rise into the skies and take out the prize, but for everyone to ascend when their day here is dead. Yes, we need to be able to sense when it is time to leave—and prepare for it, then do what is necessary without worrying about where we will land next.

This is not a country where people believe in God, but there are still some legitimate traces of deism left in the United States. Most believe in some form of God and try to erase the fact we are a nation of people created to believe America is one nation under one God, and any other version of that belief is not what we bought into when we asked to be given a chance to live here now. We still cannot accept the threat but understand the intent.

The theme of this book changed from novel to a collection of interviews—then a collection of essays about what women can do to gain power and work for the good of the nation, along the way becoming a work of inspiration. Now it's a *novel* way of teaching today's women how to change their ways in order to help others rearrange their daily work and create a better life for all—even the lowest of slaves.

It isn't doubted much that women are slaves, but most believe it occurs in other places—never in the USA. Here and now women are placed on pedestals only if a mind is cruel and the woman is obliging—willing to hide her mind and adjust her natural body and face to others' expectations. There is no greater tyranny than a woman so full of fear that she allows herself to be cut up to please others. Having been said and done by too many who wanted to be someone without doing the work required, we leave them all behind.

Driving forward into the future of women who do not fear men and can rear children once again without fear of what a man will do to them, you will be the one to judge them. Don't be surprised if you discover you cannot always love those who come after you and do what you never wanted to do. Excessively aggressive women waste time and energy working alone, forgetting they can't run for public office without being *'electable'* and interesting to others.

A pessimistic way to study women in education is to say most cannot figure out what it takes to work with others. They work alone in classes—like most traditional mothers but are not as well-liked. Thus, if educators cannot elect each other to positions of power, who can they aspire to be?

Reach out to girls and teach them what they can be. That change of attitude alone would change the world. If a woman came forward today and said she could sell you anything—and get men to vote for her, would you give her a moment of your time? No! You would not know what to say or even know how to think about such a woman now. Thus, men continue to dominate and rule in these uncertain times.

You want to be told everything is okay, but don't have any confidence in what women can do, thus you continue to let men take over and control everyone even now. The moment for action is now!

Right now, we can easily spot ten women who could run the country easily, if the community was willing to agree. What would it take to get these women to commit and run, as if their political careers were a business— and something they can have fun with now? To consider running for office, what would you wish to gain?

The ability to stun and hit-on-the-run is necessary when fighting a larger, more powerful army. You have to learn to dominate the scene at night, because you are not as frightening to men then. You must be ready to speak when everyone else is drunk. Get whatever is said quoted by others present and repeated over and over again later. You may even make the morning papers. Remember, to be noticed, you have to do something different from what men always did well.

Women who started out posing nude in order to get noticed by men are now overlooked for obvious reasons. Being conceited, they need to think things through a lot better than others. For starters, when nude or posing provocatively, you look ridiculous to others who are fully clothed. If you want drool all over you, dress conservatively and excel at whatever business you do, without frowning a lot and looking down on others, as too many women still do. Clowning around is preferable to snobbery, but it still isn't seen as a respectable way to win the day. If you smile more, it helps you forget to frown and scold like a mom—so practice smiling even as you read.

Keeping the *'Decency Factor'* in play is always the best way to run for office today. No matter how indecent a country may be, it wants to believe it is basically honest and honorable—especially when it is not. That is why you can run on a reform platform almost anywhere and at any time and easily be elected to some position of authority right away. All you have to do to be elected is appeal to other women and be able to sway a few men not to vote as they might have done in the past. It's really not that hard!

After working all day on the bios of several women I interviewed about running for public office, I could see no cohesive way to pull it together without providing a few distractions to the readers. I'm now fully aware that anyone who reads this book is also into things they are unwilling to address now.

The mess we are in today isn't just about what men consented to and maintained over time, but also women's reluctance to take their own lives seriously. Women want to remain naïve as long as possible—not speaking out when another doesn't get what is due and right, instead blaming men for what they don't like about themselves or their lives. That has to change before women can take each other seriously again.

Once women can more easily consent to being wrong and having made mistakes—not being afraid to admit them, we will make progress. Present ignorance can disappear, but not in a year. It takes a lot of enlightenment to brighten what has been blighted all this life, and for many previous lives, but it can be done.

In the work of Percy Bysshe Shelley and others of his style and grace, we sense they did not want to be men as they were supposed to be then. They wanted to enjoy life and examine what God created, taking delight in it. Only now can we grant men the ability to love and be loved in return for what they desire—not what we demand them to be. Women set up guidelines for fools to follow throughout their lives—and their fools are usually men, seldom their daughters.

You may deny you are a wife and seek solace with others who also lie, but you cannot fool your children. They know who you are and why you lie. That is why the first requirement of a mother is to produce children who can love her. If a mother cannot prove this to the satisfaction of the public, she should seek an office far from the public eye—which is easy to do!

Without a doubt, most women today cannot keep men in office simply because they are good fathers, but they keep women out of office because they are not great mothers. That kind of logic is no longer allowed! To make a nation great you cannot be contrary and divisive. You would go against the polls, instead of reading them to see what others want.

You may agree with the President who said he would lead by doing his own thing, but women won't get into the Oval Office if they talk like that. Silly talk is expected when men campaign, but one not-so-smart remark and the average woman cannot run for anything ever again. Be sure you don't overstep your rules. To succeed in politics now, you have to think about what you will say and which tasks you can do fast, because you will be expected to do whatever you say in a most excellent way—quickly.

The way I see it now, I'm about to give away my power again by treating a man to dinner and helping him get along with his family better than me, so I can learn what the other side of his life is like. I don't really want to marry into a clan of adults who do nothing for themselves or their kids, but I like to see what makes some still follow that path. I enjoy talking to people with strong convictions, but it has been at least six years since I had such a conversation with a member of the opposite faith and party, so I doubt it will happen now—or maybe ever again. What is happening to us—or is it just me?

You must know why people do what they do! It isn't the purpose of this text to test partners of people not running for office. It comes into play when you think about what it takes for you to be elected to public office one day. Fortunately, millions of women study psychology today, which makes it easier for them to ascend to power once again.

☯Chapter Six

The radio was playing while I was talking, so I felt like I was competing with some unseen force. Think about it, because this is how we live now and how we must think whenever we meet another. We aren't just talking, we are communicating on many different levels—like wordless music playing in the background.

When the rapper finished his rant, the beat continued. I felt like I had to talk just as fast as he did to keep on target—or lose my audience. Why on earth would a woman of greatness want to listen to such trash?

"I see you don't approve of my choice in music!" The woman sitting opposite raised just one artistically-arched brow, laughing so I need not reply. "I like to listen to what the kids are up to—keep up with the times. You know, keep in touch as they age and all that stuff.

"I had two girls who once called me 'mother', but now all they call me is 'bitch' if I refuse to sign a check over to them. I just don't get them anymore, but then I guess I wasn't really thinking about what they were doing back then. I took for granted they were like me—perhaps a bit too narcissistic, which really didn't apply to me. I had thought they would copy what I did, because I was immediately a huge hit when I went into business. Unfortunately, they don't take after me."

Shrugging, her blouse slipped off her boney shoulder just enough to expose a breast that would stand out on a woman twice her size. She looked like a walking ad for those who make a lot of money from women's insecurities. I said nothing, just smiled and waited for her to restart her monologue.

"I can see you're used to successful women. You don't rush to ask a lot of silly questions about kids and husbands, and what we want to do next. You wait, as though I will tell you all about it in time, but I won't. I hate bores—and talking about such mundane things is boring! No one really cares what you do at home or with your kids—unless they're bad. Then it doesn't matter what you do with *your* life, someone will drag out your kids or their kid and bring it up again and again. I see it all the time— even Jimmy Carter isn't immune."

Jimmy Carter? What does he have to do with one who paints herself in flaming colors as a pseudo-guru?

"I see you're surprised that I admire one who was elected to the highest office in the land. I was once naïve about how the government trains people to live. I voted not to reelect him then. I've never regretted anything as much as that one vote!"

She almost spit out the words, so I debated about which line of questions was most suitable to follow. If my goal to persuade her to consider running for public office is wise, how would it fly? Trying for a sincere smile I could somehow maintain, I waited in silence—rather than lie outright.

While puffing on a thin, brown cigarette, her fluid motions reminded me of an old movie star, or a young

Lauren Bacall, and it did nothing for her. It called attention to the fact that she didn't look good. Her huge breasts heaved as she breathed too deeply. Her face grew pinched with each inhale, and when she exhaled she expelled an indecent scent far into the room.

As she continued to stare into mid-air, I motioned toward the terrace. "I was wondering if you could open the sliders for me. I'm allergic to smoke—especially tobacco, and I don't want to have to leave without enough material to create a great chapter about your life and work, as well as what you want to do for your country."

My trite speech produced a pout, but she did reach over and toss her lipstick coated cigarette butt into a potted plant standing beside the sliding door. Then with minimal movement she threw open the door to the terrace with a flourish. I made a mental note that she has to be a lot stronger than she appears to be. Personal trainer, perhaps?

"How will you remember today in words, Ms. Worthington? Are you going to work hard to devise a plot in which I am just another pretty face operating a huge business empire alone—without the love of her children, or are you going to say I'm a woman of today who has it all? No one has ever gone deeper than that! Are you any different?"

Apparently, she did not mind being characterized as either type of life failure, so I smiled and said nothing. When she remained silent, I decided it was time to lay out my plan for her to examine and decide if she wanted to work with me or be excluded from this book.

"While traveling for several months all over the country, I've gathered a lot of data relative to women who never seriously thought about running a business or a country, let alone local politics—simply because no one ever asked them. Personally, I don't think it's good to ask anyone without business experience to run a company but running the county or the country isn't that hard. Actors can do it better than some experienced politicians, and certainly better than most lawyers, so it can't be that hard."

My audience of one appeared agitated, so I wasn't surprised when she interrupted. "I beg to differ with you! Acting is the most difficult job there is. I have to do ads for my company, and I put on an act whenever I go out to socialize. Everything I do or say is scripted—and I'm graded later on how well I played my role, because I'm not supposed to be me! The world doesn't expect it. The art of being an artist or writer or actor, without letting others know who you really are, isn't easy. It takes years of practice! In the process, you gain constant fear—and lose confidence. I know all about that!"

Stunned that this worldly woman would admit in a minute to being insecure and unable to believe she could lead made *me* feel insecure. It's contagious! Stuttering, I said, "Whhhat are you saying? That you don't enjoy sitting at the top of the table and having everyone listen to you?"

Shaking her head, then stomping her foot like a defiant child, she said, "I'm a puppet! I say only what I'm supposed to say. If I act like things are great and say we have even bigger plans for the future, many take it at face value and buy our stock. If I act like I'm tired and not doing great, people sell out, and I won't be able to change their minds. So, I have to always act like I'm perfect and live a dream life—and frankly, it's degrading to have to live that way. I don't have as much freedom as other women. I can't just do my thing—have PMS days, and sing if I want, or talk on the phone all day to my kids…That's why I listen to rap."

So, we are back to where we started—at last! How to begin again? "Yes, very interesting, and I think your reasoning is sound. We all need to keep in touch with every strata of the country if we are to overcome the latest phenomenon harming us now."

This seemed to intrigue her enough to stop and look at me—perhaps for the first time. Smiling she moved closer, so I smiled before saying, "I think you have a brilliant mind and just want to exercise it a bit more—And rap seems outrageous enough to scare off those who might not want to report what they see or what you're thinking about. Am I right?"

"No, but then, how could you know? I never reveal who I am—to anyone! I keep the past closeted and have ordered others to pass by it whenever talking or writing about me. I've taken pains to tell my story in plain English, so people can easily repeat it, purposely leaving out the hard parts and adding nothing recently. Although I don't always tell the whole story to one person or another, my entire biography is out there, but no single individual has pieced it together so far. Do you want to give it a try?"

I shook my head and said, "No, I'm not here to write about you, per se. I'm here to talk about politics and the need for women to lead our country now. I want to know if you're interested. If you are, would you want to fund someone else or be a front-runner? Would you want to talk for others or stand back and push others to change their ways today?"

Ignoring my challenge, she said, "I'm amazed! I am truly amazed! You want to talk politics—with me? You don't want to talk about me personally, but want to offer me a job that may or may not be something I always wanted to do? I'm astounded!"

What that display really meant wasn't clear, so I sat and watched her toy with her hair while she brooded. She took longer to respond than anyone I had previously interviewed, but then again, she was richer and smarter than everyone else—so far. Then with a brilliant smile she announced, "I think I'm interested."

Not wishing to get into a guessing game with her about her intentions, I waited.

"You know, Ms. Worthington—and I use that form of address because I greatly respect you and using your first name would sound chummy or too familiar for the business I want to do with you. I want to be completely honest with you, but I don't know you well enough to be that direct. I don't want to end up martyred or put on the stump, yet want to see what comes next."

I nodded, but said nothing. Not hard to do, since I had no clue what she was thinking or wanted to do now.

"Hard to believe, but I have only been asked once or twice in my life to do something new. I refused both times, and probably refused a few more times due to being a moral coward. I was afraid of failing—not being seen as great. What a drama queen I used to be!"

Her laughter vibrated through the huge room, but I could only sit and watch—saying nothing, because she definitely was not happy!

"I think you have wisdom that comes from some other world, Ms. Worthington, and I think you know that."

I nodded, but said nothing.

"Yes, you are aware that what you say and do isn't always what you previously thought about or wanted to say, yet it's usually better. Why is that?"

Not waiting for a reply, she said, "I think we are guided by those who are always with us. I think we have Guides who help us do a lot more with our lives than we would otherwise achieve. I think our Guides could be those who died, and we wanted them to always be with us—and some come to this world along with us when we're born. Does any of this surprise you?"

"No, I believe The Holy Spirit that Christ spoke about as he ascended on a cloud that morning centuries ago is with me always. I even think at times I can see inside the mind of another who also believes that." Stunned to have said so much without first thinking about its impact, I shut up and stopped smiling.

"I see, Ms. Worthington. You are one of us. You are here today to tell me it is time to begin the climb!"

What could she be talking about? I'm unable to feel right about this interview—or about her. Is she the silly, vacuous movie star-type executive, or a woman of power and spirit who works for The Lord?

"You work for those in power. You might think you work for the lords of industry, since you were originally hired by the biggest, most powerful newspaper in the world, but you're not. You are a reporter for a very special reason. You were born to write!"

Without any reason to agree, I nodded, but said nothing and waited for her to continue.

"I have been around longer than you."

This was a surprise, because according to my records she is at least three years younger than me and easily looks ten years younger—even in daylight.

"I'm older than you think. Long ago I changed all my vital statistics to reflect the woman I wanted to be now. I changed my face and rearranged my body, so men would not be able to say I wasn't beautiful when they attacked me for making so much more money than they. Now I regret all those attacks I made on my mind and body—and the extensive surgery, but I can't go back. I'm stuck with Barbie—and a lot of Kens who only want to play house. I aim to end it now, but can I?"

The way she stopped and looked at me was no longer coy. She was not being dramatic. In fact, she looked sad. With her mind in another place and time, I wasn't at all sure who she was—which came as a shock.

"I'm never quite what anyone thinks I will be, but then again, neither are they. But you, Ms. Worthington, are an image that will not fade once you go away, and I like that! You can say what you want, then sit and wait until you get an answer before going away. I see no hatred or meanness in you, and never heard that you mistreated a client or informer. That is why I was predisposed to be interviewed by you. I, too, want to learn more about my life—my real life, and my real work. I was not at all aware you would be the messenger—and would ask me to drop my work to follow you."

Shaking my head, I managed to say, "I'm not asking you to drop what you're doing and follow me."

Laughter shook her shoulders as she crossed her legs, as if to control a faulty bladder. "I think you're right, Ms. Worthington! You're not the woman I thought you would be. You're better! Because you don't sense your power over others—especially women. We all shake in our boots when told you're in the waiting room."

She continued to laugh, but not as loudly, until I said, "I guess I am The Press, and The Press doesn't always play fair. So, it would be hard to know who is friend or who is foe, but I'm not acting as a reporter now. I'm creating a book about Women of Today—*Women of Destiny* who can rule this country tomorrow. It's not exactly what I set out to do—and changes from page-to-page, but it is approximately what my publisher wants—at least for now."

"You're writing a book about women of today who can run the world tomorrow—and I run the world now! What can I contribute to your book?"

Amazed that she would not immediately see what she could do for her country—let alone other women, I stuttered to say, "You can do a lot! You can run for public office right now and not be pushed around. We need you to take a stand and decide what is in the best interests of this country. Show us how to gain respect back from those who so willingly trample us due to misbegotten envy and hate— eager to mess up our collective image here and abroad."

What a waste of interview time! I was inarticulate, unable to speak as if I knew what I was doing. Nevertheless, something did happen!

My host talked non-stop about *her* life plan—for two hours! It was the best speech I've ever heard. She was astounding, and the best thing was I knew it wasn't previously prepared. She could not have remembered half of what appeared to be a stream of consciousness—a recital, rather than a monologue. Really good thing I recorded it for later!

☯Chapter Seven

Most of the women were excited about meeting for the first time to decide what they would do as a group to promote better understanding of what can and cannot be accomplished by a well-run, organized, and effective government with the good of its citizens uppermost in its plans. Everyone strolled from one table to another as Spirit moved them, asking questions of those prepared to field them. Each table was manned by someone totally unrelated to the group, and unaware they were providing cover for the real agenda.

The real reason for the meeting? All wanted to see if what they put together in theory could be worked out in reality. They had to find out who fit in and who did not.

A high-pitched voice rose above all others. "The way I see it, the Far East will be fine. They have a huge population and no longer require our assistance. From now on they will be treating us as customers! I think they will be better at serving our needs than we are, but we need to be on top of technology and invention—creating innovations that save *them* time. We can do that, and they can buy from us, and so on, but we can't maintain as large a population as we have unless we begin to farm as we once did, doing all sorts of things that once fed families and held communities together." Her well-rehearsed opinion was met with sporadic argument.

"I can see you wish to return to an agrarian society, and I seriously doubt it would interest anyone alive now." This loud disagreement caused others to pause and check both women out. What the delegates saw did not impress them, thus an audible sigh arose when they were both ushered out of the room.

Not a good start, but as it turned out, neither woman had been invited, thus easily eliminated from the experiment—a good thing!

As if to fill the void, a chunky woman with sheared off black hair announced in a shrill voice, "I think Madeline is on to something. She has a lot of knowledge—and a lot more power than she seems to be aware of—which is great for all of us. Women who assume they are brilliant are often heartless and cruel—stupid, to boot, but I like Maddie! I spent a lot of time with her in the Adirondacks. She was a great hiker. I liked that. Do you hike?"

The woman standing next to her looked surprised and barely managed to mumble, "No, I never go outside my apartment. I stay at home and watch TV. Try to keep up with all the tripe the charlatans in Washington foist on us daily. If I can avoid it, I don't even walk in Central Park." Her smile faltered and died as the extrovert appeared about to speak, but hesitated.

To fill the gap developing between them, she said, "However, I think you and I must share something in common. Why else would Madeline have put us together? I want to figure it out now, rather than wait years to discover that we actually have something in common—maybe a lot."

The shy woman's tentative smile disappeared as she studied the much younger woman. Was she preaching some kind of metaphysical mumbo-jumbo, or was she a psychologist? They talk like that, too. Without further delay, Jennifer Gibson introduced herself, speaking with unusual precision. "I don't think you and I met before, but as you say, we must be connected in some way or Madeline wouldn't have suggested I talk to you. She was confident we would get along, but unfortunately never said why. Seems astonishing, doesn't it? Based solely on appearance, you and I seem to be the most oddly-matched pair here, except maybe for the nun and the woman wearing a strapless gown."

The two would-be friends laughed as they looked at each other more closely than before. The need to determine why they were selected to work together drove their conversation forward. What could they do together? What did Madeline expect would surpass their present curiosity about the other?

Questions surfaced for ten minutes or more before they finally discovered they both firmly believed there was a world of trouble waiting for today's children. Both possessed a burning desire to train teachers and help others provide children with a better life than their parents did for the past 25 years or so. The desire to help children here and abroad excited them, thus their enthusiasm ignited an energy that engulfed women manning nearby booths.

Strangely enough, a booth and table had been set up beside them that was dedicated to women helping mothers raise their children alone. Opposite was a table detailing how to train welfare recipients to run child care centers. They had not noticed these tables and representatives until now, which ignited an idea—perhaps everyone was parked in front of tables or booths representing what they could or should pursue together?

The duo newly dedicated to child care and supporting their welfare looked around and watched the nun and socialite as they passed in front of various booths while handing out literature on feeding the world and teaching people how to garden and preserve food better than most do now. For the two newly-found, but now old friends, this odd couple appeared to be the most unlikely duo to prove their theory.

They checked out another pair or two before sensing the nun and socialite might be well-matched after all. Maybe each pairing would separate later to meet others who could or would work with them, too? It seemed likely, based on what they could see developing all around them.

Watching other women closely, smiling all the while, the woman dressed all in black and the biker who was a hiker talked as though they had known each other forever. They finally approached a couple standing nearby to tell them about what they believed was the reason Madeline asked everyone to attend, as well as why she wanted them to meet each other in a specific order.

Their pronouncement surprised other women, because they had known each other for years and found nothing unusual in being put together for the first hour. Being wise women, they did not admit they found Jennifer's theory weird. Instead, they put it away to sort out later in the day—or never.

Once delegates checked out each other's appearance, as well as the caterers and various company representatives, they forgot about how others looked.

This was wise, since appearances can be managed but friendships can't. The event ended before some women met the top echelon, as they now called Madeline and her Board of Directors, but no invitee felt left out—or missed talking to everyone on the Board or those there to work with members. Each group of volunteers and paid participants from well-intentioned international charities said it was an exciting day and they learned a lot, but none fully realized it until later. It was that kind of day!

As Maddie ushered the remaining Board members toward the front of the room, she said, "I think the caterers can easily take care of cleaning up and informing us if anything was broken or mistakenly taken, so we might as well leave and talk about what we can do over coffee and tea."

Raising her hand, Maddie suddenly stopped and whispered, "Do you hear something? I thought I heard a noise that isn't supposed to be heard? You know, the kind of noise that wakens you in the middle of the night? Anyone else hear it?"

The only response was a murmur, then a loud thumping like something bouncing. The women looked at each other as an icy breeze descended over everyone as if from an open window. The cold draft swept across the room—not exactly a wind, more like a deep chill. Three women blessed themselves, several others smiled knowingly, and one giggled nervously. What was it? Who was it? Was it a warning of some kind?

Maddie looked upward and spoke with quiet authority. "We are here today for peace, prosperity, and all good things—for all good people in all nations of the world. Can we do something about it or not?"

A door at the front opened and a man walked in who seemed out-of-place, as though looking for someone. When he smiled, all laughed with relief. Some were prepared for a monster or maybe an angel to appear, he obviously was neither. The stranger appeared so serene that the nun was immediately pleased to meet him, and the socialite wanted to invite him to her next dinner party for eight.

The women stood at attention as he said, "Hello! So sorry I'm late. I was outside—just down the hall. I was pulled into another party, and for several hours thought I was supposed to be there—until they asked me for my invitation."

Almost laughing, he said, "I guess they thought I was a free-loader or whatever. They tossed me out! Then I rechecked the address and realized I was in the wrong gallery. I'm so sorry to have missed what you did earlier. It was never my intention not to be here, but I must admit I never understood why you invited me. Am I too late to find out?"

Mystified and eager to find out why this man who had entered with a chilly breeze would arrive exactly when they were leaving, Maddie spoke with an air of detachment, unlike her usual warm manner when greeting strangers. "You seem to have a message for us. Because we haven't issued any invitations that were not accepted, and everyone arrived when expected. I think you were sent to us, so we would all love to hear what you have to say. Can you join us at my apartment across the street for coffee and tea?"

When he smiled and eagerly agreed to accompany them, the biker was unimpressed and wondered aloud if he had tried doors until he was invited to stay. She decided to remain close to him—just in case he tried to get physical or do something funny. Her plan was to drop him immediately if he even thought about harming anyone, or damaging Madeline's home.

The nun stood out from the crowd, and her presence immediately attracted the man's attention. He asked what she was doing so far from her village, which surprised her. How did he know? He also seemed to recognize she was not in common Orders.

Softly, she said, "Are you from Mexico? There was an aura around you when you opened the door—and a way of holding your head, as well as your slight accent. Are you a *Man of Destiny*, as they say, or just stopping by on your way home to see if anyone else is ready to go or not?"

Nodding, he spoke softly to her so others could not hear, "You are the one! I was given this Park Avenue address and told to speak to a nun. I wondered why a nun would be at a party here. It's a mystery to me, since I don't feel I'm in the presence of one who grew up in the Catholic belief system. Am I wrong?"

If surprised, the nun did not show it. However, those standing nearby were surprised to see the two talking rapidly in Spanish—intimately, as if old friends with much to share. Maddie observed their rapid-fire exchange but did not approach them. Although wondering who he was and how he had found them in a hotel holding many weddings and meetings that day, she was eager to discover what the newly-appointed Board members had learned from the day's events and decided to put aside her concerns about the stranger for now.

☯Chapter Eight

Everyone fit comfortably into Maddie's spacious living area. As each found a good position to view others, yet still able to participate, two women covered the bar, so no one would even think about drinking. Combining wine and women at any time is not a great idea—most especially when work is required.

Smiling at two women who offered to help her, the nun closed the bedroom door located adjacent to the living room. New York apartments usually have weird layouts, so most present had not expected anything so grand as the living area with its windows on the world framed with golden, gossamer drapes that must look gorgeous in sunlight.

Everyone either sat or walked about, shifting their ideas and opinions as they talked to those they had previously met at the forum. An obvious way to quickly gain a consensus, but no one noticed. Even Maddie did not realize she was being pulled out of the kitchen and into the center of the group where she could do nothing more than she had done at the meeting—helping all settle in and be as happy as they wanted to be.

The room's high ceilings easily accommodated the noise from many voices as the lighting gradually dimmed. A perfect way to end any revolution getting underway, but it did not. The stranger was not as easy to understand as he was at the hotel, but they willingly listened in order to later dissect it with claws or not. This was his only chance to gain their attention and make friends among this collection of women working together for the first time.

Maddie made a slight motion and the women hushed so the man could address them. "I can see you are very busy. You all work hard. You do not like to sit for even a minute, but ladies, let me say work is not why we are here. Work is what puts our dreams in place and keeps us going when everything seems bleak, but it is not what is actually happening here and now. We are mere actors. We do not have casts to support us, and we do not have plays that last, but we know what parts we are playing. Right?"

Some nodded, some did not. The atmosphere was not frigid but could ice up quickly if he did not soon explain why he wanted to influence them now or later.

"I see you have never thought about how to help women of every age—and in every country close to the United States, but I have. I spent many years here and there, and I worked to prepare the natives of the Yucatan for the time when angels would walk over their land. They have now landed!"

A gasp could be heard, but he did not stop. "We have angels everywhere, and we are not aware of all the work they do for us, so we want more. We want more women from America to join us in the Yucatan to work for the good of the common man and woman there, helping them develop their art. We want help to free the Maya of the yoke that has held them back for many years. We want you to help us drive away bad work being pushed on us by those who have never wanted us to be there." The women remained silent—not one nodded.

Maddie realized this was the man she had heard about—once, and not recently. Who had told her about him? What was his name?

As if he heard her thoughts, the stranger turned to Maddie, speaking slowly so everyone could hear him. "My name is Jorge Garcia. I have used that name in The United States for many years. In the Yucatan I am known simply as *Jorge*. I do not use other names there, because it is too complicated. It tends to make people want to find you. To live an uncomplicated life, it is better to use just one name." When he smiled this time, the group thawed a bit more.

"At the hotel I was in the other room and did not reach into my hat to find anything to say, so I am afraid I am unprepared to say anything of great wisdom or wit now. Thank you for not expecting it. In my homeland they sit in anticipation of whatever I say, and I cannot talk mush, gibberish, or worse—joke. I must always be serious— channeling wisdom. It could be worse, I could talk wise and no one listen."

Meanwhile Maddie continued to struggle trying to recall what she had heard last year about this man. Whatever, it remained unclear, so she said, "I think we all have heard about you, Jorge, but some of us remain unsure about how we know you. Can you tell us more about yourself and explain why you want us to help your tribe?" Smiling broadly, she added, "We would also love to hear anything else you have to say."

Everyone was smiling now, and Jorge seemed to relax more. His hat was ditched when he entered the apartment, and now he removed his coat to reveal a traditional shirt worn by Mayan men. He had not seemed to be large, but upon shedding his overcoat, all became aware of his manliness and confident way of taking charge, and no one resented it. This was truly an amazing change for those who had lost faith in men and wanted nothing to do with them.

Smiling broadly, the senor said, "I am not so hot as in my hometown, but I feel less constrained if I do not have to wear Western wear. I am not afraid of the cold, but I would like to have a warm cup of tea, if that is allowed."

The ever-present murmur intensified as everyone looked to Maddie. Quickly peeking into the future, she knew it was time to stop and offer everyone tea and whatever to eat, or the evening would not end happily. Many would want to leave before this man said his piece.

"I think we can offer you something a bit stronger than tea, but no wine. We are all off it until we know what we are going to do next. This is like a tribal meeting, and we are not going to do anything until we all know the score."

Looking expectant, Jorge waited for whatever would come next. Maddie, however, was struck dumb. Unable to speak, she hurried to what was thought to be a closet but was actually a small kitchen with enough gear to make a pot of tea, but not much else.

Jorge did not notice. He was not concerned about the problems his simple request produced. He was used to women doing whatever mysterious things they do to make a pot of tea, and never thought it was something he would like to do, so he said nothing while the other women sat or stood in place and looked at him.

Realizing their meeting would not end for a few hours, the women finally settled in for the evening. That was the signal for peace or understanding to drop like a vision into the midst of the group. Everyone suddenly sat erect and some began to chant: "Om," while others prayed openly.

Meanwhile the Mayan man sat still, not blinking or speaking. His presence alone centered the women's thoughts on their various charities, as well as worries and concerns about what common cause could benefit them individually if they combined all their energies. Silently, a thought pervaded the room and prevailed in each mind. They must all concentrate on the Yucatan and its Mayan clans.

Maddie was surprised to see many eyes closed as she reentered the living area. How often did a group of women sit and listen within—especially with a man present? She decided Jorge Garcia must be the shaman she had heard about who has a commune or whatever in the Yucatan run by a group of women she never interviewed, because they were unwilling to travel to LA, Tucson, or New York to talk out their problems with others and take money back. They seemed to have disappeared, but some still made money doing something weird there. Maybe he would talk about it?

Startled by giggles from a few women, Maddie realized she had been talking aloud—not just thinking it! Some were surprised when she mentioned a commune of women living in the Yucatan or Guatemala, who visited the city every now and then to raise money to support their work. The nun was mystified, so she asked Jorge if he was Mayan or a shaman of another tribe like the Huichol.

"I am Maya, whether or not I am a shaman is not decided by me. I guide others to places where they can express their faith in God. I help friends who are women develop and do well in work they were unaware they could do. They buy, sell, create, and participate in all the women's lives of the Maya. I cannot. I am not able to enter that world. I am merely a Mayan man.

"Fortunately, one who is very dear to me can bridge both cultures, and often does. She is from New York and a famous woman in her own right. She left this life for a better one in the Yucatan. Perhaps you know her? Her name here is Amanda Sheridan."

The whispers erupted into a kind of hysteria. It was all over momentarily, but Maddie was shocked to realize everyone knew Amanda Sheridan—and she did not. What had happened to her? Where did she go? Was she some kind of renegade or a folk hero? Questions jumped from her mind as the tea kettle screamed in the other room.

All jumped at the shrill alarm, but not Jorge. He was not prone to notice things of a domestic nature. In fact, he relaxed and sat back in a chair near the windows as the last light of day faded away, shrouding his face. Shadows lengthened his face even as he smiled. He now looked like an ancient warrior transformed into a man of today. No one said that, because each thought it a figment of her imagination.

"I have your tea, Jorge. So no one faints, we will have something to eat as soon as I can order it. My refrigerator is empty, because I've been traveling all over the country the past month or two, so what do you all want to eat?"

She expected a deluge of requests, not a universal burst of one word: "Chinese!" No one deviated from that simple cuisine. How could that be? Another miracle—and another way of knowing everything was going right.

Maddie called in the order while several women made preparations for when the food would arrive. Everyone else stayed seated, chatting with new-found friends until she returned to sit beside the strange man and take over the meeting again.

"I've asked all of you here in order to discuss what we as a group are to do next. I'm a woman of faith, but have noticed that when women don't follow up on meetings immediately, they never get started—even when everyone believes in a project. Today we had one meeting, and this is our second meeting on the same subject. Therefore, we have to meet one more time to cement our plan as we conceived it. Is everyone in agreement that we meet here next week, then we can meet wherever you want after that?"

All but Jorge looked surprised until the nun said she would like everyone to visit her convent next. She wanted them to personally witness women working in faith, doing a lot of good for the human race. It was quickly decided that they would move their next meeting to the convent. Surprisingly, everyone could make it— another miracle!

Looking at the clock, Maddie realized time had stopped. She asked Jorge if he was a Mayan Timekeeper. He agreed that he knew of such things, but no one can say they are a Timekeeper—others might proclaim it, but no one can say he or she is a Timekeeper. He took Maddie's questions in stride, but she was now in shock. What was she doing? Who was he? What is a Mayan Timekeeper anyway?

As before, Maddie's thoughts were transparent to everyone—especially Jorge, so he talked about Timekeepers in his slow and measured way. When the doorbell chimed, everyone ran for a dinner plate, so he did not waste time or energy talking. Although unused to women feeding themselves first, he became quickly aware that he had to get his share or have nothing to eat. Obviously surprised at how quickly everyone ate, he said nothing about it then.

Each one explained their haste to him. "We eat take-out right away, because it is better hot than microwaving it after it gets cold." All said little until they were sated, which he thought very strange, but having been trained that when with natives of another race or tribe, do as they do.

For perhaps the first time in his life, Jorge ate with speed, dining on cuisine indescribable as Chinese or anything he had ever eaten before. He wondered why they liked it so much, but ended up asking for seconds.

As the feeding frenzy ended, a bag was passed around and everyone—even Jorge, pulled out a Fortune Cookie and broke it open to see what it foretold. They were all amazed! It was as though the baker knew who would be there and had arranged for a mystic to write personal messages.

The beautiful model said, "I can't believe it! It says I will go to a foreign country and work for a woman of the world. What is going on here? Jorge, did you arrange to send these messages?" For once she was not afraid to eat the cookie, because she wanted the fortune to come true. Nevertheless, she was shocked that this was about the same thing Jorge had said before they began to eat.

The woman teamed up with the nun said, "I think we're being given a sign." She could not sing well, so she tried humming a tune as if delivering her fortune via a singing telegram, but to no avail. She ended up reading it as written, without worrying about the effect it might have on everyone else. *'You are a beauty. You will not have to worry. You are going to leave your city in a hurry and be given a wonderful career.'* I'm serious, I did not write this or even pick it out. It just popped into my hand. Here, check it out yourself."

She tried to hand the slip to the nun, but the nun was unwilling to double-check the message since she believed whatever was going on now was a kind of miracle—and she was eager to read her own message. "I seem to have misplaced my glasses again. Can someone read what is written on my slip?" She handed her fortune to the woman who made huge profits selling whatever on E-Bay and had written a best seller about it.

Scanning the slip, she stared at the nun before reading: "You are going to be a nun! You are going to take Holy Orders! You will lead everyone…How can that be? You're a nun already. What's wrong with this? Is anyone else told something weird?"

Immediately the nun said, "I'm a nun by choice, but I never took Holy Orders. I am, however, appointed to run the nunnery where you will all visit next week. We don't call ourselves nuns. As Jorge would say, that is for others to judge and label us, but we work as nuns do, and we pray as they may pray—and always dedicate our work to The Lord."

The youngest present sighed and said loudly, "I'm to do something new. I'm to do it without thinking twice about starting it and am to do it all my life! How can I commit to something I've never done or heard of—or studied?"

Laughter swept the room, some saying they live that way now. She didn't like it and said: "I'm surprised successful women like you can say you didn't know what you wanted to do—and it just happened. That is what you're all saying, isn't it?"

Jorge said, "Yes, because God does move in mysterious and weird ways when we take the wrong path. You never know until you look back at how easy life could have been if you had just believed and sought help and guidance, then followed it—and worked hard!"

A woman sitting behind Maddie spoke for the first time. "No, it's not like that! First, we all run after men to fulfill whatever goals our mothers set up for us to do, which usually ends in competing with our own kind. We never seem to learn, but today I received a message that we are all over that. Really! It says, *'You will be able to do what you want and do it along with many admirers.'* Admirers? That has to eliminate men. I'm not pretty enough for men to say I do a great job."

The model resented her statement, but could not speak, because her voice mysteriously disappeared. Instead Maddie entered the discussion and asked Jorge to read his fortune to them.

Without hesitation he read: "'*You will lead a country.*' That is all—very short. Perhaps they knew I would have to translate it into Spanish, then Mayan?" Jorge laughed, but did not reject the message.

No doubt surprised, Maddie said, "That is a pretty tall order, Jorge—being the leader of a country. We're meeting tonight to center our minds on how to bring about changes in this country. We've been urging everyone present to run for some kind of public office."

If Jorge was surprised, you could not tell from his facial expression or eyes. Smiling, he nodded and affirmed that he was in favor of women taking on the responsibility of running the country. That was why he was here—to help them.

That was not what the women wanted to hear. The mere idea of a man telling them what to do was enough to make three women stand and ask for their coats. Maddie interceded by reminding them that Jorge merely dropped in and was not sent to tell them what to do. She described him as a kind of ministering angel or guide. Her choice of words was truly amazing, but Maddie never let on to those carefully watching her that she was shocked, too.

"I think we can safely assume Jorge is here to help us get started right now—today. He has worked with other women who have done similar things, but they felt they had to leave this country to work with women more interested in social progress. Can we do the same thing here and now, or will we have to leave the US and work somewhere else, because we think this society is a lost cause?"

An older woman who previously said little stood and cleared her throat before loudly proclaiming: "I'm not here to start a war. I'm here to do work that will free men and women from fears of each other. I want to do something new—and I want to do it quickly, because I'm no longer young. What I want to do isn't the same as what others want to do, so I've always worked alone. I almost left you all twice today, but I realize now that something is working through us as a group. It's not the time for the moon to rise, yet it's shining around Madeline like a halo now. To me, that is a sign! I can abide by whatever is decided, but I have to catch a train. The last one leaves in half an hour, and I can't make it unless I run."

That was the signal Maddie knew would end the meeting quickly, so she escorted the woman to the door while assuring her she, too, would be at the nunnery next week. The others waited silently for something more to happen, but nothing did.

The last woman to leave expressed her delight at being able to talk at length about her pet project; however, it was now well after one o'clock in the morning. She knew no one else could possibly understand her position as well as the two women who listened attentively after asking her to talk until she was through. While waiting for others to identify the areas of life they wanted to work now, her work solidified. She never before had heard so many wonderful plans—and so many beautiful ideas! By comparison, hers was not easy to describe or execute, but suddenly she felt she could figure it out.

"You will do it! You have a lot to do, but you can do it once through with the planning. Any plan is easier to create if you don't think about all it will take to do it. Do you understand?"

She smiled at Jorge, radiating charm even as she pulled on her sweater and stepped away from him into the hallway where she whispered to Maddie, "Is he going to be at the next meeting?"

"I don't know. I never expected him to be at this one, so you never know. We'll wait and see." As she said this, Maddie gave the woman a bit of a hug before pushing her toward the elevator waiting at the end of the hall. Another miracle, it seemed, since elevators are never there when you need them.

☯Chapter Nine

"The work we do isn't new, but most of the women present never met before today." Maddie smiled as she spoke, thinking she had dropped a bomb on this mysterious man who just happened to walk into her life a few hours earlier, yet now seemed like one of her oldest friends. Maybe he was?

Jorge spoke softly, but with serious intent. "There is nothing new about what you do? I think you underestimate what this civilization has done to women, particularly in your country. I think you do not see what someone like me can see easily."

Before he could say another word, Maddie interrupted. "What do you see? What have you noticed? Can you give me some insights into what I'm doing here and now, and why I feel strange when asking others to help me do something new? For example, I started out to write a book that changed my life so much that I now want to leave New York and go to Mexico or Guatemala. I want out of this life now! Why? Why now? When did this idea take over—and when will it leave?"

Jorge pushed back further into the soft chair and said nothing for a minute or two before taking a deep breath and looking up at the ceiling. He then moved to change his seat so they both could look outward into time and space, just as Maddie moved her heavy chair toward him with little effort. For the first time in memory, the chair pivoted to face the window where the moon had appeared earlier. A cluster of stars seemed to beckon her from afar now. She just had to stare at them!

"I think we can now enter your work more deeply than you ever explored it before. I want to warn you that when we land back in these chairs, it may not be tomorrow—anywhere."

Since Jorge looked serious while making this absurd declaration, Maddie tried hard to believe him, but could not. Nevertheless, she decided to leap into time and follow this amazing Mayan man wherever he was going. She let go of this reality and her mind was immediately out of time.

Jorge looked out at the city skyline and relaxed more deeply into the chair as he said, "Let go of your intention to make sense of all this—in order to write about it later in life. Let it all go! Don't forget, you are going to find your present mind is not without a life of its own—and that life is not what you decided it should be. You fight with yourself to write what you like, but now time will not oblige you with neat little ideas every day about people and places you want to write about. You are going to leap into space and try to convince other women with words to use their minds like you are, so they can leap into time beside you."

Although Jorge appeared to be sleeping, Maddie felt she was intruding in his space. Feeling strange, she wanted to leave and let him sleep, but she could not stand, and her voice didn't reach her ears as she sensed the room disappear.

The sun shone brightly, its rays slanted from the west when they opened their eyes and looked at each other again. What happened to the night and day they left behind?

Smiling, Jorge said, "I think you have landed as well as anyone can after their first time in flight. How do you feel?"

He seemed different from the man who barged into the conference room announcing he had been invited and got sidetracked by another group. She could not see into his right eye, but his left eye emitted a glint of light far more brilliant than anything she had ever seen in a human being, but she was wise enough not to speak.

"Your life is changed. You are a different woman, and your friends will see you as a brilliant being now. You will not have to explain it, but at times you will not feel as good as you did. You will pick up static and need to learn how to keep at bay the evil ones who come forward when they think you are without any agenda."

This was shocking news to Maddie. She wanted to acknowledge that she did not need more change now. She thought it, but could not say it aloud, so she sent Jorge a message. *'Thank you very much, but I don't acknowledge that evil ones exist!'*

"You are wise to put your mind on a positive light wave and ignore that others can cause conflict and bitterness—neglecting the work they are here to do in order to possibly disrupt your life or put out *your* fire. You can now sense evil better than ever, which is why we had to leave this space and travel into time."

Jorge paused for a few seconds before continuing. "You are being used by some who want only money. You are not seen by them as the woman to change these times—and never will be seen that way, but you will work for them anyway. You will live to see women of today change and begin to accept each other as mentors and helpers, even teachers, who can tell them what they do not know or want to hear."

As Jorge chuckled at the idea, Maddie did not wish to interrupt, so she aimed a smile at his heart.

"You see, Madeline? You can telecommunicate with me without using a telephone or television, or whatever they dream up to prepare people for the time when all who want to learn will be able to transmit thoughts."

"Amazing! I thought you were kidding when you said we would go into time and awaken in another day. I wasn't sure what you would do when we traveled together. You scared me into following you throughout the entire process, and it is a process—is it not?"

Maddie could not talk further. Her thoughts were returning in what she imagined was their usual pattern, but they were not. She just did not know it yet. Her mind had been in time and was being given a lot to think about now. She was not yet back in this work and time, able to continue what she was doing with the women's group and wanted to do now, too.

"Take time to think about what you saw in that other time. Don't be afraid. You were in a dream state to protect you from losing connection to who you are here. You are back now, and your mind is unable to comprehend what happened and wants to say it never happened. You will find that you will want to let go of the entire work we did there, or you will start working much harder here to listen to your fears and erase them within three years."

"Three years? Why that long to erase fears I have of time traveling or whatever it was we were doing?"

Jorge said nothing.

"I think we will be able to talk about this in my other mind. Can you help me find it and get back into character? I would like to be able to continue to explore this earthly world more, and let go of it, too, but not before I know what is going to happen today."

Nodding, Jorge said, "You want to see if seeds you planted actually take root and grow. That is understandable, but it is not in the plan. You are not here to plow fields and help plant seeds, so others can weed them out. No, you are here to reach the next work they can achieve only if you open the door for them this year."

"Aaahhh, I see, a year, three years. What does a year mean to you?" Maddie was not smiling, but she nevertheless felt silly mentioning it.

"You are very wise, Madeline. You remind me of another of your tribe. She was also very upset to leave this time and place and was not interested in pursuing another line of life this time. She wanted to live in New York City! Imagine that? She was stubborn, as you are. She is now living with The Maya and the Mayan tribe that still exists outside Merida."

Nodding, as if wise and open to news about others, Maddie said, "I've heard of this woman you call Mandy. I'm not as aware of her as others who were here last night—or whenever that was, but I now have a sense she is going to become a mentor of mine. Is that right?

After a few minutes, or moments, or years, Jorge spoke with definitive wisdom. "You are not going to work with Mandy. You are going to work here in this world and stay as you are. You have come to the top of your career by way of diligence and hard work. You are a star. You do not have to work hard to stay on top for the next few years, but you are. You are going to do something she is unwilling to do. You are going to remain here and do whatever comes to you to do, then move into a different part of Earth and live with others who do not always want to live as you think they should. More on that later."

Wondering about his lack of accent when talking, Maddie was now aware he could channel someone of great wisdom—or he was a great man himself. She said nothing as they sat quietly and waited for the sun to set.

The phone awakened Madeline from her slumber. She was not sure who was on the phone when she answered it. Her mind was not functioning properly, but she felt okay and thought she was fine, until she realized she was sitting in the same chair as last night and Jorge was gone. There was no way she could have been staring out the window behind her and have rearranged her chair twice. She knew that for sure!

"Hello! Madeline? Are you there? We're having the meeting and wondering where you are. You were supposed to be here by now."

What meeting? Who is calling? She could not believe a week had gone by since she had talked to the women about getting together again. What would they talk about? If only she could remember…

"Madeline? Are you ill? Do you need help? Where are you? Is this your cell phone or your landline? Are you at home or on the road? Let us know if you're on your way."

The phone clicked before she realized she had not answered the phone and it had gone to her answering machine. What could she do about the meeting now? They were already there, and she didn't even know what day it was.

Without another thought, Maddie rose from the chair and ran toward the bathroom to empty her bladder and take a shower. No time to waste! She did what she always did after waking from a deep sleep and was ready within a few minutes, even packing her bag. No need to call a taxi. She would drive.

"I'm sorry not to have been the first to arrive, but you know the traffic coming out of The City." Maddie said nothing further, and everyone let it go. Why? She would never know, but some were surprised she had to explain, since she had called several times enroute to say she was encountering problems and not to worry if she was late.

"I think we can wait another day to discuss all we are here to do. You look strained by all the work you did on the plane. Take off your sweater and rest on the couch." As the nun addressed Maddie, the others nodded and then took off.

Maddie felt fine, but was stunned that she had been on a plane—and how did the nun know she hadn't been at home?

"I think those who work hard on their own work, then go out and work for others are saints. I was once given a prayer card with no one pictured on it. It was said to be an unknown saint who was doing great work in the world. When you turned it to the other side there was a mirror that reflected your image back to you. I still have it. It reminds me to keep trying and to work hard. You, Madeline, are an acknowledged saint, and I want everyone to know it!"

Maddie could not speak. She smiled and opened her mouth, but nothing came out. Since she remained silent and the others were no longer hanging about, the nun continued. "I'm not Catholic. I never was, but when you came to call and looked at all we had done, you assumed we were Roman Catholic nuns—and we let you believe that. Why? We didn't want our cover blown until we were sure we were doing what was right with God. We aren't like others. We know that, and are frightened by it, but you aren't. You talk as if everyone is as courageous as you are. You talk as if we can do whatever we want with this farm—and I now believe we will. That is why you are our patron saint—whether you like it or not!"

Totally embarrassed, and unable to stand it any longer, Maddie tried to explain why she was there, but no words came out. Nevertheless, the nun was happy with what she thought.

"The way to congratulate women today is not to praise them to their face. How we talk now is so out of touch with sympathy, empathy, and humility that we seem to hang crepe instead of express faith in those who are great. We really need to elevate our minds and keep them centered on the prize."

Someone murmured loud enough for Maddie to hear, "What prize?" She realized no one had spoken, but she was getting inaudible help from the audience. Were questions not allowed? They now asked questions through a cloud of energy surrounding them all.

"I think we sense what the prize represents, but for some it's not that easy. Why? We want everything defined and hashed over several times, with lots of laughter—or none permitted, depending on the subject. And we're supposed to be able to tell everyone all about it then. That is why no one wants to talk about what they seek now."

The crowd in the room remained silent. They were neither upset nor despondent, but did not seem to grasp what was going on, nor why they did not want to leave, even though they were not being entertained as they had thought would happen.

"You are here seeking something you think is going to make you feel better, which is all about ego—really. You need protection from those who are also ego-bound and trying to stop you from moving in and taking over their town.

"That is why we are here today. Are you able to communicate and open gates by yourself? Are you able to talk to Today's important decision makers and encourage them to shed light on what they're trying to do? Do you know what to say if asked to talk about your platform?"

That stopped one woman in the back of the room from leaving too soon. She stopped and looked at Maddie, then smiled as if unable to know why she was suddenly happy. Her mind returned to the class, instead of acting superior to everyone there. In an instant her life was transformed and only Maddie and two others were even aware she was there.

"Yes, we can see some are unable to decide what to do—even why they are here, but once we are done working and getting our work out to the public, they will wish to explain how to do it, and why we are here now. Please resist doing that. We want this to be *our time*. Our time to be friends and help others exist and move on, so we can see tomorrow from our plane and planet somewhere else. We don't want to blast off without keeping some people working hard teaching future generations how to exist— and possibly one day ascending. That is why we are here again—as friends."

No one said a word. Some were puzzled, others wanted to smile, but no one attempted to leave.

"You know me. I've been writing and selling my work to *The New York Times, The Baltimore Sun,* the LA papers, and so on, and won prizes for investigative reporting once or twice, even the Pulitzer Prize, and you know I don't fall for gags and frauds, yet some are worried that I ended my career and am crazy to be here. It isn't true!

"I will begin now with a prayer you all know, then you can leave. But remember, you are not who is here, I am, and I'm going to prepare a place for some of you to work alone, as well as a place for others to set up a kind of group home to help others who can't continue to live as they do now."

Maddie's practical agenda caught the attention of two who were about to give up trying to figure out what she was talking about. They smiled at her and let the rest of the group disappear as they walked out into time. The mood of the group did not move or change, but only a few remained when the meeting was over.

"How can you talk so well without any sleep? You must be exhausted! Flying all over the world in a time when the airports are ready to explode and everyone searches your bags— "

With an enigmatic smile, Maddie said, "No one bothered me. I walked in and out of planes as I always have. I'm not a problem. I was, but I'm no longer a problem to anyone on a plane." What a weird thing to say. Weird enough that she stopped talking and noticed no one was listening. Everyone appeared to be in a state of suspended animation. She alone was walking, talking, and moving in this time zone. "I guess it's easy to do, or I would never have been able to do this."

"What did you say, Madeline?"

The nun was smiling as she motioned toward a door that suddenly appeared out of nowhere—as far as Maddie could see. She walked toward the exit then and did not look back. The nun did not move. She, too, seemed stunned and unable to figure out what to do now.

☯Chapter Ten

"The work we have to do together is easy! In fact, we have to watch that we don't do it fast enough or well enough, just because we think it is easy to achieve. What we each do alone will be easy, but we're not meeting again, thus you must achieve this work alone. You will decide what you will do with your life, and that is not easy, either. Some will want to give up—but those who do not will win! Even those who give up will have learned a few things—mostly about themselves." Looking around the room at everyone busy at work, Maddie smiled and sat down.

"Thank you, Madeline! We really don't have enough room here to work in groups—then gather to talk things over as a large business would, but we have computers and can meet daily by phone, as well as many evenings when we're alone." The Mother Superior stood at ease, looking at each woman as if she was their new best friend, as she said, "How do you want to set things up?" Everyone watched, but no one spoke.

"I would like to take a few moments to cover what we talked about last night over work we were doing on the new home. I want to fill everyone in and see what you all think we need to do next. When it should be done, and so on. Can you all lend me your ears for at least sixty minutes more?"

There was no moaning, but plenty of sighs, which the nun did not like. She made a face to indicate she expected better. Only when everyone set aside their pencils and paper to look at her did she speak.

"I think one thing, and some of you don't agree, but when it comes time to do something, we need to be together on what we will do, as well as who does what and when. Do you all get that now?"

Everyone nodded, some jotted down notes, only then did she continue. "I think we can move on without any problems now. We have met as a group and joined together with several members leaving because they were not into political action and building things that last, but they will be back. I know that for sure!"

Murmurs arose, but none loud enough to pinpoint where they were coming from. "I think it amazing that we merely gathered together once and in one day we made so much progress that all here are ready to go to work and do it on your own immediately—no waiting! That is truly amazing, but what is more amazing is that we will also be guided daily in what we will do as a group.

"Guidance will come to us as a group—sometimes one of us will get a vision and others will be able to work with it as if their own, then it will all change and someone else will move the work ahead for a day or so. We will all be able to say we led the group and contributed something— and participated continually. That is why we're going to make a huge difference in the way the world today is rearranged. Do you all agree?"

A resounding 'Yes', came from everyone in the room, even from down the hall where a computer was tracking the group in order to make copies of the meeting for participants to review after they departed and went back to their private lives. It was going to be a long night, but everyone was excited!

After hours of working on the agenda each group would follow, including what individuals within each group would do, they stopped as if all were watching a clock. Yes, they had argued a lot, but never got into heated battle. Lines were crossed and mended before anyone got tossed out of a work group.

After a few attempts to end the session, one of the men who had been willing to help said, "I think you women are truly the most amazing bunch of people I have ever met! Never, ever, have I witnessed a group move mountains of work and do so much in an hour or even ten hours. You've organized a huge enterprise, elected officers, decided what you can spend, and the agenda is already set for the next meeting!

"How did you do that? Men love to talk about whatever until they find common ground based on what they admire in each other and may want to do in a week or ten weeks. You all moved so quickly that I'm unable to comprehend what it is you *really* intend to do. Are you planning on moving me out of office?" He smiled, but no one corrected him, so he sat down, as if stunned.

"Thank you, Senator, the Commonwealth of Pennsylvania isn't going to be run by women and men who are not empowered to make big changes. We want men who know how to govern to continue as you do, but we are going to work hard to elect more women in order to introduce a lot more social reform than this state has seen since its inception. Not since Ben Franklin and his clan met here has there been anything like what we intend to do now—together. We're not meeting in Philadelphia, because it's effete and powerless to defeat poverty and crime. All it allows now is done in the name of greed and ill-gotten gains. However, we can change areas that remain the best agri-producers in the country—growing crops and holding folks together while steadfastly working for God."

The senator appeared to be growing angry, so a woman at the back of the room stood up and said with a smile directed at him, "I think you're surprised that a group of women—and a few men, could change a state, but that is exactly what you said on every stage you stumped for votes last campaign. Don't tell me it was simply rhetoric and you never really believed anyone would want to change the state—and that there are ways we can clean it up together now?" She smiled at him more than before, but he did not return her good will.

Women and men located elsewhere noticed the electricity dip just then, thus some of their conversation was not picked up. Since they could not see what was going on between the Senator and the woman happily talking with him, they wondered aloud: "Maybe the senator intends to help us?" Everyone laughed at that until it carried down the hall to where two mental combatants sat without talking. It was enough to make everyone else smile and say it was time to break for lunch—which it was.

'*There is a lot of work to do*' became the mantra that afternoon, so the men left. Once they were out of earshot, some women started to make fun of them, but it was stopped before it could become a habit. It is not good to do that! It is not fruitful, and just what men of such kind would like to prove we do.

The women respected the work done so far by these men, but decided farmers were gaining too much power over the tax collector and getting way too much money in welfare payments—which is how they all described crop subsidies. Unproductive farmers were making more money than all the welfare mothers in the state's three largest cities! How could they claim they were conservative? How could they claim taxes were too high? They did not pay taxes to any large extent, yet collected huge sums yearly for playing around with their farms. This had to stop! The farmer who lived and worked on his farm daily would be given his fair share of responsibility, and taxes would be used to help get his goods to market, but not to raise hogs, chickens, hay, and corn for his own consumption. That was a waste of taxes and not going to be allowed to continue.

The men did not hear the agenda, because they were unable to accept what had to be done to pay for the work these women wanted to start. They went away thinking it was merely a utopian ideal that would fail, and all would be out of business by next year. They decided it made no sense to say so, and best to *'let the ladies go'* for now.

When that afternoon ended, work for some present reached the point where they could go home and do it alone, yet no one wanted to leave just yet. They wanted to stick around and talk—a lot. This was not condoned, because some wanted to take political action immediately that would not help them all. Each woman had to keep her mouth shut, which was the most difficult work assigned that day. So many ideas popping up, their minds wide open, and time was standing still. They all were expected to maintain silence from six to seven o'clock every day thereafter, the same as the nuns on the farm, and it worked. The imposed silence cleared their heads—collectively and individually.

The nuns who were not party to the group's work prepared a meal stunning in its simplicity—and fun to eat. Everyone had corn on the cob with butter so thick and creamy that some asked what it was. The dining hall was filled with the aroma of roast beef and a bit of sweets no one could quite identify when served later with their coffee and tea. It wasn't a trifle, but contained cream and fruit mixed with pound cake to perfection. No one left hungry, and all claimed they would not be able to eat for a week.

The next morning a large group of nuns gathered in the auditorium to see what had been accomplished the previous day. They were from a convent on a neighboring farm—part of a religious order established in a previous century—not at all like this one. Their Mother Superior said she was pleased to be invited, but their breakfast was such that her nuns would want to live there instead of in their convent. Everyone laughed, but one.

"I see you have noticed how easy it is to completely renovate a farm…." Said Mother Superior Mary Michael, who was hosting the breakfast. She waited for applause, but none came, and no one smiled. She suddenly remembered that women generally thought others would recognize their sacrifices, so they did not crow about them and taught their daughters to never seek notice, as well. That had to change!

"First, I want to say I dreamed about today for at least ten years. It became crystal clear to me as I sat in board rooms with many men. Every one of them thinking about making money with chemicals that might possibly save a few lives, but more importantly—a lot of money for our guys. Everything was easy for them, but not easy for women to arrive at that stage in life. It took a lot of work in college to gain enough chemical knowledge—then it became easy. All we did then was figure out what to spend and when to spend it, so it would not be taxed.

Today those men are no longer in charge. They were given golden parachutes or handcuffs, you be the judge, and pushed aside with nothing to do too early in life. So, I think we can tap into these men for help, whenever we like. Let's begin by making a list of contacts and people who will benefit from our work. Is that too much to expect as the first task of the second day of our Congress meeting here for the first time?" Mother Mary Michael talked quickly, without any idea of what they might say, so when greeted by silence, she backed away.

When Maddie noticed no one moved to start work, she added that it was their most important task of the day, thus establishing the tone. They could relax by sitting back and letting names and thoughts pop up all day as they played games and worked on their interpersonal skills. Everyone smiled then, because it was not hard to make lists, let alone enlist people who would help the group, if you didn't think too much about who they might be now.

The group continued to work at the breakfast table while others cleaned up the dishes and put away all that remained from one meal to the next. It would become the accepted routine whenever they worked together: After eating, they continued to sit together and work non-stop as the table was cleared.

"This has been a day of greatness! We intended to stop and play—and do something to help meet others and get to know this work better, but instead we followed the will of God and got down to business right away—doing the hardest work first, and all was done in just a few hours. I think we deserve a lot of credit."

Having said this, Maddie sat and only then noticed no one else saw it as being time to end the day. So, she waited as they continued writing and talking quietly, ignoring her hint that it was time to close that door and do something new. This pleased her very much.

"Today was slated on our agenda to be a day of work and play—and we did a lot of work. We didn't stop much, and didn't even eat at the usual time, because no one was hungry then. So now it's time to go into our silence and watch how our work declines or grows within our minds. We will meet again in an hour, so you can tell me what you think then."

The clock was in another room so as not to distract the nuns when they prayed or meditated, but strangely enough it was as if all the nuns began and ended their prayers and meditations every day on the same stroke of the hour. Thus no one said a word now, but some of the new workers in this world of spirit could not sense time as well. They either waited for others to talk or remained deep within their dreams.

A chiming bell rang softly to awaken those unable to feel the presence of others waiting for them to awaken. When those few came to and looked around, they announced they were totally refreshed. Those who did not relax were tense, but not hungry, while those who relaxed were eager to eat and do something unique. A clear demonstration for all to experience relative to the power of an hour spent alone with God at the end of the day—even longer on Sundays.

When the day was over, all food was much appreciated. Everyone prayed their work would not end tomorrow without knowing what to do and where they would go next. It is not easy to start a project no one conceived or believed in before then—and done with friends known only a week or two.

The biggest obstacle for the modernists among them was having to trust and believe in others. The rest could easily slip into modesty and humility without any problems, but new age women did not believe such behavior was needed, and as a result were not as well-liked.

Turning toward the Mother Superior, in order to look at her closely, Maddie said, "How do you get women to work with you?"

"I just do the work, then wait for them to ask me what needs to be done…"

Another nun stepped in and said, "Mother Mary Michael is too modest to talk about all she does to inspire us every day. She's a born leader! She always figures out what to do when things go wrong, so we all learned to follow her and not worry a lot. It usually takes a long time to respect others that much, but I was raised on a farm—and my father was just like her. He knew what to do, and just did it. He never talked a lot, either."

A woman sitting behind her said, "I need to be told what is expected of me, and when it's due in order to do a good job. I don't like working on things that aren't organized—and hate to work for people who are stupid."

Before she could go further, two others joined in and said in unison, "No, that isn't right!"

Before they could fight or argue into the night, other nuns hushed them with sounds of love. It was not hard to do since everyone present now loved each other. From now on their work would center on how to transfer this love to the outside world and toward men who had misused their power or previously abused them.

❧Chapter Eleven

The crowd was gone and only Mother Mary Michael and Madeline Worthington continued to sit and talk about what needed to be done. They were drinking tea and celebrating the harmony and intensity they had observed in the group of women and men about to celebrate the birth of a nation once lost and now about to be put back on the map.

The two women spoke softly, smiled a lot, and then went outside to look at the flowers growing by the side of the road. Would this simple display be enough to entice crowds to come to this part of the globe to see what they were doing here? Their talk began and ended with plans—many of them. Would any come to be, or would it be a mere flight of fancy?

"I think we're going to accomplish more than we now think we can, but I'm not sure who will actually work and who is all talk. Do you have any way of knowing who is telling the truth and who isn't?" Maddie did not notice the nun blushing.

"What you want is a certainty, which can't be. We can't know what others will do, even if we watch them do it over-and-over again, because each of us changes constantly—especially our minds. I think the women here will do the work, if in charge and held responsible for it, but I also think that if they can get out of doing some things, they will. It's human nature."

Maddie grimaced and spoke more slowly. "I think we have a lot of people trying to find a way to make a lot of money, and I wonder why that is. Why has it been like that for such a long time? Why would they want to pursue spiritual work only to produce income? Isn't it enough to know God will provide all our needs—and most likely keep us happy? Why are so many now demanding compensation far exceeding what they are willing to do in the world or earn on their own?"

Mother Superior shook her head and said, "The United States is a capitalistic nation, so why try to make it otherwise? People want it to grow, exceeding what it has learned, like so many Asian countries. They want to let everyone choose better leaders, yet don't want whomever is elected. Why? Such people want advice but won't listen to it twice.

"You are too American, Madeline, to ever want to be a democratically-elected official. You won't feel comfortable telling others what to do. You would do a great job if asked, but really don't want to do it." By this time the nun was laughing, because Maddie looked stunned.

"What do you mean? I want the US to be as great as it can be. But honestly, I'm not the one to straighten it out. How can I do what needs done and still be able to report on it?"

Staring into space, Mother Mary Michael mumbled something under her breath that Maddie could not make out, so she said nothing as they walked toward the front door. Suddenly Jorge appeared and asked if they were through with their chat—then he laughed.

"I'm amazed to see you, Jorge! You weren't at the conference—and many asked about you and why you weren't here. We wanted you to tell us what to do, and you knew that, yet never called or came to see us. Why?"

"Well, Madeline, I was in Mexico doing what I do best—eating, meditating, and having a bit of rest from all these tests. I was going out of my mind and out-of-time when I arrived here, met you, and talked about this adventure. I did not get any message, so I decided to slip out and go back to Mexico. I stayed with Mandy and her women at the ancient site of many decision-making conferences in the past. We decided we would help you all now. We are going to build a convent kind of thing right here in Pennsylvania. What do you think?"

Mother Mary Michael smiled, then laughed, but Maddie appeared stunned by the news. Jorge pointed to a man standing by the gate. She noticed he was not the same man who pruned the wisteria last week, but possibly his twin. Who was he—really?

"Angels come in various shapes and sizes, Madeline. You have ten working on your business plan—all unaware that one of them is an angel and the other nine are his friends for life. Ever wonder about such things?"

Maddie smiled, and the nun looked stunned.

"You need help. Right? You asked for someone to come and help you get the farm into productive operation—and men arrived. Right?"

Mother Mary Michael nodded, remaining mute.

"You go to the top of the world, then work your way down. Right? If you start at the bottom, you never get anything across to others."

Maddie looked at him more closely and was surprised she could see the wisdom of what he said more easily now. She was ready to listen to Jorge, but the nun was not.

"I will talk at length about how we work and what we do on Earth, but you must not let your faith get in the way of God. You do know that happens. Right?" Jorge smiled, then chuckled as Mother Mary Michael straightened her back and marched across the yard to greet the new gardener.

When the stooped figure looked up, she said, "How are you? I have wanted to thank you for all the work you've done on the yard, and how well the orchard is doing now. You have a green thumb, and it's obviously going to be a wonderful year for us as a result. We are going to have more crops than ever before and more products to sell to the world. Thank you so much for lending us your touch."

The gardener smiled, but said nothing. He seemed a bit tired, not much aware of what she said, so Jorge nodded and translated into Spanish the nun's compliments. Now beaming, he said he was honored to be there. He was not able to say much, because he knew little English, nevertheless he said he loved the nuns. They were all so beautiful, and on and on, until Jorge stopped him. He was *not* a man of few words.

"I think our man can take care of your garden and all you want to do around here, but he thinks he should do more, then leave the door open for a younger man to come in and help you. It would be his honor to establish the orchard and move the yard back further—over there, rather than where you planned to put it, but it is always up to you."

"He really did say a lot! I thought he just said thank you and added a few charming remarks." Mother Mary Michael looked at Jorge, winking at his additions to the conversation.

"Aha! You do know Spanish, but you wanted to be told by me that you are surrounded by angels. I think it is you who needs watching!" Jorge laughed, then added, "You are not a nun. I am aware of that—and if you continue to act like a wonderful, caring, loving woman, you may be thrown out of the convent."

The nun didn't like that and said so. After correcting him, she left them to stare at her back. Maddie did not speak, and Jorge could not talk.

Once the three settled down in the refectory, they talked over tea and scones until the slightly frosty atmosphere cleared. Jorge was never going to jest about religion and the Catholic faith again. He was chastised, but wise enough to know he had to take sides. There was no way he could walk the middle path and last with this woman of the cloth. He suggested they talk business now, and it was accepted immediately by both women.

Jorge's work that day accomplished more than all the work done on the administration of justice proposed by folks who had worked together for days before they left, and he arrived. His work in Mexico went unnoticed, but he intended to make the convent the seat of much justice and hope for the people of this community. Best of all, he knew what to do.

Maddie jotted down notes and started working on her Palm Pilot as though she had never dropped it the other day and forgotten about it. Suddenly she noticed her words did not appear exactly as she thought them. They were more organized, terse, and full of energy than anything she had written in years. She was amazed.

"Look at this! I was writing a note to myself about this meeting, but when I read it over, I saw it was much better than what I thought as I typed. What a wonderful thing is this little computer! I think it could write history and make everyone sound bright—and interesting."

Jorge laughed, but suddenly realized others did not know what to say whenever she talked like this. They were unaware Maddie was now a Spiritual Scribe. He was not sure how to tactfully tell nuns something they must know, should know, and had most likely talked about for years and years, but he tried. "I think you now have the gift, Madeline!"

Maddie looked surprised and asked, "What gift? Yes, I can write, and I learned to use a computer years back, but this little gadget produced a masterpiece out of a few fragments of my imagination. It's not really me."

Mother Mary Michael suddenly stood and ran to the door, bolting it so no one could enter. She motioned for Jorge to continue speaking and not stop until everything was explained—very quietly.

Dropping his voice, Jorge said, "The ability to write and live the life of a Spiritual Scribe is a gift, Madeline. It is not something you just decide to do—and it doesn't require a computer. If you can go inside your mind and sit for a minute—then ten minutes, maybe an hour, you can *Write in Spirit*, but that kind of writing is half what you are and have been doing, and half is the gift you are given by those more powerful and wonderful than any you have ever been allowed to know so far. Neither of you has been given knowledge of the powerful ones running this country. Right?"

Both women nodded emphatically, and the nun mumbled they usually did not delve into conspiracies, but something was really wrong, and no one allowed to talk about it. Maddie agreed with her.

"You see? Usually you do not even know what is going on above you in your own world, so how can you know about the real world and what is happening to everyone and everything now? You are unable to comprehend it, because you cannot meditate deeply enough. They do not wish you to go within now and discover God is alive. If you did that, you would not need much in the way of a tribe or leaders who hide their greed.

"You would simply live as is and have a big family—take care of all your own needs and not be upset by whomever is in power out there. That is how it was, but now you and I and others can know there is a power within that is going to provide us with gifts and extrasensory perceptions that will change nations—change the world. We are going to be able to scribe, work intensely in our minds, and skip over time—and we can do it now!"

Smiling, Maddie stared at her handheld computer. She was not sure if what Jorge said was right or wrong but was aware she had not really written the beautiful prose staring back at her. She was not happy or sad, but aware this could be the greatest tool God ever gave man. She was also aware she had to decide what to do with it, and would she be able to use it for her own needs, too?

Glancing at Maddie, Jorge motioned for her to read the text. She laughed, but said, "I'm not sure what I intended to write, but this is so great that I'm going to keep it and submit it without telling my editor I didn't actually write it. See if he notices anything or likes what I write this way better than my usual style."

Mother Mary Michael took off her glasses, settled back, and folded her hands over her waist as if deep in prayer. Jorge did the same, as Maddie read to them.

"I am the means and the way to work today. I am the computer, and I am able to work for you, but you better be able to use all I give you this way."

Reverting to her usual tone, Maddie added, "I think it's talking about giving me all this work so easily. I won't be able to keep up with it—and where will I publish it, and how? Anyway, it's a bit long, so I'll read nonstop, and you can discuss it later." Suddenly aware they were not awake, but in trance or somewhere else, she read the text aloud.

"I am the work of your mind magnified many times. I add the grace of God to it, and it becomes a process that is prophetic and wise. You cannot imagine what you cannot comprehend. You cannot comprehend what you cannot see. You cannot look at anything until it is described, and you are accustomed to seeing it.

"You have to work hard to design a machine that will take away pain or sorrow, but it is not going to happen until you all decide you cannot provide it yourself. You each want cars, houses that have no work for others, and to be able to sit and moan. You do not say so, but you do not want to do any more work. The country is spiraling into debt faster than it can possibly make enough cash. What will happen next?"

Glancing at her friends, Maddie stopped reading. She was unable to speak, because the nun was no longer in her seat. She was levitating and appeared able to spin in space. Jorge was slumped over, not saying anything. He looked to be in a daze. What had happened to them?

Barely able to continue reading, Maddie managed to say: *"Laziness is not the best way to see God. All primitive peoples place work right up there beside their worship of God. Why do you think of them as primitive? Because they truly worship, and you can see how well they live without all the modern-day conveniences you are sure need to be in order for you to succeed. You will never be able to build muscle working-out that outlasts what is produced from working in the fields. That is why you are effete and unable to compete in fields of endeavor that require physical work.*

"The fields lay empty in the United States. Why? They are no longer able to produce anything, because it has been seeded with houses that will not last a century, then it is time for the country to reseed the fields,"

Maddie continued reading and elevating the prose as words flowed, but she was no longer able to hear what she said....

☯Chapter Twelve

Addressing the cat, Maddie said, "Somewhere around here there is a list of people I want to contact. Anyone know where I put it last?" She looked around and the list appeared as if by magic exactly where she just searched. "How do you do that?" Maddie looked at the cat who winked and yawned before pretending to go back to sleep. No one gets ahead of a cat!

As the day wore on, Maddie felt her nerves unravel and her neck loosen—the opposite of what usually happened after writing long hours. What made this work so much more powerful and positive compared to what she normally wrote? She wanted to write so others could use it, too, but what happened then never entered her mind— until now. She immediately sat at her computer once again and wrote feverishly:

You must breathe more deeply than you normally do when writing. You have to enter the room of your other mind and release your imagination, then never use it again as long as you are inside that space.

The imagination is not helpful when it comes to spiritual work. In fact, it can damage your relationship to God. It can build up such a framework of immaterial garbage that you never know what you are doing, who you are becoming, or what is the right way to live today, thus you can fail at whatever you want to do or say.

The right mind is not what creates your most dramatic pieces. Neither is it the left, rather the ether that exists between the two spheres and reached only after years of practice. You must be balanced and even, not partial to one side or the other, to meditate to a level in your mind where it stops telling you what it finds and lets you use what you want.

The great libraries of the world are nothing compared to what you have within you and link to when you can walk in time. What would you do with all this power if you were given it to use every day? Would you use it to better mankind or do something different? What would you say to your mind if it decided to lust after others and be like them, instead of letting you run and do your work of this time as you are supposed to do it?

You do not want to hear that there are things out there you are required to do. Discipline is not something you want at this time. The spine might be stronger and better aligned if you were more disciplined in mind and body, but you think about it so much that you will decide to alibi out of doing it now.

The mind is a wonder. It can make a case for any outrageous thing you can pretend to think up, then turn against you and blame you for things you had no part in doing or creating today.

Let your hands rest now....

As you sense there is nothing to be said, what do you do next? You placed your hands on the keys and gibberish was erased and powerful words came onto this page. How?

What made you smile? What gave you so much power that you wanted to shout?

Now understand that if you win a Pulitzer again, you will not be able to say it was because you used your mind and hands to create it. You will have to acknowledge you have done it with the help of someone else. Why not do that now?

Maddie sat still, poised to write a few minutes before finally relaxing, because her mind refused to accept she had written something without using it. It was amazing, but how did it happen? What did it say about her ability to write? Is this writing automatic and anyone can do it? What does it say about her present work and the inventory of stories written over her career? Was she stupid then or out of her mind now?

"What a day to be alive," Maddie said as she looked out at the New York skyline and saw a hawk. Enjoying its flight, it was unable to sense being spied upon by others all the time. Doing its thing, while people below walked or stood looking up at it, the hawk felt nothing. It was doing what it came to be—a hawk, a predator that preyed upon the weak and ate anything smaller than it. Maybe that is why hawks appeal to so many now?

As the sun rose, Maddie left home to take part in a love parade. It was not called a love-in or anything like that, because everyone knew that never worked in the 60s when it was used as an excuse to get sick on drugs. Now they proclaimed it was love that made people with no interest in what others wanted feel the need to protest. So many causes today, so many people afraid, so many up in arms about nothing at all, but Maddie loved them all and tried to carry a banner for whichever cause they espoused. In addition, it was a great way to gain interesting interviews with people she thought were going places.

As the parade or protest assembled and fell into place, a mounted policeman approached Maddie and bowed. He looked regal, with a manner suggesting a knight of olden times. In fact, she saw by the glint of his helmet that he was not a policeman at all. He was someone allowed to pose as one and infiltrate the crowds without being stopped. He kept his horse in the Central Park stables or a garage. It looked like it wanted to run the range. Imagine that: A wild horse in a crowd! Not a thought she wanted to contemplate, but his presence did make her smile.

As the day passed, the crowd multiplied, and women began to cry. How humiliating to be associated with so many who felt powerless, yet you knew they had it all. In fact, that would be her banner for this edition of the paper.

She would make this piece stand out from all other protests and any other article about people who caused similar commotions. She would point out that you need to watch when others say they are unhappy and want change—yet never be afraid, since such protests are guaranteed to make each person feel less afraid and more willing to do little.

While examining what she had written, Maddie noticed a strain in her back and thought it was her thoughts that made her suddenly feel tense and nervous. What about speaking truth to power interfered with being able to relax and laugh? That is what she thought, but instead she pulled out her old typewriter from the closet and wrote:

The parade was not something anyone wanted to write about, so press was not present. I joined the crowd in support of the work they were doing for children and left afraid for the work not done while we walked, yelled, and generally had a lot of fun. What made us so sure no one else is supportive of what we want?

Because when you really do not do much, it is best to think of yourself as being oppressed. That is why we support such parades and protests now. Is it not?

Maddie looked up at the ceiling and thought she saw the man on the horse smiling down at her. She gave the page a tug and placed it in the basket, letting her fingers run over the keyboard once again. This time she put all thought out of her mind and relaxed, barely noticing her hands as they typed rapidly.

The majesty of a parade is such that many who are unwilling to confront their own feelings privately will speak up and even protest loudly in a public way that day. It is a time when you can understand the fear that comes over people who are unable to speak to others or fear each other. They come together and see that each one has the same thoughts, which is liberating. It frees them to be themselves—if only for a short time.

How many New Yorkers march in such lines? Not many! Most participate because it gives them a sense of community and humanity. They can feel they are part of a bigger work of art and liked for what they think. They can feel the power of uniting with others!

Where is the power when the parade passes you by? What exists in the work of the wave of energy that seemingly increases, then fades as people leave? What is the nature of pageantry that produces so much energy for youth, as well as love and interest in others, but is never actually used much later?

As the letters faded, Maddie's mind became clearer than ever before. She could see many things. She felt like she existed as another woman in another time somewhere else, but not sure why. The day was not as young as when she stopped for lunch, but she had not used even half the calories from that meal and needed to exercise her body as well as her mind. She felt she had been touched by someone and was loved, but who, and where did it go when it left her there?

Day was not over when Maddie disappeared into her room for another night of watching life outside and reading about people she would never meet. She felt as if this was the end of a long siege, and she would be able to go out and about and work—no longer stuck at her desk typing. She could now work and type without thought, and it was better than whatever she once wrote.

Thinking back, she realized it all came to be when she went to the nunnery to see if anyone there knew a woman of distinction who might want to run this country or a county somewhere. That day produced a sense of entitlement to work produced in many other lives—not just this one, in this time. She never felt as weird as when she sat in the garden under the arbor and wrote words in her palm-held computer she had never before thought about.

Her mind back at the arbor, she realized she had never transferred that material to her office computer's hard drive. Retrieving the Palm Pilot, she worked for half an hour getting it in line with her office computer so she could send it to clouds and store it forever, as she liked to say. That work took only a second to move from one life to another, which she thought might be like what happens when you die. Maybe you have to take time to align one computer with another, then any file can be instantaneously transferred from one to the other.

Fearing that what she had written in that sphere would not survive or be used in this life consumed her mind for a time. She sensed panic was never a friend, rather a fire that enflamed your desires, in order to help you focus on what you wanted to do, had to accomplish, and so on down the line. Fearing her words from this moment onward would be forever lost was enough incentive to open the file and read it for the first time.

You will join an order of women from all over the world who work on what needs to be done to segregate the good from the bad, in order to make what is needed last. You will laugh. You will not get angry or go mad.

You will always want to be strong. You are not able to write with dignity every day of your life, but you can gain peace of mind. You are free to be and to conquer worry that consumes you now.

The work is coming and going. You will write without thought. Your life is now able to explore You more.

This is your life, and you never provided it. You are who will need to be happy more. You need that energy.

The work you do is going to produce an audience, but Spirit provides you with the minds of those who are also able to work as you do. You will reach many and then teach all able to scribe. Your work is divine.

Maddie relaxed as she smiled and closed the file.

❂Chapter Thirteen

"Thank you! I'm all caught up! My work is no longer piled so high I can't think straight. Be glad that all you have to do for me is done." Maddie spoke with a straight face, but her eyes shone, and a smile pried her lips apart ever so slightly.

"Well, thank you. I wanted to be sure you got your shipment and all that was coming to you. I didn't know for sure if it was to be mailed or left for you to pick up, so thanks for driving this far to pick it up. We really were wondering about how best to ship it." The old nun's smile crinkled her cheeks from ear-to-ear, revealing beautiful teeth that no one had wired, straightened, or pulled to make them align.

"Therese, you have the most beautiful smile, and I can see it whenever your name comes up. Isn't that strange? I wonder why I see your smile, as if imprinted on my brain."

"Well, Madeline, it might be. I was a model for toothpaste in the 60s. Chosen over many others with prettier faces, because I had my own teeth and they didn't have to be airbrushed or anything weird to make them look better. I guess I owe everything I have today to that particular set of genes."

Maddie suddenly realized this woman was not the nun she thought she talked to when she entered the convent a few moments ago. This nun looked much younger. Who had she talked to then?

Realizing Maddie could not figure out what was going on, Therese laughed, then said, "I guess I did another morph. I change so much that people don't know who I am—and I'm not aware of it, because I remain the same inside my head."

Puzzled, but not wanting to ask questions about something never seen before, and would never have been believed in the past, Maddie picked up the large box and started to carry it out to her car before asking, "What do you mean, morphed? I thought that was a sci-fi term for shape-shifting or something. Is it really a fact? Does it actually happen, or is it a trick of the light?" Therese laughed merrily and did not stop giggling even when Mother Mary Michael opened the gate to peer at them.

Speaking a bit sharper than she otherwise might have spoken to a guest, Mother Mary Michael said, "What's going on out there? Who is raiding our house?" She tried to make light of it but was not sure who was removing boxes and why Therese was laughing so loudly.

"Oh, Mother, it's just us—Madeline and me! She drove all the way from New York just to pick up the preserves, and we're loading them in her car. Do you want her to stop by and talk to you when we're done?"

Mother Mary Michael was shocked to discover it was Sister Therese talking, even though it had sounded like her. She put that thought aside in order to help them load boxes of peach, elderberry, and cherry preserves, jams, and jellies into the car's trunk. Only when they finished did she stop and invite Maddie in for supper.

Originally Maddie planned to leave immediately, but now realized time had slipped away during the long drive there. Since it was almost night, she expressed her gratitude for being invited to dine with them. What she would do later about driving back to the city was not to be decided now.

"Whatever you did or said made a huge difference in our business! I can't thank you enough. On the other hand, I think we might have to buy more from the grocer than planned for our own eating." The model nun grinned as she shook Maddie's hand. Her present concern was based on her past work in the convent—not her present position as Manager of Production and Shipping. Unable to talk without looking down, she worked at it now, but her eyes would slip, then jerk back to look at Maddie or Mother Mary Michael.

Maddie wanted to laugh but could see the others were not in as happy a mood. Leaving without complimenting their work in other areas was something she never did, but this time she left and did not speak about the woman running for President, nor what she said and did to increase women's work today. It was not something she wanted to skip, but it just didn't fit. The nuns worked constantly and did not ask others for advice, nor did they get upset when simple people did not listen to them. It seemed better to just drive away after saying once again that everything was going great.

Once on her way to the Interstate highway, Maddie signaled she was going to turn right just as a truck flew by so fast it shook her heavily-laden car. She could not imagine why a truck would travel that fast on a road built for vehicles no larger than hay wagons. Shaking her head, she turned to check the road again just as another truck flew by in the same direction as the first. This time she choked on dust thrown into her open convertible.

"What's going on around here?" Maddie spoke loud and clear, knowing no one could hear her talking to herself when driving alone, so it was a shock when she thought she heard someone nearby respond.

"Hmm, did I hear someone clear her throat or make a comment?"

Feeling foolish for talking aloud—and even worse—answering, Maddie began to work her way toward the Interstate ramp. There was a cough or little noise. She definitely heard something and turned to see who could be in the car.

Sitting beside her was a small woman wearing no scarf, yet her curls remained perfectly in place, as if plastered on her head. She was too perfect, but not a classic Greek statue as Maddie thought at first. What could she do about a doll that talked and appeared to be alive? These thoughts arrived rapid-fire and never left until the drive was over and she was safely back in her Manhattan garage. Once parked there, she reached over to pick up the doll—and it was gone! How weird is that? How strange can any day be?

Angry at her mind for convincing her she had a passenger who over time might be marketed, Maddie realized why it happened. She obviously needed such a being or doll to talk to at times. Such a flash of intuitive insight defeated her mind. She wondered if it would ever come back to her in time to reveal what she should feel and believe in—and begin work on by spring.

I think I'm losing my mind, but then again, I don't know if others do the same thing and just pretend they don't see children or dolls where there are none.

She thought it over while transporting the cases of canned goods from her car to the elevator. Only then did she think: 'The garage is empty, yet the elevator doors are wide open, as if expecting my return right now? Elevators are never waiting when you need them. Are they?'

Just then a bell rang, and the elevator stopped waiting and closed its mouth, disappearing into the regions where they do their thing. Maddie did not care, because she still had a lot of work to get all the boxes unloaded and into the elevator and out again, as well as carried down the hall to her apartment. She was in no rush to get it all done.

While shelving the canned goods until they were sold on line, Maddie wondered how many times she had ever known *for sure* what would happen next, like who would come through a door or call her on the phone. When did she first notice it?

What she looked for was not where she left it, and she was annoyed that her helper must have relocated—again what she had explained was not to be touched. Every so often people seemed to just walk out and not come back or stopped listening to what she was talking about—or so it seemed to her. Maddie was not as easy to live with now, because she knew immediately who would leave and who would never do what they promised. It was much easier when she just went along with liars and others as though she totally believed them.

"Yoo-hoo, is anyone in the kitchen?" She knew no one was home but liked to act like her mother lived with her and just went out for a minute or so. She never mentioned it to others, because it was better to keep some secrets—especially when they involved a woman dead many years and not about to walk in now.

Air seemed to be flowing through the rooms around her, and she wondered if a window had been left open. None were open! She checked the sound system to see if any speakers were in play—all were off, and nothing was going on in the hallway.

Maddie stopped and looked at herself more closely to determine if she needed to see a psychiatrist. It certainly was beginning to look like she was seriously losing her mind. How else can you explain being able to hear things at a much higher frequency than other human beings?

☯Chapter Fourteen

I guess I have to get used to being used. The words are not flowing like they used to....

Watching the computer screen, Maddie was amazed at what she wrote. She thought it would never include anything she thought or wrote on her own, because it would be stupid to do so. Imagine all the time she spent in college, then working years to get recognized and win the Pulitzer Prize. It was all for nothing if all she had to do was sit back, go into trance, then type as fast as possible the wisdom waiting to be downloaded.

She no longer worried but could not keep up with all the material flowing and growing every day into numerous manuscripts, articles, and journal entries. Her old computer could not keep up, either, and the internet dial-up had to go. It was way too slow!

How did it happen? Maddie was aware it began long ago when she was not the same person, but it was not apparent until she visited the nunnery and sat quietly by their arbor and worked on something she could not later remember. In fact, she could not remember much she wrote even now, so she called herself a scribe—just so she knew it wasn't exactly what she would have written or even thought. Others might not notice the difference from her usual prose, but she felt her style was very different from how she wrote for so many years. So far no one said anything about it, so why did she need to be sure it was she writing now?

The days were over when she got up and worked for hours reading stories and looking at what others wrote in order to get a good idea of what was happening elsewhere. Now she went to her computer and sat there— and just typed. She could not stop herself until a lot of material appeared on the screen, all properly phrased, and at times words appeared that caused her to hurry to her dictionary. Her daily work now was more like that of an editor rephrasing or replacing words no longer in common usage or out-of-style.

If you, too, sit and write, seeing everything come out just right, do you constantly say, '*Wow, that was great! Give me more,*' or maybe, '*Praise the Lord*'? I guess you would do a bit of both, too, if it happened to you. I want to tap into what is out there and publish it without fear of becoming a laughing stock or whatever; but what do you do when a book is ready, and no one wants to publish it, because it's not what they want or expect from you?

Last year I started with a book in hand and the means to make a profit from selling it to the best publisher ever, but quickly crossed over to another wave length— organizing a foundation and working harder than ever to help the world. What happened to me then? Why am I now unable to do what I set out to do? Many women I talked to initially are good friends and moving ahead in politics— three are in big-time businesses of their own design. What happened then, and is it happening to me now?

Maddie reclined on the couch to read a mystery meant to take the edge off her curiosity about what she could write or do to follow-up on her last book. Her life was no longer as easy to define as when she wrote for *The Times* or *The New Yorker,* or others who appreciate literary works. Even now she felt compelled to sit and write but had no idea what it would entail or if a book would appear as the last one did a year ago.

Being able to write a book in Spirit and see it cheered by those she had ignored most of her career was not exactly what Maddie wanted to hear, but it was fun to be endearing to some and hated by others. Why would people say she had no faith? She never wrote about God before—or in that novel, but everyone claiming to be Right, and the only ones going to heaven, aligned against her wherever she appeared. Why? What made them so angry and upset all the time—and not just with me?

The fear that you may be used by God is totally unacceptable. They say they honor and celebrate *The Bible* as written—but it, too, was scribed and written in the same way I write now! Why would anyone hate spiritual scribes? I'm no different, yet they believe I am. What is it I do that they cannot?

All these thoughts idled in her mind while reading a few lines about an Indian tribe and a detective of sorts. She studied how the writer inserted her thoughts and beliefs into every line. No one said she was Satanic, yet she was talking about pagans! No one said she was disenfranchising Indian tribes by taking upon herself to write about their lives instead of letting them do it themselves. Perhaps Indians spurned her? Maybe that is why I'm not getting very far with certain Christians who say they are the only true believers. Is it because I despise them?

I dislike people who create religions to suit themselves, setting up sects that entrap youths and women who believe in them. I especially dislike men who say they are preaching the word of God when what they really want is a bigger house or car. So, if I despise them, "Why am I being used by God like this now?" I can't believe I just said out loud: "I am being used by God," and I believe it!

The book Maddie had been reading slipped to the floor as she dropped into a deep sleep and did not awaken for hours. During that time, she became lost in a dream. She was unable to stop and leave it all behind and forget why she was in it. She sensed the dream was not true—just a way to teach her truths.

Upon awakening, Maddie felt the moon peering into her eyes. She rose and got a drink before settling down in the same spot, so the moon could continue shining on her in this strange and mysterious way. As it moved, she moved. It was a strange ritual that came easily to her. Why? No clue, she just wanted to do it now.

Somehow, I feel like I'm living in another time. I must be sick or out of my mind, but I think I'm doing something no one else ever did before—which has to be ego talking. Who could do something no one else ever did even once?

As the evening blended into shades of city nightlife, the moon disappeared. Only then did Maddie move to make supper. She felt it was wise to eat something light, but instead made a lot and put out two places, as if expecting a friend.

As she finished, Maddie heard a knock, then a key being inserted into the lock. She was not upset but did wonder why someone was using a key to enter her apartment. She was sure she held the only key, having never given the Super one, plus she changed locks frequently. Who could this be?

"Hello, Madeline! Hope I'm not disturbing you, but I was in the vicinity and thought I would stop by and go over your manuscripts before taking a few back with me to Mayaland."

Maddie was amazed to see Jorge! What was he saying? What could she say? She was not at all upset, even okay with his entering this way. Why? Who was he really, and when did she get to know him so well that he was a partner in her work?

Smiling and nodding toward the chair standing at an angle to the window, Jorge said, "I see you have been following the work and doing your exercises with the moon. We will make a Mayan shamana out of you yet."

He walked away from her, so Maddie could not see if he was smiling—perhaps putting her on. Why would anyone without permission or a mission assume such things? She now wanted to know how to stop what was going on, but only until she was prepared to let go and know what was happening now.

"Oh, yes, Mandy said to tell you your latest work is fascinating. She is very much aware of what you are trying to do, but is unable to do it herself. Her attempts to organize women and men have not been accepted yet. She will do it, but not just yet." Jorge smiled and winked at her.

Maddie fought back a laugh and managed to say, "Poor Mandy, unable to sell others on what she loves. Yeah, I bet!"

Jorge said nothing but went directly to the kitchen counter and looked at what she had prepared, as well as how much food had been placed on plates. He was not surprised, and neither was she.

"I think we need to pray and ask God for help in getting many others to do what they love and follow the will of God. Can you do that over food, or is it better to pray before or afterwards, so as not to infect the food with energy that might consume it?" Maddie thought about what she just said and wondered about it. What did she mean by that?

"I think we had best eat, then talk about business. Before we leave today, we will go over the needs of the nation and pray that all we said is wise and right, and if not, that we get news soon from our Guides on what we need to do."

Maddie was surprised. Did Jorge pray?

"I pray all day. I wash my hands and pray I touch nothing that is not of God or do anything with my hands that is not worthy. I thank God for all we have—even the cabs. I walk and talk to God a lot—not out loud, but I talk a lot. I also think over what we talk about and ask for guidance from angels and others who can help us now. You may not believe the Catholic Church has much to say about God, because it says so little to converts and followers, but it has much to share once it decides you are equal and able to understand."

Mystified that Jorge would talk about the Catholic Church, she wondered if they, too, attacked her work.

"You are not being attacked in Mexico and Guatemala—but not accepted by Maya of today's tribes, because you are not liked by the women. They do not yet believe they are taking over the tribe and must learn more than they know now." Nodding, he added, "You will help them do that—and do it well."

Perplexed and excited at the same time, Maddie dropped the ladle, letting it slip into the soup without rescuing it. Her thoughts were such that she was no longer hungry. Jorge reached in and picked at the end of the spoon and pulled it out with two fingers. He rinsed it off, so he could serve her, which was unexpected and not what she had in mind, but she let it slide.

Jorge put the bowls of chicken soup on the table and got out some crackers, since she preferred them to bread. He did not lower his head, instead looked upward and spoke as though addressing a bug on the ceiling. Speaking in Mayan-Spanish, his words were a blur. She did not hear them clearly and could not translate, so she said her usual prayer out loud.

"I like your prayer. It is so beautiful, yet you seem shy about saying it. Why?"

"As the youngest, I was the one who had to say grace at the table every day. Having been the baby, I feel this simple prayer is all that remains of the faith I had then. I no longer have anyone who reminds me of my mother and father, but when I say that prayer I feel I am their child all over again. I know it sounds weird, but there it is."

Jorge did not speak but smiled as he began eating what she had prepared over the past two hours. He did not appear to be surprised she had set out enough food at this late hour to feed a tribe. When she asked why he had stopped by, he registered a blank stare.

Speaking hesitantly, Maddie said, "We must have set up an appointment, and I must have given you a key?" She looked at Jorge to see if he would respond, but he said nothing, so she let it die.

"That was a great meal, Madeline. I think you will like living in Mexico. You have a flair for using ingredients most Maya use daily. You like your food a lot less spicy than most Maya, but not that different from how my mother cooked. Do you plan on taking your household goods with you?"

Surprised that Jorge would ask her such a question, she said nothing until she felt an urge to talk without thinking, and what came out of her mouth amazed her. "I'm ready! I have my business together and can write from anywhere in America, and hopefully as easily in Mexico. I have no problem living out-of-town for a while, but hate to give up this apartment just yet. It's not easy to get an apartment in mid-town that doesn't have to be ripped down or enlarged. I would hate to have to come back to a rat-infested tenement and pay the same rent I pay now. Maybe we can write it off as a company expense?"

Jorge gestured at the walls and said they should be insulated for shock. He spoke without a sense of how ridiculous it sounded, but then, she had not yet considered what she had blurted out to him. What garbled ideas she had put out to the universe!

Never one to fictionalize her life or dream in front of others about what she wanted, Maddie was astonished to hear herself talk to Jorge for several hours about her move to Colorado from here, then to Mayaland for the rest of her life. She was astonished. Never had she wanted to move to the mountains, and Colorado was now way too high. Everyone was running there. Why go there to sit in the sun?

"I know you have a lot of work to do, Madeline, so I will leave, but you must not talk so loudly. The walls hear, because they are bugged. I think the Left and Right are not happy about anything—so they might pick you apart and decide you are not their friend—even though you are. Please, take care. I will be back when you are prepared." As he spoke, Jorge walked through the door, leaving Maddie to stare at where he had stood before this latest weirdness.

After a few moments, she said to herself, "I'm sure he was sitting in that chair while he ate my soup, chicken, and a little bit of this and that, but why do I think he got up and walked through that door without stopping to open it? Am I going crazy? Was he even here?"

Right then she remembered his warning and stopped talking. She locked the door, because Jorge had not done so when he entered. Relieved that at least one thing fit, even though everything else was not what she ever expected could happen to her.

☯Chapter Fifteen

"Madeline, do you want to go to the mall and get the few things we need—or wait until tomorrow and do everything at once?"

Maddie paused to think, then replied. "I think I'll wait until tomorrow, Jenny. You never know what all you need until you leave the house to do one simple errand that turns into ten things you should have thought about or need to buy. I want to be sure I have everything in place before we ship—So can you help me another day, too?"

As she turned to look at the young woman assisting her with packing and printing shipping labels, Maddie thought for an instant she looked very different from the girl who appeared at her door earlier that morning. Glancing at her again, she decided her mind was overworked and imagining things—again.

"I was only going to help you for an hour or so, but it looks like you need more help than that getting all these boxes down to your car. I would love to help every day, but I have no way of getting here." She tugged at a hank of blond hair dangling over her ear as she smiled hesitantly.

Maddie could not imagine what she meant. If Jenny didn't have transportation, how did she get here this morning? It wasn't like she still lived in Manhattan and everyone walked or took taxis wherever they went. This is 21st Century Colorado, for crying out loud. Anyone who visits others here has to have an appointment, so they don't miss you. So how did she know I would be home and need her help?

Puzzled, but trying to remain calm—as though she knew who this young woman really was, Maddie said with a smile, "You know, Jenny, I could use an assistant. I don't have anyone now who can run errands and such. I was going to advertise in the Sunday paper. By the way, how did you know I needed someone today?"

The young woman wiped her brow and spoke without hesitation. "I came because you prayed. You were talking about needing help and said it out loud the other day in the park. I was on the jogging trail and your voice traveled to me like a radio beam. I thought at first it was God talking to me. You see, I'm religious and was asking myself why I couldn't get a job that wouldn't be too taxing while I work on my Ph.D. I can't handle crowds and rude people, so that wipes out working in public places."

As her voice trailed off, Maddie noticed something a bit odd about the way Jenny looked at her, and how she moved her hands—nothing conspicuous or really weird, but was Jenny crazy? Was she? How could she argue the case when she opened the door this morning and welcomed the young woman into her house, only because Jenny asked her if she needed help? That was not something wise women did, nor what wise women did for others—walk in and work without knowing the situation or if they would be paid.

"You know Jenny, there's something about you that makes me want to hug you and say everything is going to be okay, yet we've just met. You're such a pretty woman—and obviously very smart—not in need of a hug from me or anyone else, but..."

Before Maddie could finish, Jenny jumped in and said, "Everyone needs a hug! I'm not that pretty, and men are pests—never interested in love. They just want sex, then think you should say they're the best there is. That's why I can't stand being a beauty queen, but my mother insisted."

Now Maddie was truly puzzled, wondering what it was about Jenny that was so appealing—so revealing, yet reminded her of someone she did not particularly like. She thought for a second, then said, "Are you the daughter of a beauty queen or one who wanted to be one?"

"Oh, my mother is the queen of soap operas. She's famous and everyone loves to hate her! I get tired of hearing about her, so I moved out here. And guess what? Everyone here knew right away who I was. I can't get away from the unloved. I have to listen to them talk about my mother, as if she was the woman on TV.

"Why don't they get a life—or lives? I just want to get married and have a couple of kids and write a novel—then write the best book ever written about something people will ponder and think about forever. Do you ever feel like you just want to run away?"

Once Jenny got started, she did not stop even to breathe deeply. She rushed through her thoughts like water tumbling over a cliff—and almost as loud. Meanwhile Maddie was beginning to place her mother, but not sure if she was making the proper connection or not. Could this be Jennifer Gibson's daughter? Could she be old enough to have such an accomplished daughter? Obviously, Jennifer has had a lot of surgery, so who knows how old she might be, but I did think she was younger than me. Maybe she had a baby as a teenager? Such a thought forced her to speak, thus breaking up Jenny's ongoing stream of words. "Are you related to Jennifer Gibson?"

Jenny nodded and immediately began to tear up, so Maddie added, "You look so young—and so does she. I would never have thought of you as being her daughter. I worked with her at one time."

Appearing stunned and overwhelmed, Jenny gasped and said nothing intelligible until she caught her breath. "You mean you work on television scripts, too?"

Now it was Maddie's turn to be surprised. She said, "I'm a writer, but not for television. I write for newspapers and magazines, and recently wrote a book about prominent women who could or should run the country. Did you read it?"

Jenny screamed, "Read it! I had to read it ten times to get over the part about my mother being able to support the work of others—and actually wanting to help the world. I never, ever thought she cared! She's always so dramatic— and into herself, that I never thought she thought about anyone else—except maybe to yell at her agent. I grew up on her rage."

This was something Maddie did not want to hear. She had come to respect the drama queen, as everyone dubbed her now, but hadn't thought about how she related to family and others. If what Jenny said was true, this could hurt them all. No one running for public office can afford to lose their temper or be bored, at least that is what they used to think. Maddie smiled at the idea now, which apparently caught Jenny by surprise.

"I guess you think my mother is a beauty who eats women for breakfast—then goes out to lunch with every handsome man she stars with?"

Unable to guess what was intended by this latest turn, she stared back at Jenny and waited for an explanation.

"I think you're really smart, Maddie. You have charts and do math as though it's your second nature, but you act kind'a dumb on the phone. I guess it's an act to get others to open up and be honest with you—or get a better deal."

Shocked that this beautiful woman could be so full of surprises, Maddie spoke perhaps too swiftly. "I don't intentionally act dumb, but when someone knows more than I do about a subject, I let them tell me about it, and what I need to do. Don't you?"

Appearing puzzled—perhaps stunned, Jenny said nothing.

"Are you going to work for me, or do you want to find another job? Your references are good enough for me, and since you read my book, you know why I feel compelled to finish this work."

Wrinkling her nose as she spoke, Jenny said, "I don't get the part about women of all nations coming together to do more for the world than men ever could. That's not racist, but it's sexist, and I've been taught that one is the same as the other."

"You have a point, but we are neither racist nor sexist. We are calling on women everywhere to do more than their ancestors did for too many centuries.

Women have to unite to get the job done in any country where they are held back, imperiled, or threatened with imprisonment if they speak their minds. You should be able to express yourself, and mind your own business, if it hurts no one else."

Moving away from the beautiful blond with the ice blue eyes, Maddie wondered how many other women criticized the book without having read it. Would she ever be believed? Would women instead say the concept was too difficult to understand—let alone get involved with—because they didn't want to lose men's attention?

Walking around the scattered boxes, Maddie spotted a newspaper on the floor meant to protect the rug and thought of how she talked now and how much she left out of her last few columns, because she didn't want to be attacked by the Far Right. Was she doing it out of fear or just being strategic and wise?

Without thought, she pointed at the paper and asked Jenny about the column staring back at her. She obviously had no right to expect that Jenny had read the paper, let alone her column, but she had to ask.

"I read it. It's okay, but not like your others."

Flabbergasted at this quick but accurate assessment, Maddie did not smile nor look away. In fact, she found herself staring down the young woman. Who was she— really? A plant? Someone others used to see if she was who she claimed to be? That was paranoia moving in big time, but not about to get a place to stay.

Turning her head, Maddie's eyes dropped to an ad and suddenly realized the model in the ad was her new assistant. This totally surprised her! Why?

"Oh, so you see my picture, and now you think—dumb blond, stupid model, not a good idea to have her working close to me. She'll be after my guy! She'll need a lot of stroking to get through the average day—not to mention when things go bad. Go ahead, you know you're thinking that. I get it all the time—except when some guy is staring at my chest and talking out of his head."

"I don't think you're stupid, and I doubt you are ever taken advantage of by anyone. Models seldom ever are, but some are so vain they forget God created the faces and bodies of the young—not a doctor or even an artist. You may be a beautiful woman and able to study hard, but you're tired, Jenny. I see it in your posture."

Jenny immediately straightened up, stood erect, and started breathing more easily. She was no longer looking quite as tired as she had the past two hours. Her mouth screwed up into a small smile as she said, "You really do have a lovely way of talking, Maddie. You say so much about life—and women who aren't liked, yet should be, that I want to talk you out of what you believe—just to hear you argue. You really are a great debater. Right?"

Noticing the change in phrasing and behavior, as well as her way of enunciating each word once she stood erect, Maddie decided to write an article on the power of posture as soon as she had time. For the moment, she smiled and walked away without commenting on what Jenny said.

Once they loaded the last box in the car, Maddie decided to take them to the post office today rather than tomorrow. The atmosphere between the two women was now clear of constraint or complaints. They were much more at ease and happy to do this bit for all the women of the world. They agreed on that much, at least.

As the day worked them over and left both tired, happy, and feeling fulfilled because they completed what they set out to do, Jenny asked once again if Maddie wanted her to come back and help every day. This time Maddie said yes and did not think twice about suggesting she stay over if she liked.

"Madeline, you are way too good. You should never ask a woman like me to stay over or people will say you're a dyke or a geek or someone they don't like. Instead, you need to be more observant of how men talk down to women—a lot, and how so many women try to be like them. That's what you should write about next."

"No, Jenny, I'm too old to care about what men think. I found out years ago that men are not basically mean and cruel, but if you let them, they will be. Do women have to stand up to them? Not necessary, *if* they never let them get out-of-hand in the first place. Do you ever let men walk all over you?"

"I'm not sure. I think I shock them a lot. When I'm around straight men, they seem intimidated by me and want to go on a date or can't say two words straight. I don't think they would ever beat me up."

"That is a misconception. Most men are like that with women they find attractive, yet most men will misuse their power if permitted to do so. Women misuse their power, too, so we don't complain, seeing it as some sort of weird trade-off."

As though confused, Jenny looked at Maddie and said, "Are you saying women would make as big a mess of things as men have?"

"I'm saying women do not have to allow the degradation and rage too many think is normal today. If you don't permit anyone to hit you, they find someone who will, if they're killers. If they're lovers, they will straighten up and fly right. You have to be the one to set the boundaries—and it's not that hard.

"Our grandmothers never suffered half the degradation women of today needlessly suffer. Why? They had a place in society and demanded that men provide everything they needed to keep it in place. The men never did that much to actually settle this country. They just made money. It's women who decide where the money goes once made by men. If they don't, the money is spent on stupid things like sports arenas and what makes no sense to sensitive, let alone sensible, minds."

Nodding slightly, Jenny said, "I think you may have a new idea that needs to be put on the screen—men having to court women again. Men having to escort women to their cars and look after them, as if they are easily damaged if they aren't careful enough."

With force Maddie said, "No! That is not what I'm saying, and it would be stupid to type-cast American women as Hollywood did in the past. We are not fragile, and we certainly aren't dumb! We own homes, have plenty of money, and enjoy much easier lives than ever before, but fear men. Why? Because men are more spoiled than ever before."

Jenny shouted, "Spoiled? Men are spoiled?"

"Yes, look at your father. Who is he to run down your mother, then ask for alimony? What honorable man would expect that of his wife after threatening her with suicide if she didn't do what he expected? You weren't that young that you didn't learn from his example to be afraid of losing the love of men if you didn't do what they wanted—right away."

Maddie was embarrassed that she had alluded to gossip she never admitted to hearing before now. How could she do this to Jenny? Who was using her now, and what would happen to this budding friendship as a result of blurting out such negative rot?

"I think you know a lot, but you don't know my dad. He was always treated like he should be making a good living when he couldn't—because she was too famous."

A laugh burst forth from Maddie, then she giggled and continued to behave quite badly in front of this childlike woman. Who was she to critically analyze anyone, especially the father of a woman considered by many to be well-behaved and happy, despite all the changes in her life? She could not help wondering how she suddenly had so many insights into this young woman's life. Jenny appeared as a stranger at her door only that morning, yet she now thought she knew all that was hidden behind the model's lovely façade. How was that possible?

"I guess you know a lot more about me than I know about you. Having interviewed my mother, you're aware of what she thinks better than I am, but my father is off-limits for now. I love him, and he's so fragile I think he might actually commit suicide this time."

Without thought, Maddie blurted, "He's joking. If not, he's a serious fraud. Your father isn't going to leave this Earth when everything is the way he made it. He enjoys complaining too much! You're the one I worry about—definitely not him."

"You're worried about me? Really?" The way she smiled, anyone viewing the two women in the darkening room would have thought Jenny had won another crown or tiara instead of being told she was in danger.

Maddie pondered what to do with her, but was aware things were no longer in her hands. Someone else was standing in for her—talking through her. It felt like it might be someone nearby, but not of this time.

"I guess you're surprised that I'm such a pushover for anyone who worries about me, but that's because it never happens. Everyone flatters me, or is so jealous they act mean and hateful, but you're nice. You don't sit and cry about men, yet you could marry any one of ten men in this town right now."

Maddie stopped what she was doing to say, "Come back on me with that. What did you just say?"

Giggling for the first time, Jenny said with a slightly overdone sweetness, "You love to be flattered, too. You really do! You want me to tell you all about the men in town and what they're saying about you all the time. Right?"

Unable to follow their conversation any longer, Maddie sat quietly and thought. Who would notice me? When do I even go out? Am I being watched? Do men still watch women? Who can you trust if you're being watched? The paranoia that came with fame was not letting Maddie enjoy this sudden bit of news.

Meanwhile Jenny found it quite confusing to be ignored just when she was getting used to being supportive of another woman, so she said, "Are you not aware you're *The* New Woman in Town?"

When Maddie did not respond, Jenny said, "You really are too good to be true. You're not gay, but you're not into men much. What do you call women who are content to just be themselves—androgynous or what?"

This off-the-wall comment made Maddie laugh. She looked at the beautiful young woman and pointed toward the car, as if to say she would drive her home—wherever that was. Before Maddie could lock the front door they both lapsed into laughter, now confidant and sure this day would be repeated.

❧Chapter Sixteen

"The world isn't going to stop just because you can't do what you want!"

Maddie was startled to hear the message spoken so clearly that she might have been in the next room rather than in bed dreaming. When she realized she was not dreaming but awakening from a great dream—and not happy about it. She sat up and listened intently but could hear nothing more. What was going on?

Creeping out the bedroom door into the hallway, she could make out Jenny talking on the telephone. Jenny must have accidentally hit the speaker phone button, which resulted in her mother's famous voice echoing through the house. Maddie walked carefully to the top of the stairs, then thought better of it and returned to dress as though she had awoken without any help from the call.

As coffee and tea dripped or brewed according to the taste of each woman sitting at the counter, their newspapers dipped and bobbed, but nothing was said. They sat still for a few minutes after the beeper went off announcing the coffee was just right for one. The other stirred honey into her tea, waiting to see if she needed to add sweetener or not. This was going to be a day when being sweet was what she needed to be, so Maddie thought a lot about what she might say now.

After a few minutes of silence, turning pages without thought, Maddie announced she was ready to know what was going on now. She waited, but Jenny said nothing. That was not the best way to get on Maddie's best side— especially today.

"I guess you plan to just steal away in the night to go and visit your mother, then tell her what all you had to put up with here?" When she got no reaction, Maddie raised one eyebrow and slowly let it slip back into place.

"You seem to be more moody than usual, Jenny. Is something really wrong?" Maddie spoke without smiling, but was joking in her mind, thus the reaction was not what she expected.

"I guess you're tired of me, too. I'm so upset about you, and what you want to do—and that I just couldn't do what you wanted. I still think you're great—and really going places, but I can't seem to do enough for you. Do you want me to leave?" As she said this Jenny produced a tear, then three more spilled down over her cheeks to her chin where they hung and did not seem to want to drop.

Not interested in this latest tactic to gain attention or sympathy, Maddie spoke with ease. "I guess you and I aren't cut from the same cloth. Are we?"

Now Jenny wasn't sure what to say, so she continued to look glum while trying to produce more tears but couldn't do it as quickly as usual. Her face contorted into a kind of grin then, but it did not fool her employer.

"You certainly aren't a ray of sunshine today, are you?"

Now tears flowed, and Jenny snorted and wrinkled her nose as if she were losing control over her face as she wailed, "Oh, Madeline, you are my mother of this life! I've never had a mother—really. I mean it! Mine's a scream, and I mean she is always screaming at me—and is usually sad. I know you think she's a great woman, but she isn't, and if she runs for politics, she'll come undone and everyone will find out just how evil she's been to me."

Sensing a threat, yet unwilling to believe it, Maddie moved away to a safer spot before she said, "You might be the only person who has a mother like her, but everyone dislikes their mother every once in a while. It just doesn't get the respect now it might have gotten at one time. Look at Crawford's daughter, and the Reagan diva! You don't really think people read that stuff and believe it. Do you? Everyone wants to be famous, and some want whatever their parents have, so they rat on them, which usually ends up making all who love the adult mad at the child—believe it or not."

Just as Maddie motioned for Jenny to wipe her eyes and nose and get on with whatever she wanted to propose, the phone rang. It was not good timing.

After a few moments on the phone, Maddie turned to Jenny and motioned for her to pick up the extension. It was her mother—calling back about when Jenny wanted to be picked up at the airport, as well as her flight number, so she could send someone. Maddie did not laugh but was happy to know her employee was going to fly away and not come back.

The day flew by fast after that. Maddie did not have to say much, because all the lies of the past could not be buried in a day, and Jenny could not maintain her con any longer. Once discovered for being a fraud, and the daughter of a woman who wanted no part of her because of her lies, she could not figure out what angle to work and what flattery to apply now to keep the door open for the future. For perhaps the first time in her life, Jenny had made a contract that was not being broken as she wished, rather being given away to another because she was not wanted.

Their distance grew longer as they worked on packing the last of the preserves, jellies, and jams left on the shelves in the back of the garage. Jenny was there to see one major venture end, yet unable to guess when it started and when the next one would begin. This seemed to bother her more than leaving a good job.

"I guess you and those nuns are going to make a huge killing on this other stuff?"

Maddie was unwilling to discuss business with others in the best of times, and certainly never with someone she didn't trust, so she remained deaf and dumb to all outward appearances now.

"I'm going to miss those nuns. They were pretty naughty at times. You know that?"

Disgusted at this latest line meant to undermine her friendship with the nunnery now converting to a convent and business of its own kind—able to create its own lines without any further help from her, Maddie smiled and said nothing.

"You don't believe me. Do you?"

With her back toward the whining girl-child, Maddie fought to maintain her cool and remain calm and not spit back a word in defense of the nuns, because it wasn't necessary and was just what this wanton woman wanted her to do.

"Are you going to join them? I mean become a nun? You don't seem to like men. You never call them."

Stunned at this personal attack, one that could be used against her by one who had few scruples or ability to see people as they are, Maddie spoke rapidly. "You really do have an evil mind, Jenny! I wasn't aware of how evil you are until several of your *friends* called and told me not to hire you. I guess I never trusted what models said about their friends, but maybe they were right?

"I think your mother will be able to keep you from losing every friend you ever had, but will you listen to her wisdom? No, and I doubt you can. When the mind is so preoccupied with itself and what it does, plus how you look and who can be used, you can't look ahead and see what others are planning, too.

"You might like to repeat what I do here and now, but you can't. Anything you say will be used against you! Understand? Whatever you say, I'm the one with the pen. I'm the one who can get in the last word and bury anyone who is evil toward what I am. You can try it and see what happens—or forget me as soon as you hit the street."

With her coat thrown over her arm and her purse tucked away so she could carry the last box to the car, Maddie opened the door. Jenny did not want to move that fast, so she stopped. Maddie did not and backed her out the door.

"I guess this is it then, Madeline? You're kicking me out. You're making a big deal out of what I didn't get done, and now you're going to tell everyone I was a failure. Aren't you?"

Stung by her accuracy—shocked that it was true for once, Maddie said nothing. She merely nodded to Jenny to move out of the way and close the door behind her. Jenny did not understand, or she pretended to miss the message.

"Jen, please put your coat on and get going. You're not going to stay in my home. I heard you on the phone! For goodness sake, what did you expect? Congratulations, you got laid and the guy isn't worthy of your name and expects you to let him have the child now? This is a small town. Whatever made you think you could move in here and act like a wild child and not get caught?"

"Madeline, Madeline, Madeline, you really are a sight! Look at how good your skin is now compared to when I arrived? It didn't look great then, and I got you to finally lose weight, so you can get a man, but do you thank me? No! You go into rants! I just can't handle what you can, and I want out—now!"

Unable to keep up with the change of attitude at every whim, Maddie shrugged and pointed at the truck as she said, "You drive. I have a lot on my mind—so you drive."

"I'm too much of a nervous wreck to drive, and I can't fit in under the wheel the way you have it now."

Maddie reached in and adjusted the seat before walking toward the back of the little truck. Jenny abruptly started the engine and almost threw it into reverse. Was it an accident or was she a psychopath? The thought made Maddie laugh.

Obviously annoyed to hear Maddie laugh loudly when she was trying to throw a scare into her, Jenny sat still and waited for her now ex-boss to climb in the other side and gab all the way to town. It never happened. Maddie said nothing and didn't respond to anything she said.

"Well, Madeline, you might as well take me to the airport now and send my bags later. I don't think we have anything more to talk about. After all these months of you being the chatterbox to end all talkers, you suddenly have nothing to say. I guess I know why!"

Stunned at the inference that something nefarious was under way, Maddie let go a stream of words without one curse. Too bad for Jenny that she did not swear, because that would have been easier to take than to hear about what a mistake it was to believe anything a psychopathic liar would say—before she really got started. It was a long trip, but Jenny endured it and ran in the house and grabbed her bags when they got back. She wanted to call a taxi but didn't want to use any of her mad money—the money she had tucked away for just such a day.

Jenny suddenly realized she was being told to leave behind money she didn't realize had been missed. She was given ten minutes to replace the silverware and trophies she had stolen, too. It was quite a sight! Maddie took great delight in acting as if she had been aware of the thefts from Day One, but actually she never realized Jenny was a thief until she mentioned it unwittingly in her final tirade on what she believed would be her final complaint.

"I guess I'm going to be called out and scolded like a child now?"

They entered the house, and between the two of them they dragged Jenny's huge suitcase up the stairs. Maddie said nothing as she went over the stacks of little things that grew in number once removed from the big suitcase where they had been tucked away in among dirty clothes. What a trickster was this beautiful model! No one should ever be taken in by her again, but there was no way short of blackmail to make her stop—until an angel dropped by.

When the doorbell rang, Maddie stopped staring after the departing back of this stranger, or monster, or thief, or would-be daughter, depending upon how she presented herself over the past few months, and ran to see who was at the front door. Slim was standing there with his arms filled with flowers. He looked heavenly to her, so she smiled as if she had been waiting for him. He flipped! He was excited to see that this woman he had loved for many years was willing to welcome him back into her life after so many years—or so he hoped. First, though, he had to see what was going on at the back of the house. Someone was honking the horn and sounded a tad angry.

"Come on in, Slim. Welcome to bedlam. I'm losing a houseguest and sometime-employee and gaining peace of mind. Can anyone guarantee this harmony will never end?"

Surprised into smiling large, Slim said, "That's what I like to hear. You waxing poetic and using all of your language on me. It really is sexy, but what the heck is going on out back? It sounds like an angry ram or is it your Toyota sounding off on its own?"

Sighing, Maddie denied knowledge of why anyone would be angry with her, waving him in and taking the flowers. She picked up one of the vases strewn around the house, gifts from women she had helped over the years who frequently sent her flowers. Quickly snipping off the stems of Slim's bouquet, she arranged a few flowers in several vases before walking toward the kitchen sink.

Slim smiled as he followed her, but looked a bit wary as he said, "Looks like a hurricane struck the place."

"No, not a hurricane—a huge pain, but guess what? I'm getting my house and my life back today. I don't have to make up jobs and constantly try to help someone feel better, happy, or whatever. It's like winning a ticket to the opera!"

"You really are something! I would have canned the prima donna a day after she started her soap opera. You're way too kind to strays. I think you need a man around to keep them out." Slim wasn't smiling, so she let it hang in the general vicinity of no further explanation required, because she didn't have one.

"I guess…Anyway, I'm taking her highness to the airport now. When I return, I'll put all this stuff back where it belongs. Would you believe she turned out to be a thief, on top of everything else?"

He said nothing—just shook his head as if aware of it already, so Maddie said, "I guess I really was a fool—again."

His expression melted into a smile as he reached out and touched her cheek. "You're a good woman, Madeline. You just don't get out enough. Being a writer keeps you out of touch with people who are all around you, hating your beauty and ability—and your wealth. You never should trust the young. They want it all their way now."

Ashamed that she was in tears, Maddie tried to brush them away, but Slim stopped her with a kiss. It was the first time she ever found herself in such a relationship without having done anything to arrange it, and she liked it.

The horn blared long and loud, so the two bound-to-be lovers broke cover and moved toward the back door. Slim waved casually toward the truck and the honking stopped—immediately. Jenny had not expected an audience—certainly not a man. By the time they got to the truck, Jenny was standing outside and holding the door open while smiling like she was in love. Slim just grinned.

It was all Maddie could do not to say something, but she thought better of it and asked Slim if he would drive. He said he would, and he would lock up the house—just in case someone tried to break in.

Jenny tried to chuckle, but it wasn't loud enough or hearty enough. The next few minutes would determine how she would end her time with Madeline and begin again. Angels waited with bated breath to hear what she would say next. Fortunately, she chose to smile sweetly and say, "You can drive, but I have to sit in the middle. I'm with child."

Slim acted surprised but said nothing. He laughed inwardly when he returned and discovered Maddie was seated in the middle and not about to shift. He would say later that it was one of the best moments of his life. Two beautiful women fighting over riding with him in a little truck. What luck!

As they pulled onto the highway, Slim asked Maddie to lower her window to see if anyone was coming down the road, because Jenny was sitting in the middle, grinning and shaking her head. She was so cute, according to what she could see in the crooked mirror, that she never heard the curse.

"What a beast! He speeded up when he saw us pull out!" Maddie continued to look in the side mirror, ready to make an obscene gesture for the first time in her life, but then remembered Slim was driving and would have to deal with things if her behavior got out of hand, so she said nothing more.

After driving a short distance, the truck behind them was practically nudging their bumper and not giving an inch, as though he had been run off the road and wanted to hammer that message home. He was hot!

"I guess this fella ain't gonna' stop tailgatin' us until I leave the road. So here goes, hold on to your sashes, ladies." Slim pulled a hard right as they left the traveling lane and entered the emergency lane where he stopped abruptly.

"Well, would you look at that! That guy's coming back. He's backin' up so fast I think he might ram us all into the back. Hold on."

The offending driver jammed on the brakes and ruined his entrance by being unable to control his rear end. He ended up halfway down the embankment that separated them from cattle staring at vehicles passing by. Red in the face, the irate driver was talking fast—probably saying something nasty as he hurried towards the truck.

"Now you look at me, Jen! You better not be leavin' town. If you are, I'll be in New York City on the next plane! I'm tired of all this stuff—and all your lies. I want my son, and I want you to deliver him right here in this town. You get that?"

"Son, that's no way to talk to a woman who is pregnant. If you have a problem with her, talk civil like. We don't want to run you over, but I might if you keep shaking your fist." Having delivered the message, Slim drove off, casually entering traffic once again.

"That son of—well, anyway, that guy has a lot of nerve. Talking like I belong to him. He's no friend of mine—and not the father of my child."

When no one spoke, Jenny continued. "I guess I owe you an explanation. Slim. It is Slim, isn't it? I wasn't able to conceive and tried a lot of things, then got this doctor in Colorado Springs to fertilize my eggs. He was surprised it was so easy."

Maddie snorted, then Slim laughed along with her. Jenny could not understand what was so funny until she rethought her words and realized they thought the doctor made her pregnant in the usual way. What a crock!

"You can stop laughing. I'm hurt! I know Madeline is a jerk at times and can't be nice when she's around men, but I wasn't raised that way. My mother is taking care of me while I have my baby, and she's thrilled to be a grandmother—even if it is from invitro-fertilization."

Maddie sighed loudly and motioned for Slim to slow down, then stop. She wanted to talk without interruption and stop Jenny from lying more than she otherwise might.

"You know, Jenny, you're a work of art. Your mother taught you many things, but you kept only what you wanted and tossed aside everything else. I know she thinks she has to take care of you and the baby, but I doubt she is really into your having a virgin birth. You catch my drift?" She thought she heard a snort, but Slim was chewing on the side of his mouth.

"I think you know why you have to have this baby, and why it's not going to increase your popularity with men who are wasted or shiftless, but it might make you a million dollars if you play your cards right. Is that guy back there going to want the baby if you say you can't have children? No, and he won't marry you if you say it's his right now, so you get him thinking you're running away so he suddenly wants what he thinks he can't have. All this invitro stuff was a myth, and you don't intend to fly to New York tonight. You intend to get him so upset that he takes off with you now to get a license and immediately arranges to marry you as soon as he can. Right?"

The truck cab filled with silence, even the radio announcer took a break. When the music returned, it was Wagner's funeral march from Lohengrin, weirdly enough played at weddings, just as the other truck raced to their side and seemed to be honking in time to *'Here Comes the Bride'*. It was quite a sight—and sound!

☯Chapter Seventeen

The work of the few was not as great as the many but was much better.

Maddie stopped to look at what she wrote, aware it sounded different from her usual prose. How did her writing change? When did it change *this* time? She wrote another line and checked it out, noticing how it seemed to be written by someone else. Could it be she would never again write as she had all her life? Would she change because she was now a Spiritual Scribe—not a writer? What was she to do with all this work?

As she typed rapidly, she noticed her computer was not working the same as usual and wondered why. What could cause such a machine to change—or for that matter, a brain? She thought about it, then settled back to remember when she last sat there and wrote without Jenny pushing her to do something she did not want to do right then? When did she give over her life to a woman who had no job, so that woman would feel wanted, needed, and have something to do? That was obviously where she went wrong.

With Jenny living nearby, but no longer a friend, she had to get out and make sure her reputation was not harmed. It was not something she wanted to do, but something that must be done. Why would anyone want to undermine her and her work? She was aware many who have nothing going on in their lives are prone to tear down others who work hard, and it was now obvious that to doubt this could happen to her was not wise.

Speaking quietly to herself, but intending it for Jenny, she left her office and said, "I think you and I will come to some kind of agreement." Maddie knew it would get through, so why not talk it out now? Why not argue loudly about it, and yell at the computer, too?

"I think I'm not as wise as I thought I was. I never really thought of you as a best friend, but certainly never thought you would turn on me after all I did for you—and become an enemy. Why would you do that?"

Just then a car door closed with a loud thud and she heard steps coming around to the back of the house. She recognized the sound and wasn't happy to realize she had actually summoned Jenny. If only she could escape and not have to deal with her now. Perhaps Jenny would pull one of her quickie changes of personality and act like nothing was wrong? No, that would not happen.

As Maddie walked to the back door, thinking about what she would say, she noticed Jenny was not bothering to knock and obviously intended to use her key—and just walk in! She had to believe no one was home, so Maddie backed away, slipping into a closet to watch what was about to happen.

Within a few seconds after opening the door, Jenny moved silently into the room leading to the kitchen and pantry. She looked furtively around and seemed satisfied she was alone.

Maddie was unable to breathe deeply and wanted to sneeze but willed herself to be still. She watched through a crack as Jenny walked over to the kitchen counter and opened a drawer and pulled out a recorder. It was such a sneaky thing to do! Why would she? Why would she tape me?

Pushing a button, Maddie's words as spoken only a few minutes ago echoed through the kitchen.

"I think you and I will come to some kind of agreement," a bit of static, then a click. "I think I'm not as wise as I thought I was. I never really thought of you as a best friend, but certainly never thought you would turn on me after all I did for you—and become an enemy. Why would you do that?" The tape clicked off and Jenny stared at it for a few seconds, then placed the recorder back in the drawer.

She is such a creep, thought Maddie. She doesn't even try to conceal the recorder, because she knows I never notice it. It's always been there, so I never noticed it was turned to 'voice activated' response. Why would she do that, and how long has she been doing it?

Obviously, Jenny did not think anyone was around, because she suddenly answered Maddie's questions. "I guess you think I'm your enemy now, but I never was your friend. I wasn't here to help you, and I sure didn't want to help my mother. I just wanted to know what all you weirdoes were doing with your money.

"Makes me feel funny to be seen everywhere I go in town without you around. People smile and ask how you're doing, and I have to fake it and act like you're not well now. It could backfire on me if you suddenly decided to show up looking great, but that will never happen. Anyway, you look like a hag! You're such an old bag! You think Slim is interested in you again, but he isn't. He's interested in me! I can see it! He laughs at you and winks at me. I know he secretly loves me, but then almost every guy I know does. It's women who hate me, because I'm beautiful—when I'm NOT pregnant."

Maddie wanted to gag. She had often thought Jenny was just talking herself up because she felt down, but now she realized Jenny was an egotistical maniac and not to be trusted. How did she let herself in for such a human mistake to begin and eventually take over her life and work?

"I guess Madeline's out working on her mailings. She's such a trip! Always laughing and talking like she has it made, but now has nothing left for her old age—as she likes to say. I bet she's on welfare before she's another year older. She doesn't know she isn't going to make any money from her mailings. They're so pathetic and unsympathetic. I wonder why she bothers."

This was all news to Maddie. She was never without a healthy bank account and could make a living without leaving her living room. What was going on?

"When she sees how much money I took out of the bank without her knowing I was doing it, she'll really break down and cry—leave the state humiliated. I haven't paid her bills for ages, and she thinks I did."

Her laughter was ecstatic and erratic, while Maddie was blazing hot, ready to stomp out of her hiding place and scream non-stop. She wisely decided to stay hidden to see if anything else could be learned by spying.

"I never thought about it, but she's such a dope for being a famous person. She never checks on anything she gives away to see if it's being used the way she meant—or even if they got it. I guess she thinks all those Mexicans are happy to see her. They aren't, because I never sent them a check. No money, no friendship, and she doesn't know why."

The smug young woman left the house without realizing she had left the tape recorder activated in the drawer, thus would be discovered before long. She must have thought no one else would ever hear what she said. At any rate, forgetting to erase what she said over the past few minutes would not go unnoticed.

"Well, Maddie, if it was me, I'd get the Sheriff on the phone and report her right now. That's the best way to end her vacation and get her back to reality. Once she has to pay off the bad checks, she won't be back. You can count on that!"

Slim was not bothered by the assertion that he was much impressed with Jenny. It was apparently a joke to him, but he added for the benefit of his beloved friend, "And that crack about me being in love with her? What a joke! Who writes her stuff? I'd rather cozy up to a rattlesnake than someone like her."

Maddie smiled, but did not say much since her mind was chasing after too many other thoughts. Afraid it might jam and never run again, she decided to pray and not do anything until she heard via her writing as a Spiritual Scribe what she should do to set things right. Slim did not need an answer, so she let him sit in attendance as she went into a trance-like state in order to enter her life as a pilot might.

Flying over the Earth, Maddie saw much that was perfect and a lot that was not. Raising her arm to flag down an angel, she asked for help. She wanted to know if she should take out a warrant for Jenny's arrest. The angel said that was wise, which surprised her more than seeing an angel fly by. She decided to abide by it immediately and not bother to write it out.

"You know Slim, you're right. I think I should go and see the Sheriff and swear out a warrant for her arrest—right now."

If Slim was surprised by her sudden decision and resolute manner, he said nothing and simply gave her a hug. She was not surprised, but it was not the kind of hug she was used to getting from him. It was much more ardent than she expected. Was he upset that she had been called a hag? Did he think she was upset and not telling him about it? She would let it go for now and not worry about Slim and her until later.

"Let's lock up the house and take the tape with us but leave the recorder with a new tape where it is. I think she'll be back, but if not, I want her out of my house and a new lock on every door—and a surveillance camera outside. Do you know someone who can handle this for me?"

Slim nodded and ushered her out the door and toward the garage. She was surprised to see her RV was not inside the garage and neither was her car. What had happened to both new vehicles? Why weren't they there? That was probably why Jenny thought she wasn't home. With scarce time to think, Madeline pointed to the empty spots and moaned, "What happened to my car? Did someone break in or did Jenny take it?"

"She wouldn't know how to drive the RV. She can't drive the truck or your new car—let alone that. So, who broke in and stole them and why? We need to call the cops now and have them come out here instead of us going there."

Maddie agreed, and they immediately summoned the local police. The Sheriff said he was on his way and would not say why he was not surprised. He was too angry to reply to the notes pushed in front of his nose to identify what he suspected was going on in his town now.

As the Sheriff packed his stuff, his men were busy gathering all their notes and taking care not to scuff the floor as they pushed back their chairs. It was a huge task ahead, but they each knew what they had to do.

It was Maddie who was confused. She had never heard of scams like this, nor realized she had accepted it as truth that Jenny was the daughter of the famous woman who called her '*daughter*'. It was just the kind of scam television producers would love to film. It was not easy to come to any conclusion about why Jenny did it, but it was obvious she had done it before and no one had thought it was true of her then. This time she picked on the wrong charity.

"When you moved into town I had your charity checked out, ma'am. We don't usually like people who run charities, because too many of them are carnival types— you know, looking for a buck anyway they can make it, but you checked out. You were even recommended to us as someone who could help us raise funds. And everyone loves you! So, when we heard your charity was bouncing checks, and you were obviously not aware of it. And your RV was repossessed yesterday while you were away, we waited. We wondered what was going to happen next."

Dazed, Maddie said nothing. How could she?

"Well, Ms. Worthington, we have to get this thing out on the internet and pick up our little mother now. You'll not have to worry about her ever bothering you again. Now all you have to do is pick up the pieces and get the money back to pay your bills and stuff." The Sheriff spoke gruffly. He was known to be tough, but no one could believe that now. He was saddened beyond anything he could imagine. What made a young person create such havoc for another woman—let alone decide to wreck the life of someone she supposedly liked?

A deputy broke into his thoughts then, "I think we have a psychotic woman on our hands, Sheriff, and I think we should get others to take her in now. She might not make it if we don't take steps to save her from her own hand or wanting to harm the baby."

"Young man, when you're half as old as I am, you'll understand what I'm gonna' say now. She's not sick. She's just plain and simple evil. You better not get too close to her or she'll have you up for being the baby's daddy." The Sheriff laughed and the young deputy blushed but was obviously unconvinced.

"Well, I can see you're under her spell. She isn't gonna' be good for any of us, but most especially for the young guys who think she's beautiful even after all the ugly things she's done. She's got two men in town right now fightin' over who's the daddy of her baby. Can you imagine that? I bet neither of them is, but she won't do anything about it—says she has no desire to know who fathered the baby and wants to let her child grow wild." The Sheriff let out a loud guffaw as the rest registered smiles, but obviously felt it was news that would not keep and would be all over the streets in an hour.

"I guess you're right, Boss, but she's a sick woman. Believe it or not. These borderline narcissistic personality disorders are unreachable. There's nothing we can do to change her ways." The young deputy walked away as the Sheriff stopped and gave Maddie a sad look while shaking her hand. He motioned for the other men to follow him out.

"Thank you, Sheriff, for believing me—immediately, and not making me repeat what happened several times. I can't imagine how you can work on things like this and not get upset and want to leave town. I know I want to leave right now."

"No, Ms. Worthington, you mustn't do that. You have a good name. If you leave, people will start saying you did something to deserve all this. Wait for a year or two—at least, then think about leaving, but not now. Stay here and do what you do and find out who can help you work this out. A good accountant will probably be the best one to straighten it out, but I think you might want to hire a guy next time. These young women today are too crazy to work for a lady. You got to watch who you hire."

Maddie shook her head woefully. Every word registered, but she spoke as if in shock, "I'll get someone in now. I didn't want to hire anyone ever again, but this is way over my head and needs to be fixed now. Thank you—and your men, for all the good work you did on the phone and over the internet right here in my home. The locksmith said he'll be over this afternoon and give me an estimate on what I need done. You're an angel! I mean that." Maddie smiled, and the Sheriff relaxed somewhat and returned her smile.

Just then Slim entered and shook hands with the Sheriff, promising to stay over and wait for the locksmith and show him around and get things taken care of for Madeline. The men nodded as men do and Maddie frowned, but she knew she was too shocked now to get much done. She had to let it go.

After the locksmith tidied up the wood shavings and gave her a new set of keys, Maddie handed a set to Slim to keep. He was pleased. She was happy that he was not going to refuse to take responsibility for looking after her property, too. He would not have done it for anyone else, she thought.

"You look all tuckered out, as we used to say in the Old West." Slim exaggerated his old cowboy accent, walking as bowlegged as he could just to hear her laugh, and she did.

"You're such a character—right out of a movie— an old movie at that." As she laughed, Maddie suddenly realized she was hungry—very hungry. What could she make for dinner?

"You look tired and hungry, Maddie. I don't think you should eat alone, so why don't we go into town and look around for supper?" Slim continued to act as if he was cast in a movie instead of taking care of a friend.

"Oh, that sounds like fun. Why didn't I think of that? You know, Slim, I better start getting out more. I went out this morning thinking that, then everything exploded. Now I know why I thought it. Ever have that kind of morning?"

"Lady, I have that kind of day—all the time!" Slim laughed and she could not imagine what he meant but did not ask.

"Let's eat something light. I like omelets, and they serve them almost anywhere. Where do you want to go?"

Slim opened the door and ushered her toward his truck. She did not need to know the message he bestowed. Without another word they drove to town and only when they arrived did she start to cry.

As the town appeared to rise before her, the streets seemed too neat, too petite, and too sweet, like it was posing or poised for a magazine spread. What happened to it while she was away? Did it always look this way? Did it always appear ready for tourists to arrive and leave their money behind? Was it this cloying sweet and cute to others living here, or just looked that way to her now, because it was such a serious time in her life that it would not be easily forgotten?

Did she blame the place or simply being sucked into the work of a race to own everything in the state, in order to take it back to a time that never existed here or anywhere, being set up to lure tourists into wanting to live there and invest in the mirage, never caring about who did what with taxes left behind? Her mind was one long run-on sentence—and she could not smile.

How could she ever get back to where she was when she moved here? Would it take years? Was it impossible to ever again love someone for being young and able to do much? Why trust anyone now?

The questions did not help Maddie adjust to her new way of life. Shortly she would be expected to address the local Chamber of Commerce again and talk about her vision of the future for their community—and she was stuck. She didn't like what she saw; but how to say that to those who created it?

Within minutes of being seated at the front table, Maddie saw a man slip into the back of the room and stand with his face averted from her. She instantly knew it was Jorge. What a wonderful surprise! Why would he be here? Why would he care? Maybe all the trouble last year with checks and embezzlement—and all that other stuff, made him want to check us out again. She suddenly thought she might collapse with laughter, but this was not a place where even God would laugh. This was a place where the human race was going mad.

"We want to extend a warm welcome once again to Ms. Madeline Worthington, who now makes her permanent home in our fair city and is a major part of the community, as well as contributor to the arts. She needs no introduction, so this is our chance to welcome her back again to address the Chamber."

The community of business leaders clapped somewhat enthusiastically, then settled back waiting to laugh or be entertained—or whatever, but Maddie felt drained. She felt sad and was reluctant to say she had nothing to contribute but a long list of complaints. With nothing new to inspire them to do something about the urban sprawl overcoming them all, she let God step in and take over then.

"Thank you all! I've been out of town for a few weeks, and on my way here today I thought about all the changes that occurred since I first moved here a few years ago. I wondered if we had ever expected we would one day have to pay for all the changes we made. I wondered if we ever thought about what our children will have to pay to maintain all these expensive chalets and villages we constructed anywhere and everywhere. Then in my mind's eye I could see the town in a month or two after we let go of it, and people we didn't know took over. It wasn't a pretty picture.

"I could see young people taking over huge houses and turning them into communes where no one worked on them, and the yards had become refuse spots—not spots of refuge as they are now. The trees were gone, and the hills leading to the mountains were covered with small, run-down curio shops. It looked like *we* were never here. *Our* town looked like inner cities in the Northeast look now— only ours were European old-chic, shabbily built, mostly crumbling and falling apart. It broke my heart."

The crowd sat up as smiles disappeared and many became visibly upset. Why? What had she said that was not obvious to any keen observer? Without seeming to pause, her lips parted, and she continued to speak. "I guess you think all we have to do is make this town a material success now, then die and those who come after us will take pride in what we thought was a vision of success. It isn't going to go that way.

People of each generation want to do their own thing. Like we did! We did it all! We left very little for our children to play with or design another way…What can we do to keep from losing our grand vision if we never bring our kids into it now?"

This last thought brought forth smiles from some and anger from many others. She could not imagine what was wrong but kept channeling whatever was there to say to them.

"We keep saying there is a lot of snow left on the mountains, thus plenty of water. We behave like we have a lot of water, too. Wasting it, perhaps thinking there will always be enough water if we're smart and conserve it more and more once the town grows larger? Well, that is where we are now. The water supply we have can no longer support those who want to build or convert whatever natural beauty we still have into a manicured park no one wants to maintain even now. We need to control adding golf courses, obviously, but we also need to watch building large homes with many bathrooms that will likely leak and not get fixed."

The crowd was restless—and she felt lost. What could she do to save the situation before being shown the door and never again allowed to explore mature subjects with civic leaders as she had in the past? A man at the back of the room raised his hand. She saw at a glance it was Jorge. He was wearing a headband. She wondered if he would acknowledge that they knew each other or just start preaching or maybe teach them something. She did not have to wait long.

"I think you outlined a wonderful way of life that disappeared this year. You were unaware, because you are busy elsewhere, but this past year we have not done anything for Earth—not a single thing! We have taken everything from it as we put up housing that is not going to last a century—and the ghosts we disturbed are haunting us even now.

"Is this not a ghost town? Think about it. It is not *really* lived in. How many actually live here year-round? How many, knowing the government's desire for taxes of all kinds, erect houses all over the country that are not worth the time it takes to build them? You are all here today as a result of civic pride that allows you to think that gaining a national reputation for providing skiing and summer hiking, without doing anything to protect the environment long-term, is a great idea. You all accepted the role of guardians of Earth and are meeting to discuss what you can do now—or so I assume."

Jorge was now standing in front of the group, but many would not look at him—unwilling to meet his eyes, even though he was not speaking in strident tones. He wanted some present to change their minds—not urge him to leave, so he spoke no more about the way Earth was being put to death one-day-at-a-time. Changing his tone, he smiled and began speaking more slowly.

"Yes, this is a blessed city, and was a lovely town, but it must do something for itself soon or it will not be around when houses foreclose or are abandoned and left to go to ruin. Many think every building boom goes bust, but foreclosures are few and far between around here this year. Think about it. What would you do as a community if the real estate bubble burst in a year?"

Unsmiling, Jorge said little more. In fact, he turned to Maddie and asked her to continue reciting the facts— and she did that.

"I think that after all of this is digested and your heads clear, you will all know what to do. I am confident of it! I am not here to blame anyone or take it upon myself to decide what is best, because I am merely a messenger who noticed that our town is not going to look good down the road. I want to slow *progress* enough to let people stop and really live with us now—and take care of their investments. Once they live here all year, we won't have to worry. The environment will speak to them as much as it does to us. Then we will be able to do more as a community than we ever explored before."

The remainder of the session was brief. No one stood and clapped, or sighed with relief, because most were trying to figure out what was wise and why. A few thought it was the most interesting Chamber of Commerce meeting ever. They knew now that they had to keep this writer here and not let her leave town now or ever.

☯Chapter Eighteen

"The world isn't changing rapidly. In fact, it's sitting still, waiting for someone to stand up and either die or move it to the next plane." Maddie said it to herself, then shouted it out to the world. No one was around to hear her, so she was satisfied she was losing her mind—or at least not doing much with whatever mind she had left. Her sense of humor erupted then and bubbled over until she laughed aloud and thought about what she had done to get so involved with this young woman who was now either going to jail or having to own up to all the lies she had told or written and used over the past four or five years.

Jenny was not a cover girl, as she had said, but she did appear in one magazine's year-end issue as a stand-in for a famous model who grew tired of holding a pose. That was not what was getting her into trouble. It was the fact that she posed as a student doing research on a Ph.D. that got her into hot water. That Ivy League University was not pleased—at all.

She had been given time to get her house in order and find a way to support her child but was still flirting with jail time. Jenny realized it—for the first time, when no one came forward to take her side when she was arraigned the last time, but she still was not really getting it. She was not afraid of the law or anyone who took her past sins seriously. She felt it had all been a lark and her mother would be able to get her out of this jam, too. It turns out she was adopted—not really the soap opera star's daughter by birth. The star is not disowning her, but so far has not moved to do anything to get her out of the mess she built around her like a tall wall.

"This is all so unreal! I feel like I was wrong to call her out on cheating me—like I should have let it go and said it was all just a joke. Why do I get involved with women like her? It had to have started years ago when I was a child. Why else would I not see it coming and let such a woman abuse me?"

Leaning against the windowsill, in order to peek around the corner of the house to see if anyone was coming down the road, Maddie adjusted her thoughts while resting her head against the cool window pane. She thought about her childhood, then suddenly felt as if she had lost her balance and fallen onto the street. Her mind was releasing her into time again….

Maddie was unable to sense what she was doing and what she would find but was determined to enter this sphere and find out what was hidden here. She fell in a spiral and ended up in a beautiful spot filled with lovely flowers and people who seemed very young. Those who had died were at her side. Was she in heaven? Had she died? Who was on the other side, if she was here?

"I think you're here to summon up the courage to stop looking at women, in particular, and thinking they are probably right and you are mistaken. You do that a lot. You always did. I guess you got that from me."

Maddie looked at the woman standing in front of her and noticed her lips were not moving—or at least not much. She wondered if it could be her mother. Could she be in heaven along with her friends and neighbors and everyone she once knew? Could they all be here with her now?

"You are in the World of Tomorrow, Madeline. You were an obedient child. You always wanted to please me and your father. However, we never were the right parents for such a being as you turned out to be. We were not prepared to help you this life. Our lives were too restricted and too narrow at times to let you realize what you were here to do.

"You are still in the world—not dead. What you find here is not going to be in your world and time when you leave, but whatever you do now is recorded and actually being lived by us all. You could upset your entire future now. Really!"

Suddenly aware she was not hiding her doubt about what was being said by this dreamy figure, Maddie stopped shaking her head and smiled. Her old psychology professor years ago had said to always, always agree. It lets things flow better. Whenever you say no, too much explanation is required. How interesting that her mind went to that lesson as she drifted into tomorrow or wherever she was now.

"This is very interesting to me, Mother. You are my mother, aren't you?"

"I am not your mother—really. I was there to nurse you and help you learn how to live on Earth, but I am not your mother. That was something you imagined. You also thought I was the wise one, but you truly were who told me what to do and how to make a life then. I was lost, and you found me a broken woman unable to do her work or enjoy her children. You helped me be a mother to them, but I was never able to help you—then or now.

"I want you to have a good life, Madeline. I want you to enjoy the life you have left on that side in that time. I want to help you develop your work of all time now. I can help you. I have finally studied enough about time to find out what you always wanted to know then. I will work to help you."

Maddie was stunned at how the woman denied being her mother yet appeared to be exactly like her—even speaking with the same voice. What does all this mean? Was she a symbolic personality? Was the idea that we all have a mother and father incorrect? Do we merely exist in time, and others who appear to be our parents help us do whatever they can—then we do our thing and forget them? I don't think we could succeed if we walked away from our mothers that easily.

"You are worried now. I will help you lose that concern. You are here because you are able to fly—"

Before the specter or her mother or whoever could go further, Maddie said, "Able to fly? What do you mean? Can you teach me what that means? I heard that the elite of many tribes fly, and even now some can levitate, but no one uninitiated to such rites can fly that way without breaking bones. Can you teach me what it is we need to do to fly? I would love to know. I want to fly, too!"

The specter of her mother smiled, then benignly spoke of work that has to be done on Earth before the next group can ascend to this side without dying. She was apparently doing her work, but Maddie was stunned at this news. What was going on? She must be having a nervous breakdown.

"You are fine, Madeline. You are not my daughter and never were, but we lived side-by-side all of the lives we were together. You accepted that I was there to lend you a hand from time-to-time. I was serious about what I said. You can fly—and you need to help others ascend when this time comes to an end, because it could end tomorrow—really! You never know when your time is over. The entire world you are part of is created by YOU, in part so you can enjoy what you helped create."

In spite of her mind's worry, Maddie was interested in hearing about what she often thought about when she was floating through time and lost to the world. Why had she arrived on Earth when she did? Why had she picked a time when all of humanity suddenly jumped ten spaces ahead and began doing things they did not even think about before she arrived? How did that happen, and why did she seem to have so many close ties to men who had built industry but could not keep it?

"You are a brilliant woman, Madeline, and your intelligence was never used to benefit the world you live in now. You wanted to donate this time to science, but it was not allowed. Instead, you were given the care of old people, in order to help them die in the right way. You had no idea why your parents were not young or healthy like everyone else you knew. You accepted that you had to wait on them, and take care of them, and that this death was their time to go home and not come back again. You even explained it to me!"

Maddie smiled and said, "Yes, I remember when you were dying, as if it were only yesterday—and maybe it is…Anyway, you asked me to explain to you—you who were the finest Christian I have ever known or ever met! You asked me to explain what happens when you die. I did not say much, because it was not something I had ever put into words before then. You were there, so tell me what I said. Did it make any sense?"

"You were able to help me, because I was unable to gain the momentum needed to die and leap over the hurdles I had erected all my life. I wanted to see Christ and worship him—sit at his right side, but I could not find him. Angels came and suddenly announced it was time…"

"Yes, I remember that. You told me about it when I got home from work a couple of years before you died. Why didn't you obey their urging you to leave then? Was it because of me? You said they came to tell you I would never have children—and that it was really a great gift! You were so relieved when they promised I would, however, be a mother to many, which isn't possible to women who see themselves as mothers dedicated to their children only."

"You are aware it happened? Then you know why it happened. It was as I said that day. Nothing changed. I was told to let go and fly, but I could not. I had no faith."

"You, who knew everything about the Bible, studied it every day of your life—didn't know? I doubt that even now. I bet you levitated all the time you thought you were sitting quietly in your chair."

"No, that never happened then. It took death to free me and let me breathe. Back then my lungs were so damaged I could not run. I could never do athletics or move boxes and such, but you never tired of making up excuses to hide my health problems. You would do whatever had to be done and move whatever had to be moved—including me. You moved me so much that by the time I died to you in that world, I was unable to say why I wanted to leave.

"I was wise. I saw everything around me. I saw what others did! I know you were the only one devoted to what I was there to do on Earth. You wanted me to do it and get through to the other side and not die in such a way that I would have to return to learn to fly. You pushed me then."

When the woman she called mother, or the image of her, stopped talking, Maddie said, "I pushed you? I taught you to fly? I guess I know more than I think I do, but then that is true of everyone. Isn't it?"

Her mother nodded and sighed.

"You look tired. Does it take a lot to move around here—in time? Do you need air? Do you use your heart and lungs now?"

"You ask too many questions. You always did. You want to learn everything in a day. Your mind is so much like a mule stubbornly refusing to move when it cannot see what is ahead—then pulling ten times your weight once you get started. You really are a card."

Maddie smiled now. She remembered how often her mother had said that in the past. However, it made her feel weird now. She felt strained or constrained standing there, so she looked around for a chair or bench or something to sit on.

"Come here and sit under the grape arbor and work on your embroidery."

Maddie wanted to laugh. Although never great at sewing and needlework, her mother had tried to teach her the skilled arts, as well as the ability to sort out her thoughts as one sorts through thread, so as to never be overcome by stress. Perhaps that is why she wanted the Mayan weavers to do more than they ever did before?

"You are welcome to stand, but you do look a bit tired. Maybe it's because you were sick?"

Not sure what she was referring to, Maddie smiled, then sat down.

"You don't think about being sick now, but you are overwhelmed at times with the worries of others who leave their garbage behind when they leave your space. You take upon yourself woes of the human race—and still haven't found out that it is not your problem."

Maddie tried to smile, but her mouth would not move. She felt strange, as if her back was arched and her shoulders hunched due to bearing a huge weight that had just landed on her from above. Her mother smiled benignly as she said, "I am so happy you decided to show me your wings! They are magnificent, and I am the only one who ever really lived with you in person—as a human being. Do you realize that?"

Stunned and stumped, Maddie said nothing. She felt funny. She felt overcome with something like bliss or lightness, but not sure why. As she stood and turned around to look at the sun, she realized her mind could see into time. She was upset to see she indeed had rainbow colored wings that were not at all small. She looked to be ten feet tall!

"Now, as I said, you know how to fly, Madeline. You just don't know how to be an angel without becoming involved. That is where I failed. You are back here among us all now to learn how to do that."

Arching her back a tiny bit, just to see if the wings would move, Maddie rose even taller. She felt as if she could carry her mother across the bridge to where her father was working in his garden. She decided not to do that.

"You can see your father is still working and does not realize you are here. I talk to him from time-to-time, but he is usually busy and has no time for me."

Amazed, Maddie said, "You mean he doesn't recognize you as his wife? You who loved him so much and devoted your love to him alone?"

"Yes, that is the point. He knows now that he was not worthy of my love. He found out when he arrived here many, many years before I died that he was not the one who was supposed to go. I was, but he didn't know how to help you grow, so I stayed behind, and he had to leave."

Maddie turned these thoughts over in her mind, or whatever was processing the interview, and felt a lot lighter than before. Yes, it all made sense. Her father was not as ill as her mother, but she lived, and he died. Everyone thought it was right, because he was so much older than she, but it was not meant to be that way. Her mother had not learned how to fly, and her father had not learned enough about loving her. At least that was what she could absorb now.

"I think your father labors under the belief that he is helping you over the harder parts of life. I saw him once when you were laying your cards on the table and reading for someone. He was tired and quite amazed that people would do such things. He watched and noticed that the woman across from you was lying. He said she was evil and trying to make fun of you, because you are psychic. He watched, and when she left, he followed her home. He got her to surrender her own worthless energies and not bother you again, but she tried. When she did, he stopped her from being able to ever use her psychic abilities to make a living. She suffers even now from a slight headache whenever she tries to see into the future or say things about you."

"Wow! That was something. Who was she?"

"You see, Maddie, you never know, because you let too many people who are worthless get too close. You have to know what is worthless and what is worthy of your time. That is your last lesson this life."

Stunned by the realization that she had only one more lesson to learn—and such a simple one, Maddie wondered if she was going to die soon.

Her mother said, "You have a lot to do. You have many years left to complete everything and do well in your particular role, but if you do not rid yourself of these women—even some men who use you for whatever they can get out of you, you will have to work to the very last day. That was never intended! No one is supposed to work to the day they die. It just happens that way when people refuse to obey."

Chastised in a way she could not possibly describe, Maddie moved to her mother's side and brushed away a tear that had appeared near her eye. She wanted to take her mother's burdens from her.

"You are not here to help me! I am here to share with you the information I received about Mexico and *The Ascended Maya*, then let you go back where you are working now. You will find out it is not easy to talk when you have no body, but we thought it would be easier to do things this way now. You do realize we are not here, don't you?"

Maddie felt for her wings but could not find them. She decided it was all a dream.

Imagining she saw a car approaching the house as she stood with her forehead pressed to the window, Maddie no longer felt blue. She was excited to watch the car make a wide turn into her driveway. Waving, she ran to open the door.

"You look radiant, Madeline! You look wonderful. I could easily imagine you are an angel from the glow all around you—especially your head, but I guess it's the sun setting."

Maddie burst into laughter, only then realizing an entire day had passed. She was radiant, and it had nothing to do with the nearby fireplace or the sun slipping into the horizon. It was due to having had another adventure in time—and this time she saw her Mom! How great could anything else be after seeing her and knowing she was no longer sad?

☯Chapter Nineteen

"The world outside was not bright, happy, and growing. At least not the way I expected." Maddie spoke slowly, letting her words grow in intensity until the idea took on a life of its own among people scattered about her living room. She was hosting a monthly meeting of the locals on how to change the environment without harming Mother Earth. They had worked hard, but no one wanted to do much.

"I know we still have a lot to do, Madeline, but we've already done a lot! Really!! You want impossibilities to be realities, and it can't be done. You have to realize not everyone has your abilities, funds, and connections." As she returned to her knitting, the perky blonde's lips protruded into what she hoped was a cute pout. Continuing to look down, she did not notice how many frowns appeared as she threw her bit of a fit.

Sensing the young woman was way out of her depth and desperately trying to fit in, so she could tell others what they did wrong, Maddie long ago gave her work no one else wanted to do. After all, spies deserve to do the grunt work, letting those they envy work on what they want to do—or so she thought then.

Stopping suddenly, Maddie decided to take a vote. Not sure what to put on the table, she decided to let her inner Guides speak through her. Words poured out, before her mind could stop them. "What do you say we stop meeting like this—planning massive changes, as our friend here describes them, and do something new? How many of you are ready to quit and do something different?"

As Maddie spoke, she walked over and blocked the young woman's view of the others in the room. Done so casually, the young woman never noticed what happened until it was over. She had to go! Everyone enthusiastically sought to oust her now.

This immature woman was too weak to realize she did not know enough about how groups operate and who always leads them. Obviously surprised, the girl/woman said she would leave and do it without any grief, even appeared pleased, until she realized no one supported her and she was expected to leave immediately. She was at a loss as to what to say, but later said they were making plans to do something that wasn't legal and would end up in the papers one day.

Her allegations once made were circulated for days, then died of old age. Her only thought then was to infiltrate another group of would-be friends to find out what life there was like. Angry that she had spread ugly allegations about their friends to ever want anything to do with her, most shunned her to the point that she had to wait for a new population to arrive to see what they wanted to do with their new lives here.

Developing a transient resort into a permanent village is a business today. Many different layers of society huddle together, then separate and move into new frames of reference. This town was no exception to that rule. It provided a lot of life for those passing through, but little else to entice readers and deceivers who loved to work on things seldom found in a town of this size.

"The library was to be our next project! Our friend was sure no one wanted it now—or maybe ever, but I disagree and think we can find an industry that will support it. Not a huge building, or anything like that, so individual residents will support it from the beginning. Anyone have any ideas on how to do it?"

Slim stood at attention and signaled he wished to speak, but a younger man jumped in to say very little instead. He spoke with enough bravado that some were ready to immediately follow him, but his was not what The Lord wanted. Maddie felt it within her heart.

Why did she suddenly know such things? How did it come to her now, and why? Was she to be a tribal elder and stop the young braves' progress? Why did she have to be the one to always apply the brakes when others wanted to race?

Slim knew nothing of her thoughts, but brought the group back to the table by saying he had spotted a storeroom near the heart of town that needed a lot of work done to it. It was starting to attract teenagers who wanted to smoke pot on the sneak there. He thought now would be a good time to enlist them in building a library for their use, as well as benefit everyone else.

Such a thought had never occurred to the group, but Maddie instantly recognized it would work. Smiling, she thought maybe it was because she was in love, but those close to Earth and their spiritual work felt it, too. Amazingly, everyone knew what to do immediately!

"If we do what we can—and do it better than we ever did any civic project in the past, we should be able to complete it by June. What do you all say to that?"

As Thelma and James sat watching her, Maddie hesitated, then turned and asked them to name the library and begin preparations for the first exhibition. They were floored, unable to argue about needing more help with stopping the explorers who wanted to build a large city dump. Smiling they looked at each other and spoke in one voice, as usual: "We're on board!"

That was the best meeting Maddie ever participated in and the first time she need not say much to get the ball rolling and could watch the group agree on what was to be the next step, as well as three steps after that. She felt such relief, wondering if everything in life could be this easy.

Later, as Maddie turned down her bedspread and fluffed her pillows, she thought back to what had happened, wondering if she might dream about it now. It would be wonderful if she could turn this entire world into a dream of such huge dimensions that everyone could use it and want to live through it, too. It had to start somewhere, and people often say it starts with a dream. She let her mind go to sleep on time, but no dream came that she could explain. It was an epic dream that did not make sense to her then.

"You know, Slim, how I get a lot of help from my dreams, so last night I asked for help with this project. You know, the new library." Maddie stopped to sip her cocoa, then bowed her head. She suddenly saw what she could not see during the dream.

"As I started to say, I didn't get an explanation, I got a plan. I was told what to do next, now that we're done with the library—at least I am. Not sure why that idea came up last night and everyone agreed immediately, yet today it's no longer a part of my life, because I have to leave. I have to do something new."

Slim missed his lips and dribbled chocolate over his chin as he grinned. He flipped out and grabbed Maddie by the shoulders and held her close. She was not smothered, but close to it when he put her back in her place to say, "Yes! You've finally seen the light! I want you to design a new life—one without all these people around you—like now. You need to enjoy your time while here. You're not always going to be around, and you keep saying you have so many places you want to go and so many things you want to do, but you keep on working for the same people. Let's get going now! Start by telling me your dream."

Maddie moved into the family room, selecting a soft chair where she could see outside, yet still enjoy the roaring fireplace. "I guess I built a fire this morning because I knew we would need it. Ever notice how many times we are prepared for whatever is ahead, yet we still don't trust what comes easily to us?"

Slim settled in the chair opposite so he could see the front door, then nodded and made a rolling motion with his hands to indicate he wanted to hear about the dream.

"I guess I better start at the beginning of the dream."

"Yes, that would be good. Now would you get on with it so I can get home before tomorrow?" His good-natured grin was in place, but there was an edge to his words.

Maddie did not notice, because the words she heard were more perfect than she ever thought possible when describing a dream. "I didn't write it down. Didn't want to break the spell, so I said to myself: Remember everything about this dream and don't forget a single thing. I guess I wanted to be able to tell you now but didn't realize it then. Like I was saying—"

Slim interrupted with, "Now Madeline, what did I say? I want the dream—now!"

Unable to ignore the imperative tone of this man who was now more than a friend, she decided to let it go now and talk to him about it later. Slim appeared impatient, so she moved on with her story so he would not leave too soon.

"I guess it was a major breakthrough kind of dream for me. I felt it in my bones, or my mind, or wherever you feel such things. Yes, I know, you only want to hear about the dream, but I have to lubricate the pump. You know about such things…"

Slim did not smile but made no more gestures.

"I'm on the edge of a cliff, and I can see you pushing a car toward it. You wanted me to motion to everyone below that you were going to drop this car on top of them." She hesitated and noticed his surprise that he was part of the dream.

"You said, 'Don't let it go until I say so,' and I couldn't figure out what I was holding onto that made you think I could stop the car from plunging over the cliff, so I stood there and watched as you eased out the hand brake, then gave it a push. I hadn't warned anyone that the car was going to drop, but you never noticed."

Slim was now staring at the door as if someone was standing there watching them, so she turned to look. He was obviously annoyed that she stopped talking to check what he could see so easily but said nothing.

Maddie decided to get on with the dream and stop fidgeting and irritating him. "In my mind I got this dream in line, but now I can't figure out why I didn't listen to you in the dream. I'm not really like that, am I?"

Slim looked at her oddly, so she smiled and said, "So, anyway, I was there when the car starts rolling over the cliff, but it gets hung up. It can't go over the cliff—not enough momentum or something. So, you push at the trunk, and as you push, it explodes! You get blown away—and the car shoots out into the stars. Oh, yes, it was at night. You're stretched out on the ground, not moving, and I wonder if you're dead. Finally, you slowly got up, then looked at what exploded and what was left of it. I guess it was some kind of bomb, but you didn't say anything. You just shook your head—like you do—and are doing now."

Slim stopped her by holding one finger up. She decided it was time to move along or be urged to forget it. "I guess you were surprised to find everything blown apart, instead of staying inside the car. Not sure why you looked so surprised, but you got up and dusted off your chaps. Oh, yes, you were riding a horse when the dream started—and I was in the car. I forgot to mention that."

Slim said, "Maybe you should write down your dreams—even the ones you think you will never forget!"

Without a word about his lack of tact or attention, Maddie smiled and said, "I went to your horse and tried to mount it, but I was on the wrong side. I couldn't get on, and I frightened the horse. It shied away, and you caught it by the reins and jumped off to help me get on. We then ride toward the sunset, but it was probably dawn, since it was dark when the dream started. Anyway, as we ride you talk to me seriously about life. Normally you tell me not to be so serious, but in the dream, you said I wasn't taking life seriously enough."

Slim was now listening intently, so Maddie continued. "I took a little twig and tickled you with it, but you didn't laugh. You said the forests and all that lives in them were being given away to people who were barbarians in every way, and that we needed to leave before they infected us with their hideous ways, and I agreed."

She looked at Slim and noticed he was not smiling, so she added by way of explanation, "I guess I wasn't listening to you then, because I just laughed and said not to worry. You yelled, but I said it wasn't that bad. You didn't want to talk, and rode away really fast. That's when the dream really got interesting!"

It was obvious this was not what Slim expected. He was not sure he could interpret what was going on in the dream but listened more intently than he had listened before.

Maddie's words sounded sweet and melodious to her, like honey flowing down her throat. She said, "I saw Mother Earth. She was grand and happy. She wanted us to stop bickering and just run. Run everywhere and do whatever we wanted and know that whatever was done by anyone around us now wasn't important, because she would kick them off the back of the mountains with a flick of her power and set it up so they were lost for centuries to come. All the mountains of Colorado aren't going to accept what they try to pass as laws. It will erupt into a place where only the strongest can survive, and they won't let anything more be done."

She sat with her shoulders hunched, watching the fire leap toward her. Suddenly she saw a vision within its flames. It was not horrifying, but it was not comfortable, either. Her mind was on fire with the urge to run and never look back, but instead she continued to recite her dream as if reviewing a play.

"It was easy to see Mother Earth and greet her, but she wasn't going to let me do anything new. She said she was done working with people. I heard her loud and clear! She has run out of patience with some, and never liked the others, so now she is going to make all the investments as shaky as Earth is in some places. It won't be a good thing to run the country from a palace where you can't greet everyone by name. You will have to greet people and actually run for public office again. That will be the end of the way politicians act today."

Almost whispering, Madeline said, "I can see angels everywhere now—mountains are where they love to talk. I want them to meet us at Machu Picchu and work with us, as if we are frequent fliers there—you and me. I want you to go there with me now. I want to leave this place and never again participate in what others want to do with our money."

Slim sat quietly for a moment, then smiled as if he had won the largest lottery ever amassed. In reality, he felt like a brand-new man—spotless and pure.

Noticing his reaction, Maddie walked over and sat on his lap. They did not dance, instead they sang an old cowboy song, one she remembered from childhood. It was fun! They laughed as they almost yodeled in unison, "I'm an old cowhand from the Rio Grande…" When they could not remember any more words, it collapsed into nonsense.

☯Chapter Twenty

The window on the world wasn't open, but it wasn't closed, either. *'What is going on with Madeline?'* was all the buzz. Was the world-famous author and authority on what women need to do to get into politics really quitting? Was she leaving Colorado in a huff? Was she in love? If so, anyone we know?

The talk was non-stop, and Maddie had enough to keep her busy all day just answering the phone, if she had bothered to pick it up. She did not! She was determined that her life was not to be the subject of gossip. She put out the word, but it was not what she got back.

The response was not a reality she wanted to inhabit. She did not see herself as a big enough star that others would talk about non-stop. Obviously, she wanted to get bookings and sell her work, but not be stopped on the way to the post office and asked for directions on how to live well now. She did not like being given ultimatums by those who expected perfection once they did what she said, assuming they should be elected to public office without further work.

During the time she had left behind her apartment in New York, the world had not grown nor shrunk—at least it seemed that way today. However, Maddie knew it was weaker and not keeping up with the universe. How did this world crumble so fast—and when did everyone forget to laugh?

"Look at this, Slim. I got a message from someone saying there should be a queen. Imagine that?" Maddie laughed, but then thought about it and stopped laughing. Who would even want to be queen? She quickly decided some would do it for the money and prestige, expecting others to think of them as somehow superior. It would never take off! No one believed anyone was better than they today.

That was it! Maddie laughed and said she just found out why no one wanted to actually run the government we have now. It wasn't fun! No one would automatically believe in you, or do what you said, instead you would be run down and put out of power the moment you went up against *The Big Guys*.

Slim asked what she knew about *The Big Guys* and Congress, but Maddie did not wish to comment. Instead, she left it hang in mid-air, in case he would tell her what he knew.

As the day disappeared and the air cleared, Maddie went to the store to get a few groceries to prepare some meals before they, too, disappeared. She never thought it would cost her a lot to go shopping, because she was not planning to buy much. When she stopped at the deli counter, she felt eyes on her. Turning she realized someone had taken her picture and was walking quickly toward the back of the store. She did not like it and was determined to find out what was going on.

There was a large area at the back of the store where people often congregated to chat and talk about the price of whatever. She did not stop there often, but it was filled with neighbors and strangers now. Wondering if she had missed something in the press, Maddie decided to check things out. She overheard someone nearby say she was spotted at the deli counter. No one noticed she was standing nearby, and not wishing to appear just yet, she stood with her back to the crowd in order to better hear what they were saying. It was quite a shock!

"She's lived here for years! I used to work for her—and she was the pits. You can't believe how mean she can be! Honestly, she makes Leona Helmsley and Martha Stewart look good. I had to run fast to get away from her and her big ideas. She is such a crass person— she really is!"

Face burning with rage, Maddie thought about strangling her old assistant, but figured she could never do it without feeling sorry for her. So, she stood rooted to the floor waiting to hear more.

"You're so right! I used to clean her place. She was up all night! Never had anything right. I would go in and have to start over every time, because she wasn't willing to keep her own bathroom clean—and the laundry!"

Astonished to hear she had ever had a cleaning lady, Maddie bent her head closer to the macaroni and listened to the crowd at the end of the counter.

"I think you're talking about someone else. Really!"

Madeline was happy that someone spoke up for her. "She's not about to have you in her house. I know. For years I've tried to get into her library and check out what she reads all night. She must not sleep!"

"That's what I mean! She's always out-of-sight, writing or reading—definitely not interested in any of us."

A deep voice drawled, "Who would be? What do you women have to offer someone of great compassion? You don't do anything for others—or that much for your children, from what I heard at the pool."

Astonished that someone would stop the women with only a few words and scatter them all over the store, Maddie laughed and was discovered by a few embarrassed neighbors. Wondering who had come to her rescue, she was stunned to see it was Jorge who had appeared out of nowhere to rescue her from the cats!

He whispered in her ear, "I should have known you would not stand up for yourself, Madeline." He gave her a peck on the cheek like he did not know her very well, and she returned his smile as if she did not know him. No one present knew any different.

As the group dispersed, a new voice was heard. A friend who could not stand the way the women of today were willing to put down anyone who wanted to run their town. She was not elected to the post of Mayor—twice, because she talked too much like a guy, according to the cats. What did this town need more than speed bumps? It needed a collector of exotic cats to cage them, pull out their claws, and train them to play nice. That would be the first order of business once the nation changed.

Maddie laughed, only then noticing that no one was listening to her anyway. It was so relaxing to laugh. She decided to do it every time she felt tense.

"As if you had a million dollars to waste on others, what would you do with it?" Jorge was not speaking to her, rather the group gathered around the frozen food cabinets. He laughed when no one knew what to say. Had they never thought about it before? Why?

Maddie interrupted him to say, "Too many women never think far ahead. They want to have a lot of stuff, maybe pay off their bills and give their families the best of everything, but when it comes to philanthropy among the middle class, it's usually handled by the lads—or women who never worked for a living."

"You better believe it!" Was repeated over and over again, and Jorge was obviously stunned. He said nothing and walked away from the women to ask Maddie if she needed help with her basket. She handed it to him and proceeded to shop for produce.

"I guess I blew your cover by letting you pick up my basket?" Maddie sported a little smile that looked mischievous to even those who seldom trusted her. She did not laugh again, but then no one spoke to her, either. How did she become the new '*queen of mean*' without leaving her office or computer, where she never wrote about local happenings?

"You need to leave this place, Madeline. They are beginning to become way too familiar with your reputation and aura. They know nothing—obviously, but they want to say they knew you always. If you leave and state you were here on hiatus to gather material and write a book—and now you are done, you will grate on their little nerves as much as anything you might otherwise do. Say it was the perfect hideaway and you had no trouble maintaining a low profile. That will cut the crap!" Jorge ended his little speech with emphasis and was heard above the usual noise and not forgotten. He was right, but no one wanted to agree.

As she put her shopping bags in the truck, Maddie talked about a few things she needed to think through before leaving town. Meanwhile they were observed by those who did not know either—but felt sympathy toward Maddie, wondering why so many were turning on her. Later most would say it was the usual day in the neighborhood.

When the need to flee a place comes upon you, you either obey the urge and leave, or you adjust and begin to change how you live now. Maddie did not immediately obey the urge, but she may as well have departed that day. Her seminal work was finally published, and she was making the rounds of TV hosts who talked down women and said they could not run the country, as well as the few men who thought so, too. It was not an easy task, but she laughed—a lot, and it was passed along to others trying to do something new. New motto: *Laugh when attacked!*

As the weeks passed into a month and then a few more, Maddie was unable to open the door without seeing police urging passersby to move their vehicles and keep on moving along. She had to move—soon!

Without a new idea about where to buy and how much to sell, she opened her mind and stepped into time. She could do it quite easily now and often left for days at a time and knew better than to leave the lights on now.

Drifting into a deep trance, Maddie decided to move to the couch where she could lay back far enough to see the clock, even though her mind would not register time. Once her head rested comfortably on the arm of the couch, she saw a man enter the room. He was unknown to her, but she thought he was a cop, because he looked tough and seemed to be seven feet tall. His arms swung up as if to salute while wings suddenly popped out. She thought she would faint, but instead moved deeper into the dream.

As the window to time opened and closed behind her, Maddie bowed to the winged man and asked him where she was to go now. He said nothing, merely pointing to the next room, so she left him behind to stand guard over her sleeping body.

When Maddie left that room, she noticed nothing in-between the scenes. She was taken by the hand and led to a garden where she could see herself writing on a hand-held computer. It was her past. What would happen if she were to return there and not write anything this time? What would happen if she went into that personality and did not do what came next? Would she be different now?

The world was not explained. She had no sense of time or any idea how she stayed inside the lines, but she felt she was now deeper into her past than she had ever been allowed to travel before. Why was she going back?

A person of no sexual preference motioned for Maddie to follow him or her. She did it without thought since she was not interested in anything there, or so it seemed to her then.

Shortly, Maddie felt as though she was in another century, but surely, she could not be. How could she cross from one entity to another personality and not have noticed it happen? Was it all about time or was it about the capacity of the mind to register only what was great and small—forgetting everything else?

As she rested and thought about the next step, another entity came close to her ear and whispered she was to follow and keep close so as not to disappear. This was not amusing enough to keep Maddie from doing what she was told. She hurried to comply, which turned out to be wise!

In a room where she could finally stop and look around, Maddie felt it was to be a new home and new career for her. She looked around and saw she was no longer a scribe. She was an artist—and it had to be Paris. She loved it immediately! It was like a translated thought belatedly entering her mind. Had she been beheaded and not allowed to live through that life or had she committed suicide in a garret as she had once heard about a past life? What really happened there? Would she find out now?

The woman or man, who could easily disappear without appearing to ever be there, entered the parlor. That one stood out from the wallpaper as if able to beckon her inside the wall and turn her over to another. This all transpired much faster than she expected it could and was not at all like other '*dreams*' she had engaged in over the past few weeks.

As she folded her mind into a piece of paper and put it aside in order to climb a ladder into the sky, Maddie saw she was not alone. Jorge and Mandy, as well as many others she knew well were waiting in another room. Only now could she see what they were doing and hear what they were saying. Would she arrive among them as if out of time?

"Welcome Madeline! You are now a Woman of Today. You had to slip out of one life and into seven others to find this one which you neglected twice, but now you can stay and do your work, or you can return to Colorado and think you are leaving town. You do not have to end that episode, you can let it stand and do it again."

Maddie relaxed so quickly that she gasped and almost passed out with the sudden release of energy. She managed to say: "I don't ever want to go back there. However, I will return and take care of business, then meet you all here."

Without another thought, Maddie leaped from the couch and started packing. Was she crazy? No! Was she making haste to leave? Yes! What would the outcome of all this haste present to The Press? She didn't know nor care.

Maddie packed, sorted, and gave away what was not to be hauled away. Hordes of people waited to see her leave, so they could snatch anything left behind. They sold whatever was scavenged on E-Bay, which amazed Maddie since she never thought that way. Why would people want others' old things if not to use them? Today, it seems like everything is for sale, yet the needy can't compete with E-Bay—or so it seems.

Within a few days of deciding to leave, Colorado could no longer say it was home to this famous author. She left without explanation, laying no blame on her assistant or anyone who had ever betrayed her. She left vengeance to God, trusting that God knew what she needed to do. Whatever came to those who hated her without reason, she was sure it would be far worse than whatever recourse she might take relative to their treachery—and she was right.

☯Chapter Twenty-One

"Thank you! I want to say that moving into a new country and being greeted as a friend by everyone I meet, without hesitation, is truly a revelation on how far my old country has slipped since I was young." Maddie motioned toward Mandy, then spoke to the women waiting with their hands humbly folded on their laps,

"I want to thank you from the bottom of my heart for all you've done to help me make my home in Guatemala. Really! You are so honest and brave—and have suffered so much, but your gracious ways and warm smiles never betray how life once was in the mountains. I take heart that together we will be able to accomplish things I only dreamed of doing in the United States."

Saying that caused Maddie to pause and think over the past few weeks and how much she had accomplished using what Americans ignored and put aside as Third World ideas. Here she had more hands to do less work and would be able to teach the young how to reach out to communities far beyond this one via the internet. She had great hopes of communicating with others about the wonders of this country, but still not sure how it would all turn out.

With one eyebrow raised, Mandy said, "As if we all need to be thanked for what little we have done, Madeline.

Here and now you can sleep deep, eat fresh food every meal, and drink really clean water. All your meals will be prepared and put on the table for you, so you can write as much as you like—and you can dream safely, too."

With a wave, Mandy stepped back so an older Mayan woman could present a plate of fruit she had cleaned and prepared for everyone to eat on their break. It was a fun day, yet it was not exactly what she had thought it would be. Was she losing her touch, or was it simply because Madeline was so newly from The States? Whatever the reason, something was different from how she normally lived now.

As the two Americans sat eating fruit and talking quietly, the Mayan women did the same, thus all had a break from the many translations needed to bring so many different clans together for this one special day of unification. The Mayan women did not know why their elders said it was important for them to attend, but having known Mandy for many years, they never turned down a good time, aware it would be a time to remember and might lighten their lives forever.

As if inspired, Maddie said, "I guess it's time to go back and think about what we did in the past. Do any of you wish to talk about the revolution?"

Mandy sat waiting for a minute to pass before turning to Maddie and indicating it was not yet time to discuss such things. The pain and sorrow were still much too new to let go of today.

Chagrined, Maddie realized she had been unwise to jump in where angels would never go—or did the angels want her to open this wound now? She never knew when she was working as a channel, or as a Spiritual Scribe, what might happen next, but she wasn't going to try to explain it now—especially to Mandy. After all, Mandy knew everything!

"I too believe it's time to think about such things, ladies, but I'm unable to contribute anything worthwhile now. I have no way of knowing what you experienced over the years, but if we are to do something about the past together, I think at least one of you has to speak up or let it pass." Mandy looked at each woman, then back to Maddie as if to say the subject was closed—at least for now.

Without hesitation, Maddie said, "I'm new to your country, but when I do discover what went wrong, *know* that I will step-up my work in Spirit—as well as the law, and help you all accomplish something then."

All the Mayan women laughed, even Mandy could not refrain from grinning. Unsure what she had said that made them all happy again, Maddie decided the translation could not have been what she intended. She decided to let the subject drop, but Mandy interrupted her thoughts.

"You see Madeline, we don't believe anything needs corrected, and we certainly don't think lawyers can figure out what the Mayan people need. We are doing our best to do such work—get it done and over with before all these legal types figure out we handled it without them. After all, what do they really do or even know? They do nothing but smile or harp on their greedy needs that we are not going to pay for here and now.

"In Guatemala there are few who practice law—not because the people are all law abiding, but because it doesn't provide as much money to buy big cars and homes—and power, like being a politician here—and everywhere in this world we all created. No matter, they are condemned, no matter what they do, so only a dog would want to run for public office now."

Unconsciously. Maddie shook her head. She had spent the past few years mobilizing women in the U.S. to run for public office, and here her idol, Mandy, proclaimed it a waste of time, and no one refined or nice would ever seek election to public office now. What was going on in her life that she was upset by what women she never knew would do? Why did she feel like she could not renew her life? What did she do to deserve this great reception anyway? They all acted like she was like Mandy—and maybe why she had to change her life, too?

"I have to say that when I moved down here, meaning to stay half a year as an experiment, I obviously didn't expect to stick around. I expected to take an extended vacation, then go back to The States feeling great—maybe even have a few great new ideas to present friends in high places...

"But this is so great I don't have to do anything more. Do I? Do I have to continue to work as a scribe for people who refuse to listen and read, or do what is intuitively given to them so easily through me?" Maddie expected no response, since she was not sure what she said in Spirit, thus was surprised.

The women babbled in many Mayan dialects at the same time, yet all seemed to be telling Maddie to never give up being a Spiritual Scribe. Why? What did they find within the writings and her other work that Americans could not?

"You are now able to write as a woman of this time, Madeline. You get many to open your books and read, because they admire your mind even though they refuse to admire Spiritual Scribes, per se. You made the material world easier for women without degrees to understand what your work means, which will make the immaterial world easier for these same women to understand. You know what to do. We don't." Those were the words of the interpreter, yet they did not seem to cover all that the women sitting in the little hut were saying then.

Brushing off her skirt, Maddie offered to help an older woman stand, but no one moved. Once again, she was forced to wait for her guests to decide when the party was over. She was learning, but much too slowly.

With the help of the interpreter, a smiling elder pushed a plaque toward Maddie, indicating she wanted her to read it. "You have a lovely home yet take the time to visit with women and children every day who do not have a nice place to live. That is noticed."

The plaque read: *"The Woman Who Knows"*

The message was a mystery to be comprehended and dreamed about later, because Maddie had never received such an honor. She had no idea what they expected of her but spoke of her gratitude. The interpreter did not bother to repeat her words to the seated women. "I guess you all know I'm unable to understand yet what I came here to do—so far from where I grew up, but I promise I will work hard to deserve this recognition from women who are by far my superiors. Please accept my sincere thanks, because I am close to tears—again."

As she wiped a tear from her eye, one woman stood, then the others followed the elder out of the hut. Maddie concluded that no one wanted to see a white woman cry, but that was not the reason. Later Mandy told her that the women left because God was within her then, thus they could not stay.

Weeks went by before Maddie was able to remember that day without blinking back tears. At times she felt as if a heavy hand was being placed upon her chest. She wondered about it but did not seek out a doctor. Her personal medical needs were small, whereas many Mayan towns and villages were without clean water much of the year, thus no one was immune from dysentery and other diseases. She felt weak but did not speak of it.

When the women working in her home created crafts she had no use for, she loved them too much to let any be given away. She wondered how many carpenters it would take to alter her home to accommodate the many beautiful things she had collected, then she decided it was time to learn about E-Bay and how to sell their crafts on line. Would all the women want to participate, or would they prefer to let a few continue to work with Mandy at her compounds sprinkled throughout Mayaland?

The cook was no longer into cooking, evidence being the dirty dishes stacked in the sink since lunch, and the helper who was supposed to wash them was reading. This inattention to work upset the entire staff. What could be done about a girl who did not laugh, instead read all day, unless prodded and shoved into working hard?

When the women brought her to Maddie for discipline, they shared their worries about the lazy girl. She was unsure what to do so as not to upset the entire household. For her, everything was going great, and she was having a good time, so she did not wish to make any changes—not even a maid. She told them everything was in balance, and if one left it could all fall away and no longer work as well. Thus she proposed they rearrange the way they did daily chores, letting everyone work in whatever capacity they wanted to contribute to the group—at least for now.

Since the women were still unfamiliar with how Maddie worked, they were unsure about what she expected, until they realized she was allowing each woman to change assignments and do whatever they enjoyed most. Suddenly, everyone was happy. Most had never before been given a choice and were now giddy and giggly in anticipation of making a change. The older women were aware Mandy did not do things according to how the Elders had raised them, either, but it was okay with their tribal Elder, so they decided to do what they wanted now and tell her about it later.

The disaster predicted by the cook never happened. The children were herded together and the young girl who loved to read was assigned the task of teaching them to read and help with their art. The littlest ones could draw and play and talk while she read aloud all day, and they were all better for it. Their mothers were happy and no longer nervous about what fathers might say, because their children returned home every night tired and happy—and did not cause problems.

Since the cook was in charge of the money, because she needed to shop daily for herbs and such to improve their meals, she was considered to be the smartest one. As it turned out, she was not.

When the group's accountant decided how they could help their economy while eating better than ever, she sought to account for every dime spent. She wrote down each and every expense. While stewing over the columns, she was totally disinterested in anything else. This actually made all their lives easier by comparison to the past when they had to make decisions without knowing full cost and if they could afford whatever or not.

This woman created her dream job, which inspired another to look around and try something new, but she was not as wise. She sat on the sidelines and watched what others did, then reported it to Maddie. Nothing was done without her knowledge.

At first supervision problems were unknown to Maddie, but she began noticing that this one woman had no friendly interactions or helpful connections, even though she continued to report daily on work going well or not. This one could have supervised others well, since she was wise to what everyone could do, and interested in making the work better for them, but the workers did not like her—simply because she was now in charge. Maddie noted that a wise supervisor would have guided them all without being noticed.

☯Chapter Twenty-Two

There is nothing in the air. I can see that, but there seems to be something disagreeable around me, and it bothers me. Should we move by the sea and live there, instead of with the Maya who make my life wonderful?

Maddie looked at what she had written and meant to e-mail to someone, but now unsure who to talk to about making such a move. If she wrote to Mandy, she would quickly hear back loud and clear, but maybe not what she wanted to know—at least not yet. If she wrote to her folks working in the trenches all over the U.S., they would say move and not worry about anything. They didn't realize what disruption such a move could be over time to her mind and work as a channel. So, she decided that no matter what, she would discuss matters like this with Mandy only, since she knew what it was like to move and not know anyone there.

The message sent, Maddie sat and thought maybe she should have asked Jorge instead. She had not kept up with his latest projects, because she had not wanted to be involved with politics, but now that she was at a distance and unlikely to be caught up in ego traps and power struggles, as well as everyday business and greed, she felt safe enough to start talking to him again, without afterwards feeling mad or wishing she was a different woman.

Pulling up a fresh page, she started to mentally compose a letter when her fingers flit across the keys and produced a message she did not intend to write.

I am unable to quit, yet unable to move ahead. What can I do? I want to enjoy this life, since I do not intend to come back again—but if I take off and do not do my work here and finish all these projects, what will happen to my flight? Will they all take off without me? Will I be made to wait again?

This message was a statement, yet it introduced a subject she had never gone into with Mandy, Jorge, or others. What did it mean, and why was she afraid to miss her flight? Where was she destined to escape, and why didn't she have enough patience or whatever was needed to be there waiting for the plane to land and take her wherever?

As one hour disappeared and no explanation arrived, Maddie decided to send off the scribed message and see what Jorge would make of it. She emailed it and instantly got a message via a separate messaging service. It was Jorge!

He must have read it quickly and immediately responded, but it didn't make sense. He wrote: *Will help you ascend, but you must be ready when it is meant to be or stay until the next century—or ten of them before you can enter that plane again and fly with me and Mandy and those ready to leave now.*

Jorge didn't sign his name, but he didn't need to— the address line revealed his identity. She felt compelled to ask him what he meant, then realized he was right, she did know what was right, and could decide what to do with the rest of her life—And she better not lose her place in line this time and miss the flight!

How had her mind overturned itself and become willing to listen to Mandy or Jorge—no need to write? Was she now in a place where the frequency was high enough that she need only think things to have her questions answered? Could she do her work at home and translate energy into what she was channeling from those who no longer worked on Earth? She wondered, then decided to take a walk to give herself a break and let it all collide in space and time.

As she walked through the forest preserve behind her home, she heard saws cutting timber on her left and right. What was going on? Didn't they realize the birds would have no place to rest at night if they took all the trees? What was their problem? Did they think selling a few trees would make their economy more like America's? It might, but what a blight, and at what a price. Why not accept that life is better here, and you can live well without having to work all the time?

Aaahhh, that was the price! You had to do something with your mind. You had to do something to keep yourself from going crazy, and if you had no money from your past, or education that would last, you have to keep working, imagining you cannot retire.

The price of being cosmopolitan is that they hate living in the city but aren't fit to live anywhere else and make a living wherever. This thought settled in her mind. Why did she not see it until now? Why? Because she had not been able to shed the idea of returning to The States until today!

As she thought about moving, it never occurred to her to leave Guatemala and move to another country or return to one of her old homes. She merely wanted to move closer to the sea, which seemed easy. Why the big mystery? What was she afraid to say—maybe believe?

The walk cleared her head, but her sinuses began to plug an hour later. Smoke had harmed her lungs in the past and now the saws bode ill for trees that cleaned the air in this community. It made her sad to see people did not realize their lives were being taken away for no gain. They would not benefit from the products the trees would be used for now. Nothing printed on this type of product was good—indeed never good enough to kill a tree—and they don't even read! Maddie parted her mind and let it sit for a time.

After sitting an hour trying to read by candle light, the darkness overtook Maddie and she opened her mind to time. She was not afraid her neighbors would say she was up too late, so her mind drifted back to the past. She felt herself laugh, then she thought: 'What a way to dream! Would it mean anything?'

She walked into the first scene of a dream and thought she heard someone screaming loudly. It was just a passing thought that did not prevent her from going deeper beneath the level of earthly knowledge that normally prevents humans from becoming true dreamers. Her mind disappeared, and life became clearer. She could see things as they were—not as her mind interpreted them to be.

The forest was restored and more birds than ever before were encouraged to take shelter in the hills and surrounding areas. All the world came to Guatemala to see them. More and more money than any timber baron could ever produce poured into their public coffers. Offers in abundance arrived asking for their economists to lecture other tribes on sustainable forestry and conservation.

The Maya surprised all others, because it was time for their elders to leave and take with them the work of this time. No one wise would be left once they ascended. All would remember when it was, but not know or recognize how they left. No one had ever realized they would leave, even though this was the repeated history of the great Maya of the past and present, and every phase of life on Earth from the beginning of time. Once the masters knew enough, they could stay or pass from among us and do whatever they wanted.

Enough of that…Maddie walked into the next view and noticed *The Ascended Maya* were present at a great feast, but she was unable to join in the festivity. She was not considered to be a master among them. She had to do more work than those who stood closer to the platform where she noticed Mandy and Jorge were seated at each end of the dais and apparently unable to smile. The status of this group was so much higher than Maddie had ever before thought possible, so she left the door ajar and stood outside so as not to burn with the intensity of the heat they seemed to emit and send forth into the group gathered before them.

That is when she noticed a woman who looked like her sitting in the fourth row. Was she able to see herself as she seemed to be to Jorge and Mandy? She did not know, but she was eager to please them in the dream. She did not raise her hand, but her head glowed with a halo like an old master's picture from long ago. Her mind focused on what made her look to be kind and beautiful at the same time. She was not as she is now.

As the dream faded, Maddie was afraid she may have intruded into something not meant for her to see or believe. What if some demon had introduced itself into her mind as she left Earth? Was it okay to see herself in such an elevated state and not believe she was better than she actually was?

Her faith and humility produced a deeper state of dreams. She drifted back toward that same room but did not enter it this time. Instead she walked into a view beyond that area, town, city, or compound, into a forest where she walked for an hour.

The walk was such that she was not provoked to do anything. She did not think, believe, or conceive any new reality—past, future, or personal. Her perfect vision was of a man and woman able to become one in utmost perfection and walk the Earth now. Such a person need not be either sex, rather could choose to be one or the other. They were so far beyond the usual human state that appears in this time that they often were not given enough work to do, and their hearts did not swell large enough to help them live well. She felt sorry for those who could not tell which sex they could excel in and do well even when assigned to them this birth, but she did not dwell on it.

Her assignment became clear as she aligned in her mind with time. She saw the figure of a woman sitting with a large bundle and beginning to pull it apart, as if she intended to leave a bit behind. Maddie sat and watched with interest as the woman pulled out a stick and set it aside before checking her bag again, tagging one or two things with a rag. She was not angry, yet fire appeared to leap from her mind. Not angry enough to cause a fire, but mad enough to affect her aura and what she gave out as her work.

The stick was ignored, and no one came forward to take it from her. When she grew less irate—calmer of mind, spirit, or whatever it was that was guiding her now, beings came to her and explored her more. She was able to give them many things.

Why were people angry, never able to really talk about themselves now? Maddie thought about it and decided they did not indulge others, thus others did not wish to indulge them. If you have something to give, be honest and trustworthy, then everyone will accept it.

Maddie felt weirdly proud of herself now. As this thought came to her, clouds swept over the scene and she was almost drowned by rain. *Pride almost always is followed by tears* is what she decided it meant and would write in her dream journal when she got back to her bed.

It was a long night and Maddie did not stop dreaming until late morning. She then felt bright and renewed, unable to chew anyone out for the rest of her life. Would this feeling end? She hoped not, because it was easier to get good help now, and she wanted the best.

That was a great day for Maddie. She found answers to her questions via her computer and could easily see why both Mandy and Jorge agreed she needed to sit by the sea many days to be able to see into the present she was living today. Her need to be free of the past was greater than her need to scribe about tomorrow. The tribe would keep her alive with fish and whatever she could eat. She would recover, which was the only thing that bothered her now. Was she actually sick? Recover from what?

☯Chapter Twenty-Three

"The world of tomorrow isn't going to go away just because we don't agree today."

Maddie stopped, looked up, and saw immediately that it was not time to leave, but she could not listen any longer. The speaker was talking about the same old, same old, and she had had enough over the last two days to feed on forever—or so she thought.

The air in the room was not stifling, but too many had given nothing but hot air and stale thoughts they would have been better off keeping to themselves. She did not disagree, just didn't see the need to sit and do so little while each woman said the same thing over and over again or swooned if a man entered a conversation or discussion without adding a thought to the pot. Why the need for all this discussion about life and how to live well now?

Maddie could not restrict her mind to this one time any longer. She exited through the side door and hoped no one would follow. Once on the sidewalk, she detected the sound of uneven footsteps following her, as though someone was limping or trying not to be heard. She turned to see two giggling girls and reluctantly smiled at them.

The teenagers were obviously having a great time at the conference and were now out to find food or something good to drink. They invited her to go along with them, but Maddie declined. Her day so far was bad enough without listening to two giggly girls talk about boys or whatever. It was not until she left them that she realized her attitude was sour and not conducive to eating anything now.

Without further thought, Maddie left the main street to follow an alley to the end of the block where she turned down a wide tree-lined avenue, still looking for someone to talk to about life. Anyone would be better company than the group she had escaped for the rest of the day. 'I won't go back! I'll plead indigestion and inability to sleep well last night or whatever pops up. I don't need to explain, but my mind won't let me speak plainly enough to get them to stop bothering me with invitations to conferences that age me. I don't enjoy sitting and listening to the same old mush. I want to listen to someone really knowledgeable talk about a subject she or he loves.'

As Maddie emerged from the shade, walking into the sun, she did not notice anyone else at first. Temporarily blinded, she felt rather than saw a woman she recognized standing at the side of a tiled patio leading to the street. Looking closer she almost let out a scream. It was Mother Mary Michael, whom she loved dearly, but had not seen in years.

"Oh, Mother, how wonderful to see you! When did you arrive? Are you here for a day—or longer?"

The woman stopped to peer at Maddie, then smiled and laughed as she took her by the hand. She was not wearing the habit she had worn in the past. She was no longer a nun. Her hair was long enough to touch her shoulders, but Maddie did not notice it until they sat at a sidewalk table. After they ordered something to eat, she blurted out: "What are you doing here?"

Both spoke at once. There was no awkwardness, but it would be a long lunch if they did not get beyond the moment. Nothing further was said as one looked at the other more closely than at first. The nun was obviously unhappy. She did not look as she had when Maddie first interviewed her years ago. She could not help but wonder what was going on in their country if a nun felt she had to move somewhere else. She was certain of this, even though nothing was said.

The nun was still in her order, but unable to stop Maddie's mind from jumping to wrong conclusions, but she was able to shake off her own delusions about the writer. She spoke softly and watched in amazement as Maddie lost years—age lines disappeared from around her eyes. She looked ten years younger than when they first sat at the table.

"How are you Madeline? You were in the news for so many years—then suddenly disappeared. We all feared you had been kidnapped—until your book came out last March. What was it that made you leave The States?"

Maddie did not smile, but her heart was no longer heavy. She felt happy for the first time in a week. Her thoughts escaped the prison the conference created. She could now smile as she retraced her steps back to when they first met. It took no time to describe what she had done with her life, but it was difficult for the nun to talk about what she had lived through.

"You see, Madeline, I refused to run The Order the way they wanted it done, so I stepped out. Now they want me back. I have to decide whether or not to return, yet I never really left. I had to leave them to see if I was needed and not just doing my own thing—and taking other women along with me, maybe even leading them away from God. I had to leave, but now that I'm on my own and not heading the Order, I feel like I don't have to be there any longer to do God's work. Do you have any idea what I'm trying to say? Do I make any sense at all?"

Unsmiling now, Maddie drifted into the time they had set aside for starting up the huge organization that ate up their lives and let others decide what they could do or not. The foundation they created became an organization run by men and women who were not in it for the fun or the work, but for glory and prestige they believed they needed. It was no longer functional, filled with those willing to give their all. The nun had to do something new or lose her religion soon. Maddie could easily see that, but she did not believe her friend would ever lose faith.

"As I see it, Madeline, you have no need to please anyone now. You're a writer and can move anywhere you like, but I can't. I have to stay with my order and do whatever they want. If I leave them, eventually they will shun me in public and talk to me in private about things I don't want to hear. I don't want to be food for their gossip—which is happening now. I'm always, always being called about this problem or another. They then carry back whatever I said, pretending it's their idea—and too often bungle it. I don't wish to be the power behind the throne any longer. I want to do something worthwhile! I want to commit to doing whatever without fearing I will lose all I gained while pursuing it."

"Why not run for public office? You can. When they go to search your path, they will discover you were a nun, and before that you ran a Fortune 500 corporation—and you were good at both, because you know how to give and take orders. That's a pun!"

Maddie could see her old friend was not happy but beginning to feel a lot more secure or content, for whatever reason. Why would a nun want to run? She had to think about that. Proposing that her friend run for office had leapt from her lips, but it made sense.

"I doubt anyone wants a nun to run the country, but I could work in the Commerce Department, or run some other department for the undersecretary or secretary of some state, but which one?"

Now into something that captivated her mind and spirit at the same time, Maddie jutted out her chin and thought for a minute or two. Once able to see into the future and notice a thing or two, she said without mumbling too much, "I think you could run for state office in Arizona and not have to give up a lot. Then we could meet on the border from time-to-time and talk about the world. You could do your work and not be over-supervised, and you just have to run for office twice. The first time you talk about what you like, etc., because you won't be elected, but the second time you will be elected and never again will you have to talk about what you did in the past or who you are now.

"Since your history will precede you, you have to do something about it. Can you remember anyone who was ugly while you were working at the convent? If so, that one is who you have to talk to now. Get her to let go and be able to say you were great. Know what I mean?"

"No, Madeline, I don't have a clue. I would be running for office in a state where I never lived, and you say that at first, they wouldn't want me, but then they would. Then I have to go and look up a nun who hated me and talk her into wanting to help me? Isn't that what you just said?"

"Yes! You are going to make it with the support of The Church, which will never appear to be support. You are no longer in The Church, so bigots can't talk about The Church ruling through you. You might not like the idea of dropping away now and not going back, but you can do it once you run the country—believe it or not."

Amazed at what she had said to the nun, Maddie sat still and looked at her lunch. When did it arrive? When did they order? Who was their server? She was unable to feel like herself and do whatever she liked if she could meet an old friend and leave her life completely behind yet come back in time to eat lunch. She felt strange!

"You look unlike your old self, Madeline. You don't smile the same. There is too much trouble in your mind now, I can tell. Why don't you talk about your job and let my future rest for a while?" The nun smiled and looked down at her salad but ate nothing. The worm she saw a moment ago was nowhere to be seen now. Unwilling to eat it, she decided to let the worm enjoy the lettuce.

"You look rather whimsical yourself. I guess we better decide on your new name now. We can't call you Mother or anything that sounds like your convent title, so what do you want to run under?"

"Well, I guess I'll run under my real name—the name my mother gave me. Eleanor."

"Eleanor. That's a great name—for a Democrat! Which party do you want to work with to start?"

"Oh, Madeline, you make it sound like I'm going to run for office right now, even though I have no understanding of what is required. I don't vote or belong to any political party. I never have."

"You are a liberal from the way you live now—well-educated, tactful and kind, and you don't use violence to get your way, so you're a liberal. You might as well be hated for what you are." Maddie laughed and started to eat her salad.

"You might want to check your lettuce. I saw a worm in mine and am letting him dine."

"Yuk! That's what I hate about this place. You never know for sure what you're eating, and you better make sure it's cooked. A salad today is always an adventure, unless you're eating at Wendy's." Laughing, she did not notice the furtive glances the waitress gave both of them.

"You better watch what you say now, because the waitress isn't happy to see you stop eating the salad. I wonder if she placed the worm in my salad, possibly in yours, because she hates us. You know the problem with being an American now…"

"That would be too hateful for someone of great faith, and I doubt anyone around here is without faith. Maybe it was her way of saying we should be grateful for having food to eat and money to pay for it?"

"You may be right, but I don't get that message."

This stopped Maddie from saying anything more about their lunch. She would go over it later and figure out what was needed to open to the next level and channel this old friend to discover what they could do for the next hour or two, without being hunted down by others who would interfere with what was about to happen later this year.

"Are you dreaming, Madeline? You look like you are. You have a distant visionary look that comes and goes as we talk, and I don't remember that happening when we used to work together. Has something happened to you down here?"

"I guess crossing the border or borders isn't exactly the only thing I did when I moved. I feel strange talking to you about what happened, but it could explain why I want you to run the world—or the country, or your state, rather than disappear into the convent again. Can you understand that I'm not really interested in you per se, but what you are here to do? Does that make sense?"

"Yes, it does. I know I'm here to do something, and that I have been driven to try various things and learn to use many different tools because of it, but I never see or feel anything. Are you saying you can feel it?"

Nodding slowly, Maddie said, "I think you know, but your humility is such that you don't believe you could lead. You try to put the idea down all the time, but you can see into the future what is going to happen next. I know. I've been there with you. I couldn't go into the future with you or have dreams with you if you couldn't do what I do."

"That is a very interesting, but what makes you think I can do what you do when we haven't met in years? I'm not that astute. I don't look at you and see your past or future. In fact, I'm having a hard time understanding who you are right now." The nun tried to laugh, but it stuck in her throat.

At that moment, the waitress left and was replaced by a man. Both noticed that he waa laughing. It was Jorge. How great is that!

Jorge approached with two plates and set one in front of each woman. He laughed as though he knew something they did not realize was going on around them now. He did not speak and did not laugh loudly but bubbled over with its power.

"Jorge! When did you arrive? Are you here with someone, or do they allow you to drive?" Amused at his change in attitude, Maddie lifted the plate and slid it toward him, indicating he should sit down and eat with them. He mimed that he would get his own food and be right back.

The two women were saddened for a moment that they had not finished their conversation but looked forward to talking to this most fascinating of men. Were they any different from the women at the conference then?

☯Chapter Twenty-Four

The world around them was not shrinking, but their minds were enlarging faster than at any previous time. They could almost see the explosion of ideas as they talked, worked, and thought about tomorrow. The group was going to make decisions based on what people need and what they know but was unable to figure out why they had to hold meetings with people who did not know enough to change their ideas. They met, however, because Jorge said so. His word was law!

During the time it took Maddie to write a book and enter into the group to see who was undermining the work, she was able to develop another idea. It was not exactly what she expected it to be. Her mind, having been given the usual amount of attention, and a good education, was not used to divine inspiration—or was it intervention?

She worked hard to reach a goal of some kind, then felt she had not accomplished enough and would slip back to anxiety patterns of the past. This was not as easy to see as many would believe, because she always appeared to be in complete charge at every meeting. She was not.

As time drifted into a new year and there were three more people to feed and keep with her, Maddie felt the pressure to own a house, as well as the need to move soon. When had all of this happened and why?

She sat back and decided to write out a time line and figure out what she would do for the next ten years. It wasn't a worry to decide what she would do in ten years' time, but it wasn't what she was thinking about now. It forced her to look beyond the time when the end of this world would appear, and either be well used or let go for another year doing the same old thing.

I think I'll write out what I want out of life. That can't harm anyone. It may, however, help me decide why I have three extra mouths to feed that I never planned on before now. I'll begin with the first one, then move down the list and decide which of the three has to leave.

Hmmm…. Interesting that I should decide in a moment of time that someone has to go. I never before thought about it even casually, but there is a definite need to trim the crowd surrounding me now. Who is not pulling the weight required to work on *our* work? Who is perhaps beginning to wish they were in some other place? Who would be best left here to disappear over the years?

The first name written was—Slim. She decided in a minute of eternal time that he was a keeper, and she was not about to lose him again. He was her man, and she was unable to do without him. The fact that he had not always been around made him more desirable now. She could see when he became tired of the work he had grown to hate, meanwhile he celebrated being away from his faithless fans and working hard every year on the land down here. She did not have to think much to keep his name in mind as the one she would love and be with ten years from now.

Turning to the next page in her journal, Maddie hesitated for a moment, then wrote out—Jorge. Why? He did not live with her, and he was not a problem, but his name popped up. He must be part of the future, but intuitively she had to figure out why. When no idea came to mind, Maddie decided to add his name to the ten-year line and move on for now and see what would happen then.

The minutes dropped off the clock while her hand tried to write. Her mind kept mulling over who among the tribe was to stay with the work and who she needed to drop. It was easy to see one was more capable and able than the others, but was she the one? She did not really know why, but Juanita was not of the tribe desperately in need now and did not always see eye-to-eye with any of them, but that was a good thing—usually. Juanita gave them reason to do more now, because she was not an admirer of what they did before. She thought they were less into work than they should be and too involved in superstitious nonsense than was good for them. Juanita lent an air of superiority to the world around them, but she could offend men. She did not appear to be someone we would need, but then again, we could foreseeably need her more than others, if we leave.

As Maddie started to move to the next line, her hand stopped to draw a line through Juanita's name. She knew then that she was being guided but wondered why she had to erase Juanita from the group now. She sat and waited, but nothing arrived. Her mind continued to interfere until she could see that one cannot demand the Divine to tell you why. You have to wait and see. You have to patiently sit and wait—and accept many things.

The next name seemed to her to be an obvious keeper. She wrote quickly, but just as quickly was told this woman was not a good friend. She didn't know why, but she erased the name and decided to evict her in a day's time.

Why not ask about the last one to come and live with her here? She felt it wasn't necessary, but she could handle only one thing today—so she put her down for staying a year longer. It wasn't easy to let anyone go—even harder to say so, but she knew she had to please the one who guided her through everything she did now and would do in the next few years.

Why were the men allowed to remain while the women were split down the middle and not allowed to stay? It was something she wanted to know more about, because it appeared more important to her work than having a lover. It was why she lived and thrived in the work so many admired. Maddie did not know what to think, so she decided to dream.

As she slipped back into a chair kept in her office for whenever she had time to meditate or stare into time, Maddie felt a hand pass over her face. She was scared. Who had entered her space? Who was here? She saw no one but felt the presence of another.

"I am here today to take you to another place. I am not Michael or Gabriel, but *your* friend. I will pull you up and move your wings now, so you can sit alone in this place—and no one will know you are with me." The deep rumbling was amazing.

Maddie felt a chill as her shoulders rose and seemed to expand. What felt like a heavy weight ascended and pulled her upward into a vortex of some kind. She saw a choir, or group of angels, or some kind of beings who were all light and sound—nothing you could put your arms around, and was pulled toward them at a high rate of speed. When the group absorbed her completely, Maddie felt she could do anything. She was perfect! Her life was great! She did not have to change, and her work was done.

What had she done to be able to ascend? This thought caused problems. Her mind was still with her, because she was not yet prepared to go into time, so the angels surrounding Maddie caused her to give up on her mind and not care about whatever she had once done. This formed a vacuum within her that would never fill until she was not of this world. Her thoughts could never explain it, so she did not retain it.

Thoughts were too slow and difficult to grow, so impulses where felt when she was to listen or do whatever with them. Maddie could not pause. She had to move as swiftly as they did. Her wings were not at all difficult to handle, once she stopped being afraid of flight and height.

The idea that speed and light—and the ability to fly, was what made some want to do much that had never been part of their thoughts. Perhaps if she had learned to fly a plane she would have been able to take flight sooner than now. The answer was: *No!* They were able to communicate directly, so she decided it was better not to appear to be unwise now. They all laughed at that.

The day was over when Maddie reappeared outside her home, looking totally sober. Some said she was drunk and could not be roused. Their gossip should never have been allowed, so it was given to Maddie to decide what to do about it now. She immediately fired the woman who had lied. It was that easy!

The next to go was not as quickly over. She had nothing to say, but Maddie could see she was not easy with the way things were achieved. She wanted to constantly say there were difficulties everywhere, and everyone was lazy or crazy or unable to follow orders. That was what she had to explain.

How could Maddie have so many problems with people who did whatever she asked them to do? Since she had no problems with them, Maddie decided it was due to the other's inability to work and cooperate with workers of another class. That was not an easy thing to achieve, so she removed her in an evening or two, and no one on staff was unhappy about that.

The house was now empty of those who would hold Maddie back, but she still wanted to move out. Where? Where would she be happier? This was not easy to think about. She had previously removed her mind from the world in LA, Colorado, and New York, as well as other metropolitan areas, but had never embraced rural parts of the United States. Maybe that was where peace and tranquility still existed? She was tempted to follow through, but someone arrived from Montana and told her to forget about it. Montana was a hotbed of people moving in from LA and other such places and making the locals crazy. It was not a place where anyone would want to live who was tempted to dream and meditate, instead of work all day on a problem.

The final decision was made by Mandy. She arrived in a kind of frenzy, as is her way, and decided at a glance that Maddie needed to be with her. She said she and Jorge, and others, were building a ranch in the northern part of Mayaland to do something new. She did not say what it was, but Maddie knew it was a disguise for living as they intended when they first met—with *The Ascended Maya*.

This action was just enough to let her forget all she had said and remove all regrets, yet Maddie felt leaving Guatemala was not exactly what she had intended. Would she be wise to keep this place and rent it out, or continue to use it for business? She let it go, hoping she would be wisely advised before she decided what to do with Mandy and Jorge.

The week of the Epiphany was not easy to keep, and all were happy when it was over. Kids were wishing for more liberal parents, and parents were hoping for more obedient children, so it was not going to be an easy transition from the old days to the new ways for them. Everyone else seemed pretty content when the outline of what was to be done was shown to them.

Maddie was jealous of no one but was the envy of many. How could this woman who wrote much that the world wanted to read help The Maya? Was she truly a Spiritual Scribe? Was she able to live off her gifts?

This last was easy to prove. Maddie would write and keep the profits from her books in order to supply the people nearby with many gifts they could use in their everyday lives. At least that is what she thought, but Jorge stepped in and suggested she take time off and not worry about what others thought. It was a great beginning.

When Maddie saw her style of writing change every other day, she thought it was okay. Why worry about it? When others started talking about how difficult it was to understand her now, this was not what she wanted to hear.

If channeled material isn't easy to understand, what do you do with it when you use it to teach children? You do nothing! That was said over and over again until she realized the work of The Holy Spirit was to keep adults in line and growing all the time. To do that, you had to make them stop and contemplate a thought, then use it or not. To let the mind merely scan a line of words and never retain any of it was a waste of time. This would not be allowed much longer, if you wished to ascend with The Group at the end.

The Group was gathered into a single room and many were astonished to see who was in attendance then. Those they most admired in show business were not present, but many stars you would know, if you went to the movies often, were there. Why would they be allowed and not the others?

The group was stunned by Maddie's appearance. Why? She was more spiritual in her outlook than most of them, but why were they so surprised?

The consensus of The Group was Maddie was too elite, too into what the powerful do to be sincerely interested in spiritual pursuits. They were amazed when told she had organized the change in political parties practically by herself. They were stunned when told she had written books that sold millions of copies in other countries and helped women everywhere change their ways. However, none of that was what surprised them most. She was too young to be in the room is what they all thought. What a wonderful thing to say since Maddie would never see 50 again! They were surprised at that, but few wanted to admit it then.

When you work inside the line or inside time, you do not age. You stay about the same, but you have to compensate for not moving your body. You cannot eat as much. If you remain the same and eat as you did, you will age, and your body will gain weight. That was something they were interested in studying immediately. Would they all be allowed to age, yet not gain weight? Yes, but they had to change the way they ate.

This simple thought upset them all. No one on the stage or in the audience could think about never eating food again. How would you keep your feeding tube open and bowel clean? It was unspoken but written in questions given to the panel to discuss now.

The Group was not there to discuss the human body and how to live well now, but soon realized it came first if they were to talk about how to ascend as a body of human beings when the time to rise arrived again.

☯Chapter Twenty-Five

The time to move out is when you feel you are not growing, yet everyone else is. Anyway, that's how I feel, but you might not think the same.

Maddie read the e-mail again—and then again, suddenly feeling unreal, as if floating in the world outside while sitting at her computer as usual. How unreal is life when you can't sit and do your business without strange fears about things disappearing and reappearing everywhere? She felt her thoughts could not be organized, and certainly she could not write again—to those who would think she was insane now. Better to rest and let time catch up with her life here in the tribe.

Daylight came, then darkened as if an eclipse occurred, but it was merely a summer storm. Nothing different from all previous ones, but today Maddie felt like running about in it. She wanted to go outside and see someone—anyone. How could she do that without getting so wet she would get sick? She decided to try to fly.

Speaking to no one, Maddie said, "What a ridiculous woman I've turned into!" Sighing, she sat down after trying several more times to fly by raising her arms at her side and flapping them. Laughing, her feet suddenly left the ground and she felt amazingly happy; so happy that she wanted to rise higher. Bumping her head was likely, since the ceiling was low, but she easily kept her distance from the floor.

While maneuvering around the room, she thought about brooms and how witches were said to have ridden them in olden days. She had never believed it, but now she was a witch or whatever you called such women. Could others fly, too? She was sure The Maya did in times past. She heard a lot about it from people passing through her area. They talked about the possibility of ascending as a group one day—but she had never really taken them seriously—not even once.

If a novelist and one-time Pulitzer Prize winning journalist could learn to fly, however, anyone could do it. The thought that she was only now able to do what millions did for years was not very comforting, either. How did it happen—and when would millions more do it again?

As if she was with a wise teacher, Maddie felt her mind receive information she alone could write about. She let her feet dangle a few minutes more above the floor, then said she was ready to write. The entire process took less than a minute, but she thought it was at least three hours since she stood and tried to fly.

Sitting with her hands poised over the worn keyboard, Maddie did not try to see what she typed. Instead, she read what appeared on the screen—as if someone else was writing. Although she felt it was the best of times, she did not think she was truly invested in the present. Her role was to merely scribe and write what teachers from other places and times revealed through her. It was hard on her to do it every day, but fortunately she was used to such work now and did not complain.

The printer was not working, so everything had to be saved to memory stick or CD. Saved to be printed another day—if it made any sense to do it then. She did not realize her work was not any different from the past when she thought she actually interviewed others and produced a piece that included their thoughts as well as her own. She had thought then that she was writing the same as all journalists and novelists, never knowing how many others did what she did now—channeling, merely providing a means for those working elsewhere to reach people here and now.

The text was not easy to read, but then again it was not that hard. If you had yesterday's high school education, you could read it easily and grasp its meaning. However, if you had a college education today, you might not be able to read well enough to understand its entire meaning. How much was written in code will never be known, but today's general population does not really read or listen, thus cannot know what is being said in public ways every day and intended to keep all imprisoned in their minds, unable to vote for the most intelligent and qualified people to lead them.

As Maddie sat and watched her hands type a manuscript that compared the economies of people in another country to a lesser one—showing how the poorer you are, the more you want to succeed and become rich. In this reality she was not sure what it meant, nor why it mattered. She felt time was changing and this world would end, resulting in no one having the same work anyway, but she was wrong.

The work of one generation sets up the work of ten others as they come together within one lifetime. If you consider that sociologists claim a new generation is created every eight years, an eighty-year-old has lived ten generations in one lifespan. You don't have to live one life or generation over and over again to become one personality.

American Indians look at a generation as the life span of one person and multiply it by five to get the perspective they need when making tribal plans for the future, which is much wiser than what the conquerors who ran them into the ground and killed them with plagues ever figured out. How could one country beat another as easily as the tribes of the Western Hemisphere died? Disease—and despondency.

That one thought shook Maddie to the bottom of her soul. What would be the outcome of a tribal meeting where they talked about getting vaccinated against many diseases that previously killed off earlier generations? They did not believe vaccination was any longer necessary, because no one had diseases like measles any more. They assumed they had built up immunity over the generations, and many bought into it. However, the top echelon of every country was immediately inoculated whenever a new disease appeared to be a problem.

The way to digest such material and not give out her name was easy now, but sending it out over the internet meant a few would slavishly copy it—adding their thoughts and names—and likely sell it, too. Maddie could never do that, but it made sense that God would use the internet to disperse work needed to be written and published for the public to study now. Why not?

So, at that moment, and not a second before it arrived, Maddie decided to start a new life. She would find the way to use the internet without giving her name or aim in life. Every day she would send out messages that arrived as unexplained as this article came to her now. She would not check out the documentation, or even use spell check—just send it out as is. If others received it and used it, great! If others hated what she said, too bad.

Her mind was made up, but first she better talk it over with Jorge. He might not like the idea of the tribe supplying her with a machine that could possibly be confiscated and taken apart by the authorities one day in order to condemn her.

Why she thought that way now was easy to see. She no longer felt lonely or happy, but more and more afraid for the tribe and what they might have to go through once more before the elders could ascend.

Talking about the elders produced a new view of what she was to do. She stopped and thought: 'Am I the scribe of this tribe? Am I supposed to write what I want and use this machine for me, or just for them? What is allowed, and will I harm any of them over time if I do what I like now?'

Immediately, Maddie heard feet stomping about outside her door. She rose to see who it might be. With relief she let Jorge into her office, then remained standing as she watched him read what she had just written. He shook his head and said he was amazed at how much she picked up this way. He had never tried to be a Spiritual Scribe, because that was not what he was here to do, but he was thrilled to work with her and view her work first.

"The Scribe is a role honored by The Maya as a learned person is always admired by any tribe. You are able to write what is allowed to be written now, and you are able to enter the work of *The Ascended Maya* who travel here through time. We cannot. You deliver what we often talk about and use in our work, but your work can make us stop, look, and think more than just listen to someone channel *The Lords*. Thank you for doing this work, Madeline."

Jorge shook her hand in a ceremonious way until she felt herself blush. Why? What was so exciting? She constantly was told she was *The Scribe of The Maya,* and it never was something that made her proud—until now. Perhaps she never thought it was that big a deal until today?

"You are very much aware of what is going on everywhere. You are able to smile and laugh, but you never do that now. Why? What about this life in this place is taking away your ability to enjoy it?" As Jorge stared into her mind, she felt her feet rise off the floor and her entire body ignite. He did not seem to notice.

"You can run away from your homeland and never go back, but you are still a patriot. You want to save the U.S., which is *not* why you live now. You are Scribe to The Maya. You are here for us! We know." Jorge's eyes flashed. He did not smile but spoke softly enough that others outside could not hear him.

"You are able to fly now, and I realize you can go anywhere you like and never come back, but Madeline, you were never tied down—ever. You could fly wherever when you lived in the U.S.. It is not an evil place. You could live here and never fly. This is not a sacred spot, rather a place where God is not forgotten. That makes it a place many want to live in now."

"Yes, Jorge, you're absolutely right! There is something different about Mexico, Guatemala, Peru, and other places where The Maya rule today, and have ruled for many years. You do not notice it at first, if you are a tourist and unaccustomed to living in alien places or without a lot of perks, but this place provides peace of mind for all.

"However, I do think that is an over-simplification of what we find here. Can you think of any other place where the people are shy and happy—able to live in the light, even when they are being shot down? I cannot think of any other place like it now."

"You have cities in the U.S. today that are so blighted that nothing can survive if not removed or transplanted elsewhere when it tries to find its roots. You may not realize the blight, because you think it is what happens when a civilization grows too fast, but it never before happened like that. Your people took whatever and wasted Earth's minerals, created monoliths dedicated to men who are now dead. What survives of them? You obviously are no longer in the U.S., but will find most are blind, deaf, and ignorant of what pertains to God now."

Maddie stepped aside to let Jorge pace back and forth across the small room. She did not think and did not write. She was unwilling to fly now, so she stood and watched—and waited.

After passing several times closer to her than he ever walked before, Jorge appeared to collide with Maddie, yet he did not. She felt his mind bump into hers. Was it an accident or was it an intuitive way to make a connection that helps one learn what another intends or wants to do next?

Unsmiling, Jorge drifted into the other room and spoke over his shoulder, "You really do need more space. It is a hardship for you to live this way. While talking to your Guides, you are unable to walk about without falling over what you must save for the tribe or for your business interests outside. I would like you to accept our offer to move into a new place. Can you move now?"

Without thought, Maddie said, "I've already made up my mind. I thought when I arrived here that I would not move again, but now I see my life here is not going anywhere, while time outside isn't exactly standing still. I will leave so I can attack the false beliefs of many others outside. I want to attack them from the inside outwardly, rather than the other way around, so I will go to mosques and synagogues, churches and cathedrals, and pray at each to discover who is doing what and why."

Judging from his face, Jorge was not happy, but he said nothing to stop her from following through on what she had decided to do. She would not be blocked—at least not by him. He knew others in the tribe would say: 'If she was The Scribe of The Maya, why did she want to go outside and work with others?' He spoke little after that, keeping his thoughts tightly guarded in other ways, too. Maddie could not know his deep thoughts, because he did not wish to influence her in any way now.

Without another thought about what she was giving up, Maddie made haste to leave in order to talk things over with Mandy, who was still in the compound and would be moving to another part of the country tomorrow. Since her life was beginning to resemble the life of Jorge and Mandy, she did not expect to hear any reason why she should change her mind, thus Maddie was not ready for what was about to happen.

☯ Chapter Twenty-Six

There was no way Maddie could know, but Slim was trying to reach her about a new project. He wanted her to go with him to a place they had often said they wanted to visit together and pretend they lived there back in the day. The phone rang on his side, but not on hers. It had been diverted to a place where no one heard it. The days were such that racket created by building over a ditch that was once a raging river made everyone nervous, still they persisted and built it as directed. The work was now non-stop. No one wanted to stop for any reason!

When Maddie finally got the news that Slim was doing a new picture at Machu Picchu, she was upset that he had not called. Why did he take the role without consulting her? That was when she realized she was not in close contact with him now, and it had to be corrected or she would lose her best friend to someone who kept in touch better. She immediately sent an e-mail to those who knew his location and what he would be doing next, begging them not to mention she didn't have it on her calendar. Her alibi was that she had misplaced it, and her computer wasn't working right.

As the day wore away and no call arrived from Slim, Maddie began to panic, thinking maybe he had dropped her or forgotten her, because she had been running all over the isthmus—not paying attention to her own business—again. She knew it had to stop, so she could get on with her work, but did not know how.

That evening a hush fell over the jungle and everyone stopped talking. It was not a time when silence was provided by animals dining, drinking, and locating a good place to stay overnight. Later when many were busy hunting and running, working their way through the bush and away from the light, they all felt something before they noticed a hush like no other had taken over.

"The Maya!" said one elder to another. Everyone else was quiet. Sitting in silence, they were not sure what to believe. Time spent in anticipation of this day was such that to be told *The Ascended Maya* were here was too stunning for some. They could not face them now!

As the night wore on, no one said much—and nothing happened. One man who was unable to stop talking at any time, was obviously annoyed. He said, "I guess The Maya never stopped."

The elders looked at him and smiled. They said he missed them entirely, because he never settled down and made his mind follow suit. He had not listened or meditated deeply enough to hear what was said, so he was chagrined and thought they were lying to him. That thought caused a ripple in their mood, so he was cast out into the night. He never came back, and his name was written as unwelcome to attend the parade when it came time to leave behind today.

The world was dark, yet everyone felt light and wanted to dance and laugh all night. Could they bring *The Ascended Maya* back again? They discussed it a lot, but the wisest said it was not something humans could know. It was of God and only those who could summon angels and birds to do their bidding could summon *The Ascended Maya* to arrive in time.

When no one stepped forward and said he or she could do that, the elders decided to celebrate the fact that *The Ascended Maya* had arrived—and though some were not ready, others were. How could everyone be prepared to accept the light and work together now? What needed to be done as a group or alone? Who could lead, and who was unable to follow? The time had arrived, and all had to decide who was wise and who could not do the work. It was a matter of life and death!

The Group separated at dawn. Many went off to work while stopping to meet others who wondered what had happened last night. Meanwhile, Maddie felt unreal. She did not know what to do. What if she left now—just as *The Ascended Maya* arrived from out of time? Would she miss what was happening to the group surrounding her here and now?

When the crowd disseminated material they could feel, and knew to be real, some families were united by it and others took flight, because they did not feel right and did not think the village was able to work together again as it had in the past. The materialists and fundamentalists resorted to their usual ways, demanding that only what was written could be allowed, and only the words on steles of the past were truly worthy of following now.

Maddie was never accepted by them as *The Scribe of The Maya*, so she gave them no thought until a man from the village approached her. He often spit on the ground when she was around, as though her words were not acceptable. She looked away, unaware he was smiling at her now. Her refusal to acknowledge him did not stop him. He was determined to make up for lost time with this Scribe, because one of his group's elders said she spoke the truth, and what *The Ascended Maya* said last night was in her trance-scribed work.

"You, You lady, you Scribe, you are wise! I can now accept that what you write is right. I want to be friends with you now."

Maddie did not quite understand him, but nodded as if she did. He then came forward and gave her the welcome sign and asked her for work. He wanted to do whatever she could not do for the tribe. He said he was descended from many, many scribes, but they all copied the old work. None had anything new to write now. That was why he doubted she was *The Scribe of The Maya*.

Distancing herself from others, she pulled the man away from the wall where he was standing in the shade while she stood in the sun. Looking into his eyes, she saw fire and mists, then a dim image. It was a type of pyramid. She was impressed! How did it happen? Glancing around to see if anyone was producing an image that could be reflected off his eyes, she saw nothing like it around them.

Noticing her look to the left and right—even behind, the man wondered what Maddie was doing. When she said nothing, he asked and was astonished that she could see the temple of his ancient forefathers in his eyes. He was so dazzled by it that he let out a shout that awakened a baby not far away. Everyone came running to see what was happening, while he stood still as if rooted to the spot.

The group around him worked out that he was stunned because Maddie could see his family history. All became agitated and wanted to pay their respects to her then, but she did not approve and said so. It did not stop those who had ignored her for years. Her work was finally accepted, but what did it mean to her and her work?

When the day was over, many came to the gathering place and sat quietly—hoping *The Ascended Maya* would come back, but it did not happen that night. The group could not keep from whispering and wondering—eagerly expectant. The mood was neither quiet nor right, so no one got a message—and no one noticed Jorge was repentant and would not stop Madeline from moving away and being with her lover again.

Maddie did not stop to talk to anyone when she left. Her home in the compound was given to another, since she said nothing about her work and what she would do in the future. It was as if she had never lived there.

The man who volunteered to scribe in her place was dismissed as being too ignorant to be of any use to The Maya. He was able to accept that he could work in a way he never thought possible until now and would publish Maddie's works, translating what he could into his dialect and hiring others from outside to spread the news that *The Scribe of The Maya* was alive and back in business, and going to help the tribe.

As days disappeared and fears registered higher than the Richter scale allowed, Maddie was angry that she had not paid enough attention to those who wanted to be with her, live with her, even marry her. She had ignored suitors over the years, but hoped Slim was not a joke on her, since she was finally willing to settle down with him alone. Would he be too busy and walk away, ignoring her as she so often did when he was between movies? She could not feel what was going to happen—perhaps that ability had been lost, too? Her anxiety was not yet paranoia, but it was historic in that she previously never needed anyone that much, and now was desperately in love.

Working in a jungle hut, having great luck, and being loved by many others was not enough—or so Maddie discovered. She wanted only one person to say she was the one. She now did not think about work on ascension that she had devoted her attention to for so many months.

She now felt disconcerted by all the people who constantly talked to her about what she was doing now and where she had been. Her remarks were off the cuff and not meant to be quoted, which created a problem. Now everything she said was recorded. She was watched as never before and was not sure what it was that made her discourse and actions something the government and a few others wanted. How and when had she become a threat to anyone?

The days of her life disappeared in an instant once she was reunited with Slim. He was so happy to see her that he never said a word. He just sat and watched, then sprang to his feet and caught her in a bear hug. She could not breathe for several seconds, then let go with a hiccup as a kind of verbal protest to his hug, but clinging to him more.

The Press was abuzz with all the attention given to this particular movie star and his girl. Why? What was the reason so many spies were present in the airport and on the bus to the parking lot? The Press knew them all and reported the star was involved in something not quite right.

Slim said not a word and laughed when reporters pressed him to say something about the number of secret service people assigned to every function any one of the Administration might appear and come in contact with him and his love. He knew what was going on, but Maddie did not. Slim had many friends and most of them were not at odds with the present administration, so they told him Maddie was not wanted, and he would be wise to get rid of her.

AS THE CROWD GATHERED AROUND THEM AT A MOVIE PREMIERE, A LIGHT SUDDENLY FLASHED THAT CLASHED WITH ALL THE MEDIA PRESENT. IT LIT UP THE SKY AND WHAT APPEARED TO BE ANGELS, BUT WERE REALLY *THE ASCENDED MAYA*, WHO ARRIVED AND TOOK OVER THE ENTIRE ATOMOSPHERE THERE. THE PRESS WAS DENIED ANY NEWS TO WRITE. THE ADMINISTRATION WAS PUT TO FLIGHT. EVERYONE KNEW WHO WAS RIGHT!

ALL WERE TAKEN TO THE HIGHEST LEVEL, AND NO ONE WITH WISDOM HAD TO DENY THEY WERE DOING WHAT THEY KNEW WAS BEST. THE NIGHT ENDED WITH EVERYONE SHOUTING. THE MAYA HAD ARRIVED, BUT ONLY ONE KNEW IT WAS *THE ASCENDED MAYA*.

AS THE PHONE RANG AND PEOPLE CAME TO THE APARTMENT THEY SHARED WITH THE DIRECTOR AND HIS STAFF, SLIM COULD NOT STOP YELLING! HE COULD NOT STOP THE CROWD FROM SHOUTING OUT WHAT THEY THOUGHT, TOO. ALL THE WORLD WAS NOW IN A RUSH. THE ONLY PEOPLE WHO COULD HEAR WHAT WAS HAPPENING AND DECIDE WHAT WAS REAL, WERE ON THE OTHER SIDE WHISPERING: **THIS IS THE LAST OF THE MAYA, AND THIS IS ALL WE WILL WRITE.**

WITH THAT EMBLASONED ON THE COMPUTER SCREEN, MADELINE LEFT THE COUNTRY.

☯Chapter Twenty-Seven

The mountain stood before them as they stared in awe at the way it poked through the clouds at dawn's first light. It was as bright as when the sun is in place for hours high above the Earth. How could it shine so bright and not be affected by the night? It was power, and its innate way of being a place where such power was never extinguished and made this mountain so great.

Maddie stared at the place where two mountains stood separate—not joined and thought about her life as she had lived it so far. Which mountain would she take? The one closer to her more powerful feminine side or try once again to scale the heights of power that truly belong to men?

This was her first day with Slim and no others around. It was to be their first day in a new life. She was sure she would be his wife now and live by his side and do what women have done for centuries—if not forever. She decided to let life lead her once again and see where it would take her. Could she do that, or would her ego interfere and command her to do what it wanted, instead of what was genetically-implanted and forever resided somewhere within her mind?

A group who entered the grounds in a rush, even before they could reach the peak, was now quiet and hushed. Not one spoke, apparently no need for someone to interpret or read aloud about the scene before them. It was such a peaceful experience until someone started strumming a guitar and singing as if by popular demand. Would there never be peace and quiet?

The happy pair walked toward the mountain without noticing what was happening at its peak, and what many others wanted to see. It was not for them to wonder and seek what others wanted to see. They came here to commit their lives to each other and decide what they would do with the rest of their time together.

Slim took Maddie by the hand and kissed the lines that seem to telegraph the love he felt directly to her heart. She could not take it and cried out for him to stop. He was surprised, until he saw she was not as she had been and was crying with joy—not the sorrow she usually felt for all who wanted so much from her, and she could not give them enough. Her previous life was over and done with as far as she could see now. Her mind was with his in a place where they would live and grow to know God as only two people can who live together on Earth now.

Their plan was to be alone on the mountain and roam until they found a spot where they would marry in their hearts. That was what they wanted, but witnesses began to creep into the world around them. No one left them alone!

Slim had been spotted as being a movie star, and even people who never saw any of his pictures wanted his autograph and wondered aloud about her. Then, and only then, someone recognized her as a writer. Yes, someone said, she was famous in a way today, too.

Maddie wanted to run away, but Slim held her hand as he nodded to some and walked through the waves of fans as if he had done it all of his life, and perhaps he had. It was not what Maddie wanted, but the people all around them were pleased. It was such a small thing, so she smiled at them all.

The world was now fully awake. There before them stood a shaman without anyone else nearby. He beckoned to them to follow him behind a stone wall, which they did. Why? Why not? They wanted to be blessed, and he appeared able to do that without knowing who they were.

As they turned a corner of the ancient site, there stood a crowd of ancient ones who never left this place and were visible only in the shade on this side of the mountain. Slim gasped and Maddie felt faint, but they continued and managed to hail those who were there to give their blessing, then leave before crowds pursued the couple in order to see what lay on this side of the mountain.

"You see! They can make themselves known—just like angels!" Maddie spoke softly, with awe, but Slim was not listening.

Instead, he was looking at her and saw a light he had never seen before—and was almost positive he saw wings behind her. He wondered if they had entered a grand delusion that began when they ate food the night before prepared by a man who looked too good to be true. Was it filled with magical mushrooms, and as a result they were simply out of touch with reality now? He could not figure out why he thought Maddie looked angelic but was satisfied she was now his wife, and they would not be bothered by anyone else.

"You look like an angel standing there, Maddie. I never saw anyone in my life who radiated light as you just did. How do you turn on such power? In the movies they call it backlight. You have to have an expert on hand to do it, but you just turn it off-and-on from time-to-time like magic. It always startles me. How do you do that?"

Maddie was not aware she had become angelic in appearance. Unwilling to talk about her life in another sphere, she had to try to divert his attention to something else—so she would not have to share what little she knew about it now, as well as what might happen.

The day turned out to be superior to all others. Everyone around them returned to their trains, buses, hotels, and hostels. They did not see the famous couple rush back toward the mountain to sleep there overnight.

Both wanted to do this at least once, unless the guards said they were not allowed. No one stopped them, and no one spotted them going behind the mountain that was open to those who had appeared there that morning—just in case the ascended ones decided to arrive once again in time.

As night fell, birds did not sing, and frogs did not croak, everything was strangely quiet. Even the monkeys and babbling waters were quiet. All was as it was supposed to be when a dramatic play was about to begin.

Quiet, and without a worry, Slim and Maddie waited and thought not about anything they could name. They did not work on each other or notice the walls around them, let alone single stones or mountains. They let the air stand still until it quieted them within again.

Lack of oxygen was not the problem it had been, because they walked up the mountain rather than taking a car or train—or even flying in. It took time, but they were now accustomed to the thin air and did not feel out-of-breath laying on the ground and looking up at the Pleiades and other constellations that no longer surprised them with their huge size—at least nothing like what they witnessed that morning.

Waves of clouds drifted by until the moon came out and stood over them, as if to say it was day and they could work and do whatever they wanted now. The light was bright enough for Maddie to examine the skin of her hand, noticing it looked better than it had looked in the past ten years. She looked at Slim and saw he was not as old as he had been when they walked the sacred path. She was amazed, but he was not.

The lighting gave them faith that they would now have years to live together. The time left was for their minds and lives alone—not living for others—ever again. It was time to retire and be all they could be. Able to work in their minds or in time, and not be bothered by schedules, editors, fans, and those who did not like them. It would be a wonderful time, but where could they live that no one would come by and bother them when at home?

The world disappeared and let the moon work its magic. It gave them all the inspiration they needed to make this night and others like it last as long as love could partake of it. This would be the best life, and the best love, and the only time they wanted to remember after they left this mountain. It would be their favorite place, and they would always remember it.

Several hours later the sun was difficult to discover. It came through in bits and pieces, chasing the rain clouds away before they hit this magical space. Women and children of the past arrived and spoke of what they knew and how many had once lived there, too. It was a time when all was complete—and no one below needed them.

Whatever these strangers who had slept on the mountain were able to do amazed the shaman who had ushered them into the shelter of the ruins the day before. He would not tell anyone about having seen a strange being and a light so bright he was frightened by it. This was a time he would remember and return to again and again before talking it over with friends.

The world was less intense for them, and life within was greater than they had ever believed it could be. What would they do once they could walk into the center of people of their own tribe and look them in the eye as if nothing had changed—when everything was now different?

They decided not to return to the site where the movie was being wrapped up. Let others cut scenes, add and delete dialogue. They would hide from the crowds and let everyone assume they had returned to their home.

During the month that followed their time on the mountain, the couple learned a lot about love. They were unable to say what made it the first of many such occurrences where they would greet strange beings, but they began to realize this place held many of them. Why? Who lived in this time? Who remained here to guide others to the other side? Why would anyone be needed to help you die?

The tribe who told everyone else there was going to be a change in the Earth was unable to make itself heard—or so they thought. When Maddie and Slim appeared and were able to talk and listen with their hearts, the tribe decided it was time to make a movie and Maddie would write it. She was not ready for such a commission and had not wanted to ever write again. However, Slim was pleased to see someone else recognize her accomplishments while still on Earth and give her work that would lead them to the next path and the way back. He laughed as they once again ascended to a place where others would come to dance. It was not so far away, but never obvious to those who never prayed.

☯Chapter Twenty-Eight

There were people everywhere when Maddie and Slim departed, but they left unnoticed. They had shed the aura of stardom and were traveling like everyone else now. This made things more interesting. It strengthened and improved their relationship as it enlarged their margins of error relative to what was acceptable, yet able to easily reject what was not worthy of argument.

Time was not going slowly, but each felt a different kind of rhythm from what they had lived with for many years. The couple traveled for four months without stopping to go back to The States. They never realized it until they got tired of eating exotic foods and wanted to eat something they could cook at home. That brought them back to where they had decided to run and not think about anything else.

Where would they live now? Would they hide as they had or be open to whatever happened next? After several minutes of defining what kind of life he would like, Slim turned to Maddie and winked. He said he did not have any real idea and was just thinking out loud. That made her stop and re-listen to what he had shared with her.

She could not remember all of his ideas, but felt he wanted to ranch or raise animals somewhere, and he wanted to do it without the government handing him money to not do it. He wasn't happy with the welfare distributions made to ranchers and farmers, while women and children in cities and towns went hungry. He objected to the idea that just because your granddaddy landed in the clink somewhere out West that he now gets title to millions of acres to hand down to his family without complaint from those running the country now. In fact, those who run the country are most at fault for raping the treasury for money they don't need.

As they talked more about living in the world as they remembered it, each decided to not do what they did in the past. They decided to first read *The New York Times,* then decide what to do with their lives for the next five years. It sounded kind of strange to Slim, but he was ready for action and willing to try anything. He sought out a section of the Sunday paper and began reading while Maddie did the same. She took up a few more sections as Slim slowly perused the news. What was making him look so serious, she wondered?

As the day disappeared and no decision was made about where they might relocate, Maddie decided her idea was too lame and they might as well start driving and see where they end up, paying strict attention to whatever appeared in their minds. Both then decided to disappear and drive wherever incognito. That would lend them the opportunity to go from city-to-city and state-to-state until they found someone or something they liked and wanted to explore more. Their work was not left to chance but done the same as when they previously traveled outside the country. They emailed her agent and others with no mention of where they were then.

Days disappeared, and it became obvious nothing would appear that would induce them to settle down and get to know people in a particular town. Everything was too much the same. It became monotonous—not what they thought their country was like. Every small town had a big Wal-Mart that chased the little guys out, who in turn bought franchises until the line of fast-food stops lined every major highway into every major city and town. It was ugly and distressing to artists, so most of them headed for the mountains where they depended on their success in marketing more than creating art.

Yes, they discovered artists everywhere had to market their work or be left behind. No one really cared if their art was great or not, as long as the artist promised to be remembered, so whatever they bought would sell for more one day than what they bought it for now. Artists were bored. They had to keep in mind the financial aspects of each creative effort, and time spent, rather than letting it go to whomever.

How could a country go into decline so quickly? Was it because its people were no longer excited about inventing new things and moving into new areas in order to explore more? It was a slow death that even Maddie could no longer deny.

Always an optimist, and often criticized for being unable to see things as they really are, was no longer the case with Maddie. She saw villages left behind in a race to get someplace far away. Families no longer cared if a member left—many actually kicked kids out as soon as they could run. It was not something anyone wanted to talk about or hear, so articles about the descent of the communities she visited were ignored and did not sell. She decided it was the kind of world Steinbeck was needed to write about—again, but where was John when you needed him?

Would a great literary novel set the record straight, forcing people to hate enough how they were portrayed to change how the country was moving now? She thought not, but Slim was beginning to think he might produce a documentary or two about what they observed while driving across the states in pursuit of happiness and some place new to live in soon.

His idea was quickly accepted by his business partners. They began e-mailing him from everywhere with ideas about what such a film would look like when done. He rejected all their ideas and decided to do it alone. It would either be fun, or it would teach him a lot, which was all he wanted anyway.

Maddie recognized that every documentary needed a good script, if the public was to experience what others did, but didn't talk about. She decided to create a thoughtful script and share it with no one but Slim. Their new project led them to the North Rim of the Grand Canyon. They wanted to start the story there because it was fabled to be the navel of North America, from which everything we ever wanted to be or are was created.

The canyon is full of mystery and very, very big— gigantic! It was and is a place where many gather, yet no one stays more than a short time. Water is scarce—as scarce as anywhere they could think of where people build homes now. The Colorado rapids gave them a rush and produced a foreboding that this day was fading away quickly and would not end the way many believed it should.

The documentary was not going to win a prize, but it would set things straight. It would tell the story of how American Indians had been cheated and manipulated, then killed because they knew what was happening and fought against it. It was not a story people wanted to hear, but it might help teach American history to students of advanced degrees, since it was no longer taught in most elementary and high schools. Graduate students might want to hear about real life as lived in the past, as well as the ages it took to create this magnificent national park.

That was how it all started, but they did not get very far then. It took months to decide what pictures were right for the work they hoped to produce, then the film crew was unable to do as they directed, so they did it themselves rather than hire professionals. Slim enjoyed this work more than anything he had ever done in his career. He never before realized how much experience he had picked up waiting to be filmed until he shot the rapids with a still camera perched high on the side of the canyon and one strapped to his chest, then did it again and again, each time catching another look at birds, plants, and people who made the descent with them.

Without much doubt that anyone would be interested in their film, Maddie asked her agent to get a proof made and see what experts thought it needed to be circulated through high schools. When she did not hear from her agent for days, she began to think Sheila might not be in New York then. At the end of the week, a phone rang, and she rapidly sorted through her bag to find her cell phone and answer it before it went dead.

The news was astonishing! Everyone in New York loved the concept and wanted more. They wanted their film to be distributed to movie theaters and included in the documentary category of the Academy Awards! Maddie was too stunned to say anything then.

Later as Maddie and Slim disappeared into their RV, once again assuming the identity of an older couple on retreat, they realized they were no longer on the run, and indeed having too much fun to settle down now. It was not in the cards. They wanted to go everywhere together and continue doing the same thing over and over again. But how long before people would recognize them and try to act out parts? They decided not to care—thinking it would never happen, but they were wrong.

As the Academy warmed up to the idea that documentaries were more important than most of the movies made now, artists and writers, even some actors, began to seek out those who lived lives worth repeating to others. They scouted and scoured the country for stories to tell. Those who lived by their own ideas and wits most of the time were valued most highly.

Documentaries about urban life had been overdone. No one wanted to run yet another one by audiences who now ate up documentaries like they once ate up TV news. It was a time when stories about how others lived was what people craved and wanted to know more about.

No one could do a documentary to please the thought police of this Administration, so they rivaled each other trying to rile them. It was an interesting sense of revolution sweeping the country, rather than an actual coup. Many teens, and others not much older, were busy making documentaries about their peers, trying to get into their psyches and what their home life was really like. It was a time when coming-of-age movies came into their own and owned the country once again, but it would not end well unless someone sat down and analyzed why these films were worthwhile.

Maddie decided to analyze movies from the standpoint of history and how many people could possibly document their lives, as well as how they would stand up over time in order to tell future generations about this period of time and these particular lives. She realized then that their films would never survive, and neither would their books. To last, they had to be inscribed in some kind of material not available now.

Mathematicians and research assistants battled for funds to experiment with products that would preserve filmed materials too quickly forgotten by the public now. Something that might stand up to centuries of weather and wear. One who had nothing but one thought decided what could be done. That one presented it as if a gift to those unwilling to admit one person working alone can still do much for humanity. *'Developers'* in turn tried to imprint their hands on it and were surprised when the one who actually used it was willing to ignore them and give credit only to the scribe who invented it alone for her own use at home.

This product was not named right away, but a silly logo was applied anyway, as if it was something everyone would want to use. As it turned out, it was used by everyone and released all over the world. You could enter into conversations with diplomats writing their memoirs and movie stars who were illiterate, sure that cameras never lied, now writing about their lives—shallow or not. The world was now watching itself, trying to live up to what it believed it should be, not just what was most easily sold.

One man dreamt up a product that would allow others to write about their lives and keep it in space-age style until future generations could open and decipher what it said about this time of inward revolution. Would the documentaries be seen when people could read the tiles and symbols used now?

Maddie thought the documentaries would be worth it once people saw themselves and decided their lives were not pretty pictures now—certainly not what they would want remembered eons later. Thus, the world changed because documentaries were made about life today!

☯Chapter Twenty-Nine

Thinking back over the last ten years and all she had seen and been involved with, Maddie was stunned to realize that what began as a simple exercise, and later received permission to do within the lives of others, was now over and done. Many of the women she once interviewed were now leading the country. How interesting!

As she had been able to do only so much herself, she had stepped out of her life a lot and never expected anything when she began the book that never got done. Instead of finalizing that first attempt, she launched her life into time, meeting others who were far from divine, but still able to ascend at what seemed to her a whim.

Maddie was able to travel to other worlds and live among those revered for their abilities to live well even when famine and fate deemed their lives would not be easy. What had she gained along the way—beside a life-long partner? Had she earned another star or just passed time and done nothing to garner a star for her heavenly crown?

Their days passed in reverie with no complaints. Each set up cameras, then waited and watched as others lived their lives. They pulled a kind of long-distance switch at times in order not to call attention to their work, even joined in with others then. This was the thrill of a life lived for the world and not dedicated to being someone who would rest at the end of it and say, "I'm done," which is what they both really wanted.

As days passed and people did not stop and talk, rather they praised them for doing documentaries that enabled both to work harder and become more interested in their families again. Along the way they missed the ability to simply have friends in to sit around and talk about things other than business and where they had been. This was not discussed, but the thought arose, and both immediately started pulling up camp and heading to Mexico in their RV. It was to become one adventure they would never want to film, but it would become a part of their human histories.

The time taken to get the RV in great shape, and the films back to her agent, sign off on however many forms, plus do whatever was needed to get out from under their work for a time, stretched into a month from the moment they thought about visiting friends again. It was not boring enough to make them rush, but it seemed to take way too much time and energy—or so they often said to one another.

"I think we can drive 12 hours the first day, then 8 hours a day after that, and still meet people. What do you think?"

Maddie was not watching the impact of her words on Slim, until he spoke. Only then did she notice that he did not agree. He said, "I think we need to work a bit more on communicating without words. I think we also need to get in the habit of not talking about every thought we have—like we do in The States."

Suddenly Maddie became aware that she was staring out the window into air, not seeing anything that existed in this community. It was as if the cab of the RV was free of any entailments and could fly. She wanted to just lay back and glide.

Slim drove while Maddie rested in her mind. He took the wheel nine-to-ten hours at a time, never asking her to help out, so she was able to rest, and he was able to go into his own state of reverie without any details expressed. It was a trip that ended without either remembering a single thing that happened along the way. How had it transpired and why? It could never be said they did not wonder about it, but they had taken the time required to move into the Mayan way and not look at life as Americans might.

Their arrival in Mayaland was greeted with hoots and hollers and lots of smiles, but no one they expected to see was around to welcome them to the compound. All were busy working, so they felt they were not expected. Both frowned when they realized they had arrived several days earlier than their projected arrival time. How did it happen so fast?

During this day of settling in and getting to know the crowd who worked in this area now, they both worked hard not to talk a lot. It wasn't easy since they were raised in the true American way of suspecting anyone who did not speak about what was on his or her mind all the time.

When the tribe arrived out of time, Maddie and Slim were waiting by the side of the road, not expecting anyone. Their RV just stopped and refused to move. No one knew what to do. They had taken a few of the staff from the compound to town, then decided to visit a ruin not far from their place on the way back. It was the usual side trip for some, but a place never visited by Maddie or Slim until now. It was such a powerful place that their vehicle could not accommodate the energy emanating from Earth and broke down. It would run again once *The Ascended Maya* were gone.

This day was exciting to begin with, but the entrance of The Tribe of Ascended Maya who did not exist on this planet at this time was something they had never read about or even been aware of until now. Yes, they had heard tribal tales of Maya arriving out of time and taking over, showing them how to fly and how to prepare for the end of this time, but it was not something they actually thought would take place. They could now see it was not a mystical experience for others present—only to them, perhaps because their minds were unable to accept anything that others in their lines of descent did not already experience.

The Ascended Maya arrived without a lot of flurry, and the sound of wings did not reach them, but angels seemed to be around them now. They were not angels, per se, is what Maddie would say later when trying to describe the event, but she felt a profound ability to rise and talk to them in a language she had never heard before. She was greeted by them as if an old friend, and Slim…Well, Slim was one of them! He blended in and just sank into the world encompassing them then and there. Maddie was not as able to blend in and could not lose her sense of curiosity in the event. She was trained to report things others could not understand or perhaps witness, and that part of her mind refused to shut down.

The Ascended Maya met with Slim, then greeted her as a long-lost friend. She watched how the natives acted and noticed that none watched them. They were either bent over with eyes on Earth or bowed in respect while praying aloud in a far different way than she ever heard before today. She regretted not wearing a dress and being able to bend easily now to show her true respect and love for *The Ascended Maya*.

The time it took a human to travel to meet *The Ascended Maya* was many light years, but they could come and visit Earth without thought. Their mission now was to announce there was to be a new mission, and Maddie was needed to help with the announcement. She was unable to talk. Her thoughts were jumbled, and only her fear of heights kept her from peering into the air to see if she was standing now and where.

A pyramid of light opened at that moment and Maddie watched as she and Slim seemed to conquer their humanity and walk up steps as taught in Chichen Itza many years past. They worked up the courage to enter the altar area and look at what was to be sacrificed once again—their lives as men and women of this time. Would they live to tell about the sacrifice or disappear forever in a single slice?

The absolute power spent in this event was centered in an area that could not be described. It was that holy, yet so indeterminate to men that it was not what one would ever expect to see in such a sacred place. The altar was covered with nothing you ever saw in this world. It vibrated, and with each vibration changed color, yet it was subtle enough not to occupy the center of your attention once you noticed who was presiding over the event.

The head of *The Ascended Maya*, so to speak, was no one you would have thought to see in such a place. He was neither man nor woman but seemed to be a transgender kind of man. This being was not what Maddie could describe without it sounding too strange for explanation, so she settled for '*He*'.

This holy place blazed with light. All who were on their knees, as well as those bent over, never noticed how long it took to indoctrinate Slim and Maddie into the work that was going on all over the world. It was accomplished in a moment—and no one died.

The fundamentalists of every time and creed would deny you could do such a transfiguration without blood and flesh being sacrificed, but *The Ascended Maya* never touched the heart with a knife or anything like it. That was how ill-educated ones interpreted their faith and brought fear to others. They had clearly lost their way and were doing it more and more often now, but it did not stop those who were to ascend from removing their minds and hearts and laying them on the altar and awaiting the star.

As they waited in absentia for the star to arrive, the altar ceased to vibrate. The entire scene was so unique that no one could paint it afterwards on a stele, a tablet, or a pyramid. All anyone could say was: '*King whomever ascended then, and all present witnessed the miracle of his ascent and were able to fly with him if they had prepared for it or were given such lives that permitted them to leave then.*'

The lie of the time spent on Earth is that you are only here and will never go anywhere else. That is such a silly notion once you experience such an event, that Maddie did not know where to begin with her dissertation on how to ascend and leave this life behind. That was to be her mission now.

Maddie looked at the altar and began studying its art when she felt a hand on her nape. Her mind disappeared again and retained no memory of what happened next, but when the RV started up on its own and parted the crowd gathered around the ruin of another time, she turned to Slim and took his hand and smiled at everyone. Their cheer was for a bride and groom who had just exchanged vows. It was not at all what she thought would happen in an event of this kind, but then again, she never thought anything like this could happen—at least not to them.

☯Chapter Thirty

Do you wish to be great? Then begin by being. Do you desire to construct a vast and lofty fabric? Think first about the foundations of humility. The higher your structure is to be, the deeper must be its foundation.
~ St. Augustine, 354-430 AD

Just as the taxi pulled up to the curb, the doorman jumped out of the shrubs and opened the door. Maddie thought she saw a reporter or photographer right behind him and had in mind to report them if that indeed was the case, but before she could process that thought someone rushed at her from behind and jumped in front of her, blocking her view of what was happening around her.

Within moments of being ushered out of the taxi, she felt rather than heard another move around her and pass by. What was going on? Who was after her? What had she done? The crowds around her hotel were definitely not waving banners or yelling at her, but they seemed to be waiting for something to happen. What could it be?

Now that she was safely inside the hotel, none of the competing thoughts she could view, as if from afar, could justify all the shouting outside. Who was about to arrive, and had she got in the way? Were they expecting royalty or someone who had just made a huge movie—one she had yet to see? What was going on in New York that she had not heard about?

The elevator opened, so she and Slim and another man slipped in and watched the doors close on the lobby beginning to fill with people who appeared to want to use that elevator, too. What to do? Just mind your own business is what her mother taught, so she determined to do that now.

When she and Slim entered their suite, the man following them began to usher them around the rooms and demonstrate where everything was and how to operate whatever. He was definitely not a bellhop, and did not have their bags in tow, but he acted as though he was employed by the hotel. As it turned out, he was the manager, but behaving subservient to both of them. They could only wonder if their cover was no longer effective. Perhaps Slim was once again being observed by his movie fans from years ago, rather than his recent documentaries. Mandy could not see how anyone would be waiting to see her and decided it had to be about Slim.

Their arrival that night left them tired. They felt as if the air around them was stifling and could not supply enough energy for the work they needed to do before they could run around the country again. Their appetites were not as great as they thought they would be when faced with so many different restaurants they could visit each night. They continually wondered together and separately: 'Why were they sapped of energy now?'

The morning light brought respite. Feeling it was time to trot about Central Park and view what the city was up to now. It quickly became apparent that someone was posted outside their room, and downstairs someone else took them in hand and escorted them everywhere. Who had arranged for all this fanfare and why? They continued to wonder, but let it pass. Why not? It was only for laughs. No one really knew what either of them was doing here.

The morning was a whirlwind of activity once they visited his agent and discovered they were expected to do a lot of publicity shots. Slim was not alarmed; however, Maddie wished to sit back and not be mentioned. It was not allowed. Many shots were set up with props and backdrops, then sudden silence as a model emerged from the back of the stage. It was none other than her old assistant—now returned to doing photo shoots to high praise. She was not delighted to see Maddie, either, but acted as if she were a long-lost friend. Maddie could not stop frowning whenever she was around.

The news covered by the world was too materialistic for Maddie and Slim to fit right in and share their opinions and views, too. Everyone wanted them to sell a product and make a lot of money from it, but neither wanted money. The world was not going to buy or sell them or deliver anything they wanted to do now.

This world was no longer an option. They just wanted to deliver their latest documentary and get out of town. They were now on the run. The time allotted to deliver all that was expected of them was unequal to their attempts to stay away from crowds.

It was exciting to learn that many women came to hear Maddie and wanted her to talk about their victories in minor elections all over the country. She was unaware so many would repeat her words and buy her books until she stopped to see her agent on the side.

Her agent begged Maddie to go to lunch with her, and stay for another day, which was suspicious as such. Maddie did not wish to harm her ability to forward documentaries and have them put into motion by this agency, so she decided it would be okay to meet again the next day in front of Madison Square Garden and check out who would be there. She had a hunch someone would interrupt their lunch, but her agent did not want her to know too much about it, because she would likely reject meeting them and do whatever she wanted instead.

Maddie's mind tired with run-on errands and decisions that suddenly had to be made wherever they went that afternoon. Upon arrival anywhere, someone would step up and have a picture or two taken with Slim, maybe even include her. They both lost their appetite and decided to stay inside and not leave their suite for yet another night.

The tide of women waving at Maddie when she left the hotel to enter the limo was growing larger. She felt pleasure that so many women wanted to lead the country now, but who were all these other people, and what did they expect her to be? As the limo approached The Gardens, she realized someone had blocked her window, so she could not see out, except for a little circle close to the door. When they stopped, noise exploded, and she wondered what was going on now.

Who was playing The Gardens at this time of day? Surely no rock star would be up and about at this hour! As Maddie stepped out of the limo, flashbulbs burst her bubble of contentment and ended the illusion that she could travel without a parade of strangers wishing to capture her every movement and remark.

This was to be the most interesting day so far in her new public life, but the drama never arrived and the comedy of errors one would expect from an unscripted event never happened, either. Without any idea of what she would do once on stage, Maddie sat down at a long table until prompted to move closer to the podium and urged to not worry about anything. She wondered if she was about to receive an award. Was it going to be for her writing or her photography? What had she done so far to deserve any award anyway?

Her modesty was still intact, and her humility had never wavered over the years, so she was totally unprepared when the speaker announced that Maddie had a few words to say to everyone. What? What was she doing here, and why was she expected to talk to this crowd? As she stood, the crowd erupted into cheers and shouts, clapping, and stamping of feet. She had never before realized women could be so loud!

Standing before the crowd, tears began to stream down her cheeks. She could not see anything clearly that was directly in front of her, so Slim jostled her elbow and handed her a Kleenex. The crowd went wild! They loved Slim, which was obviously why she was here. She suddenly felt stupid for thinking they were cheering for her. Maddie proceeded to introduce Slim, but he interrupted her with a note that said, '*Congratulations! You've been voted the most important woman in media today!*'

Stunned, Maddie read the note over the microphone and heard everyone sigh—some even cried. She felt so silly for being unable to understand that her time had finally arrived—and she was not prepared for it! She wanted to cry but knew a strong woman would not cry when she stood at a pulpit from which she could teach and/

or preach to all gathered there. She decided to do what she did best—just say whatever popped into her head.

"I'm here today to be of use to you, and all the world, too. I want you all to tell me what to do next. I want to be of use to all of you! Please tell me what you want."

The audience grew quiet. No one spoke. Suddenly someone contributed an idea and then ten thousand said what they would do. She had to swallow it all in a gulp.

With a chuckle, then a bit of a giggle, Maddie said: "You each know now what you want to do. Don't blame me if it doesn't get done. You each have to do your bit for humanity, too! I will do my bit by keeping up the pressure on The Administration and whoever else complains that we aren't paying enough taxes or don't understand why raping the countryside is not wise.

"We will survive! We will live to be mothers, fathers, sisters and brothers, as well as aunts and uncles to the greatest miracle generation to ever be bred. We will help each other and pass on to them our decision to be the best we can possibly be right now!"

The crowd was now quiet, so Maddie stopped to look at the unusual mix of people staring back at her. At first, she had thought it was filled with women only, but there were many men mixed in among the women and even some kids. This was to be the best time in her life, and she had more than fifteen minutes to make a meaningful statement that could help others—or not. The decision to teach rather than preach was reached in an instant.

Pulling out a slide or two from her pocket, Maddie asked to have them projected on the wall behind her. Everyone became quiet, apparently interested in the process of slides being passed to a member of tech support.

The slides would provide an idea of what she was about to say, so the crowd waited patiently, some nodding as if thinking about the famous movie star and his brilliant wife—the famous journalist, Madeline Worthington. No one moved to walk away.

As the first brilliant picture lit the screen behind her, the crowd let out a slow *'ahhhh'*. Maddie slipped out of her consciousness for the rest of the day, never noticing what was on the screen, but always aware just enough to keep the audience in a kind of trance and able to release her in time to bounce back to the past, then back to the present. Her mind never skipped a line as she recited the background script of her most famous documentary so far. She talked for an hour, then stopped as if time had been called.

When Maddie was ushered out of that great space into a waiting limo, she let herself be seen by those outside and unable to view the stars inside. Many registered surprise, because they had never seen such a woman before. She could change in a moment and still not be there. It was hours later before she was back in her usual form and able to order dinner with Slim. They decided to eat-in again.

☯Chapter Thirty-One

If we live good lives, the times are also good. As we are, such are the times. ~ *St. Augustine, 354-430 AD*

The group that wanted to meet Madeline in person was much larger than anyone anticipated, so there were some ugly words spoken and a few went away with anger embedded in their minds, but no one else cared about them. Maddie was unaware of any anger, or that some were barred from entering, so she did not realize the decision to ignore some would cloud the way she was viewed by too many in the future. If she had been aware of the crowded conditions, she would have gone outside and spoken to those who could not enter the hall, but she did not know about it until later. She paid the price of admission much later in life.

The work of a few people is all most read about in daily papers, and many who report are not paid enough to keep their personal jealousy and envy locked inside, and not hint at it when reviewing what others do or say. This was not the best of times to be in New York, because so many were even more paranoiac than in the past—if that is possible. Maddie felt strained each time she went out, because security people surrounded the area due to celebrities running in and out.

"Why did I once believe this to be a great life? Why did I pity all who didn't have enough and had to make bread do instead of eating cake? I was sure I was a benevolent woman, but I was as selfish as everyone I knew then. I just didn't get it, and I guess we never do when all you ever see is life from the outside—like visiting the zoo or a museum."

Slim extended a cup of tea to her, motioning with his free hand that she should relax in the big, soft easy chair. She did not want to relax now. She was fired up! She wanted to vent anger that had somehow infiltrated her mind today. What had she said that made people report she was unwilling to talk to '*the little people*' now that she was a star?

Pulling up a chair at the table in order to place her cup on it, she felt Slim could not understand how angry people can make you when they write such nonsense. She started to comment when it dawned on her that he was the expert when it came to being misread. No one knew who he was and most never cared. They preferred to think of him as a macho man, and that image stuck—and was what sold at the box office even now!

"How do you get over being abused in the news? I can't stand all this stuff about being snobbish, or whatever. Not caring about my readers and others who stand in the rain waiting to see me for only a fleeting second or so."

Slim nodded, then walked to the spot she had vacated in order to sit at the table and drink her tea. He looked out over the city below and smiled.

"What makes you smile? Can you fly over this town without seeing those who are down on you—hateful and moody, trying to ruin you? Are you able to forget they exist?"

"You know, Maddie, I just don't think about people who are rude. I've met so many people in my lifetime who are wondrous and powerful—great to know, so I think about them whenever I can. I think about how wonderful they are, and what a great deal I learned from them, then just walk away from today. It's all in how you remember the past and the people who made you the image you maintain today."

"Image? You mean we really aren't individuals at all? We're just images created by myths printed about us?"

As if already an ancient sage, Slim shook his head and looked at the books climbing the walls. He said, "All the books and all the scholars would never be able to top your reception at City Hall, and that was why you are going to have to get out of town now. You have to keep up the façade or fall from grace. Today, people hate a winner. It's that simple! Hate is not even strong enough to describe how they can get when they see someone made out to be great.

"Remember Clinton? He was the best President any of us common people ever had, and we acted like he was a terrible person for letting a woman make a fool out of him. It happens to every man, and happens more now than ever before, but we sacrifice our morals and become depraved trying to deprive the guy of his just rewards."

Slim nodded solemnly and added, "You can't talk about oral sex in every article you write about the President and expect the next generation to not do it. Everyone said it was shocking, and he shouldn't have done it. Described it in detail—and they enjoyed every word of it, but now the crying begins about kids doing it all the time! What did they expect? You get what you get!"

Maddie said nothing. Her thoughts were not aligned enough to think straight, but she wondered if Slim had ever had any ideas about how to run the country. Funny that she never once discussed it with him, yet sold that idea to every woman she met—or was it funny?

"You know, Slim, I never thought about it before, because we have so little time to talk about our own lives, but did you ever want to run for President?"

Before she could say another word, Slim blurted out, "Sure! Who hasn't? Then you sit down, stop drinking, and get yourself into rehab or whatever you do when you become addicted to being you." Laughter bubbled and burbled out of him at such speed that Maddie could only laugh, too.

"Are you saying you once thought about running for office?" She spoke with her eyes crossed, as if it were meant to be a joke.

"You talk like I couldn't do it, Maddie. I could, but I don't want to. I like what I do. I like talking to people face-to-face in a dark movie hall and in their homes, channeling what I think is wrong or right. I like that kind of power, but it keeps me up at nights."

Shocked at this pronouncement, Maddie stopped rolling her eyes to listen intently, thus encouraging him to continue.

"I guess movie stars are taken for granted as having big egos, but no one I know can match the local politicians— wherever you go. They talk about their constituencies as if they were all stupid, and I guess some of them are, if they elect them…"

"You know, Slim, you have a point. What would you say if we were to run for office like Hillary and Bill?"

Not at all amused or able to smile, Slim spoke softly. "I would never do that! I love you way too much to put you through all the stuff they would dig up about my past—yours, too. We would be hated by the time we got to the first state primary. It's all staged, but it's staged with hatred and a determination to never let the good guys ever win again."

"You are so bitter, Slim! I would never have guessed it. You look so unhappy right now that I want to skip to the next subject and forget this one. What will it take to make you happy—now?"

Slim shook his head and said, "That's the biggest mistake we all make. We skip to the next part, instead of getting it into our minds that this is it. This is the only time we have! This is the only time America can shine! Once we decline, there's nothing left to share with others anywhere. We'll never last ten thousand years—never be here as we are today once we lose our credit protection—which is beginning to happen."

"Credit protection? What does that mean?" Maddie could not dance away and create a diversion asking this question.

"Credit is something that reduces you to being a beggar—someone others try to avoid...Unless they're making a huge profit lending you money to go into debt over your head. Countries with wealth don't spend like we do. They keep their money close to their chests, so no one notices it. They don't walk out and buy everything China can make—and then think China has no money. That is so stupid it makes me want to end my game—but I'm only joking now."

Maddie was startled at how Slim talked, realizing for the first time that he spoke as intensely as Jorge. She never before thought much about why Jorge got upset with his government and others, because he wasn't an American. Americans are not into politics, and seldom want to run for public office, so she had put all her hopes into helping capable women run for public office and win. She never thought about the men—at all, until now. How had that happened and why?

"You look like you just had an epiphany of sorts. What's going on in your pretty little mind now?" Slim smiled but seemed to sense what she was thinking and how it got started. "You know, Maddie, you want to leave the world sounder and stronger than when you arrived, but it ain't gonna' happen—not this time. You have to come back to do that."

Shocked, Maddie almost squawked as she said, "Come back! Are you crazy? I want off this plane as soon as it can be arranged—once I die. I don't want to come back again. I want to do whatever I have to do to make it to the next level and be able to ascend, then never come back."

"Ascended Masters come back, according to a lot of New Age people writing about ascension now. Do you believe that?"

Shaking her head as if she never thought of it, Maddie said she would have to ask her Teachers and Guides if it was true or not. She had neither the wit nor wisdom to understand what Ascended Masters did or when, and if they returned to Earth.

"Well, why don't you sit there for a while and just let your Guides and Teachers talk it over, and then get back to me about it?" Slim smiled to soften his wit a bit before walking into the kitchen to start dinner.

Maddie sat deep in contemplation until she noticed aromas that announced dinner was underway—and not what she would have made. She felt herself enter another mind then and clean it up a bit, so she could invite company now. The fear she once had about going to the altar within her mind was over, but she was not so foolish as to not honor in every way possible Teachers and Guides who arrived at her request—but only if she could remain perfectly calm.

You need to think about your life so far, and how much you gained by working with your father and mother, as well as those able to guide you in your early years here. When you can see them again, you must be able to greet them with a smile.

Maddie immediately thought back to the past and her calmness lapsed. She almost laughed that she was nowhere near quiet enough to set the stage for the greatest of the great Teachers to enter her sphere. She tried again, and this time she was able to disappear into time.

The effort to do it was enough to make dinner late by a few hours, but Slim never suggested it was any the worse for waiting because he loved his chili hot and steeped in beer—a lot. She did not.

As they propped the work on the easel, Slim looked at it again and asked her what it meant. She stopped and looked at him, then at the mandala or work of art she had done while he was out of the room and she was communing within with those in her auric field. This piece was not as bright as many she created as easily as she wrote a poem or two. This one looked like a funnel coming out of the center of a whirlwind or storm cloud, and she was unsure what it meant—until he asked.

"You can see The Teachers are very close to Earth in this piece. They are circulating in and around the work of those in charge of children and others who will be future leaders. They are very concerned. We have neglected the kids. They want us to be held up, unable to ascend now."

"What? Are you serious? Are you saying everyone who wants to leave Earth now and never come back is going to be held responsible for their kids and any delinquency we may have contributed to today?"

At the look on his face, Maddie started to laugh, then embraced him as she said, "You don't have to worry, Slim. You've done a great job teaching right from wrong, and your music is never outrageous and angry, or making fun of others. You have been a good father to many homeless children all over the world. You are their father-figure, and you can make things happen that I can't begin to change now."

Slim looked at her and smiled as he said, "What are you talking about? You teach and reach women who create the babies and keep them safe through all the stages of infancy and their young lives until they can live as planned. You make the real difference. If you can help one mother see the right way to raise her family, you have created another world, and many will sense it is now better for what you did."

Shaking her head, Maddie said, "Not now! Now everything I taught women to do is going to be run into the ground, just like they did with Martha Stewart, who never harmed any one. In fact, she rather improved many a family by idolizing the old ways of keeping a home lovely and full of good food."

"Ahhh, yes, I keep forgetting about the insane jealousy of too many that is eating up this country now. Can we do anything about it?" Slim flung it out as if a challenge to Maddie, maybe even himself.

"You know, Slim, I think we need to make a movie. A real, honest-to-what-God-would-want movie."

"You know, Maddie, I think you might be onto something. Maybe we can structure it like a fairytale, so they can analyze it to death, yet not forget the message? What do you think?"

"I think we need to think about this for a week to ten days, then start writing and directing our ideas into an area that will be worthwhile and fun to work in...."

Maddie never finished her thought because Slim put her into a lip lock that lasted more than a minute and a half. They were so into it that together they began to imagine the movie needed to begin with a romance, after a lot of research to make sure it was a movie that would last— something like *Gone with the Wind*...

❂Chapter Thirty-Two

Cats always seem so very wise, when staring with their half-closed eyes. Can they be thinking: "I'll be nice, and maybe she will feed me twice?"
                                        ~ Bette Midler, 1945-

Workers were running in and out of the house as Maddie and Slim walked up the front path. The developer had assumed everything would be done by noon, but they had never shared in that opinion until now. They were shocked to see the house totally neat and clean, and nothing appeared out-of-line. Only a few men remained of the huge crew who had installed the concrete and pre-constructed modules in only a few days. This house was to be all the rage someday, but right now it was the only one like it in development around this part of Arizona.

Water pressure was the most important topic of discussion for months, but now that the work was done, their house could use solar energy and wind power to do much that normally would be carried by wire from afar. They were not going to do anything unusual or different from what they had done so far, but everyone was expecting them to hold a huge celebration to honor the community for being far-sighted and doing all the construction work required, without help from others who wanted to jet in and do it in a day. They expected to be toasted for having worked hard! It was an interesting concept, and Maddie commented on it to her husband and best friends, but decided not to write about it—at least not now.

The work was not easy by local standards, but now many knew a lot more about design than before and planned on building a number of modular homes nearby. It was something they could now understand, because they saw it unfold successfully.

When people do not know how to do something, they usually do what they were taught over and over again until their minds rot from inside where creative thought is believed to abound. These people were artistic by genetic structure, but unable to understand that money was not the problem when you lived in a hovel you never improved for generations past and present. They needed to be aroused if they were to ever change.

The idea that a house could be built and made beautiful for less than any of them could rebuild their present home was astonishing to most of the contractors who wanted to help build their house. They wanted to be able to say they built it and advertise the fact, but they could not. The concrete people did not think it was a unique building, once done. The carpenters could not rave about the modern way they finished the interior, because it was like any other house in the area. The plumbers were surprised that cistern work was still needed and were not about to advertise it, and so it went. Now finished, everyone involved was sure they could build it over-and-over again, because it was not that great.

When Slim organized the celebration, after putting men to work on building a straw barn and fencing it in, he had them erect bleachers for people to come and watch their kids ride and work hard. The local women sat on the sidelines and let him do whatever he wanted, but when Maddie tried to organize the women, they resented it. They were sure she was not the type to work hard, so they would not cooperate with her in organizing the event, so it went off without a hitch as far as what was done outside and within the barn, with lots of competition in the kitchen and within the garden.

What was so hard about holding a party? Why were so few women interested in creating a safe place to entertain and keep their families safe? What was the attraction of the local bars and restaurants where they served nothing great, and too often caused people to come to blows and loudly hate one another?

Afterward, news traveled far and wide that Maddie was a great woman, but no one really believed it until she welcomed local Indians and their families to her home, disregarding what was said about Mexicans who often dropped in, too. No one else in the area appeared to feel easy with '*those people*', yet Maddie was famous and had a lot of money and thought they were great. Other women wanted to know more about it.

Weeks became a month, then a few Sundays after that the new couple visited the local church to learn what they could do with the community that worshipped there. They were not shocked that the minister was self-ordained but surprised at how many thought he was really great.

He was not above putting out the offering plate several times during a rather quick-and-easy sermon about what he thought God was like. It was a child's version of religion, but everyone seemed happy to hear it repeated over and over again. Actually, the sermonette was much like what was spouted on television now, but his was too childish for even Slim to listen much. They later wondered about their decision to locate in this part of the desert. Why was it to be the place where they would do their best work? It no longer appeared that promising to either of them.

Once the service was over, several people stopped by their car to ask if they were going to the church social next week. Since neither had heard about the social, they said no. Their response was unexpected, so they were talked about—a lot by those who thought they were standoffish and snooty for not attending the social.

When it got back to them—and it traveled fast, Maddie laughed. True, she didn't know what life was like in a small town, but they lived so far from anyone else that there was no town, yet she was expected to do what neighbors did—or find herself without a friend in the county. Unwilling to isolate herself or their combined lives, she quickly sorted out who did what and talked to those most likely to want her to stay. In turn they straightened things out so Maddie and Slim were not only invited to the social but told to bring a side of beef.

"If this means being a member of the community, as well as being new to this area is a kind of sacrifice, I guess I'll kill the bull and take him to the altar and let them eat it." Slim teased her about it, but he was not happy when he learned the price of beef. He was no doubt offended by the decision made by someone who remained nameless that they had to buy their way into the social life around here.

"You know, Maddie, I think I have to go to Hollywood again—and you have to go with me, so we can't make this social after all. We have to work—or not have enough money to pay our bills."

Maddie was struck by his tone, because he looked serious but was laughing. What was happening? Did Slim resent the bribe, or was he more aware of what was really going on here and now? She decided to get on the phone and make arrangements with her agent to set up a meeting and get it into the paper today that she was called to California and would be there a week to ten days.

Used to traveling without having to take care of closing their home, they forgot how much they had to do to get out from under the responsibilities of owning a property that in some ways resembled a ranch. They decided they needed a man to stay on the place and were determined it would not be someone who lived nearby. Why? They wanted him to immediately start work without being aware they were skipping out on a social obligation.

As the truant officer drove by, he noticed Slim's workers lined up on the fence being introduced to a new guy. He slowed down but didn't want to act like he was nosey. Once back at the grade school, he went straight to the principal and mentioned there was something going on out at Slim's place. It looked like they were going to change things around—again.

The social circle of a few ranch families was not easy to enter, so Maddie and Slime decided not to play by their rules and do what they loved to do, without any fuss. The time to cut ties created when building the house was now—not later. They left town without saying a word to anyone outside of their employees.

The mailman stopped by to deliver a package and was greeted by a guy who looked a lot like Slim, but younger and not quite as nice. He thought the guy would tell him where he wanted a big box put, but instead took it off him like it was light as a feather. That was enough to impress the mailman.

The day ended before anyone called and left a message on the answering machine. No one asked if they were going to the party, but one did ask if the beef was to be delivered tomorrow or not.

The manager called back and asked what they wanted, and how big an order had they placed and when. He was unaware Slim and Maddie were to take a side of beef to a ranch barbecue the following day, and laughed at the idea. He was surprised to hear a gasp on the other end of the line and responded a bit unkindly, "What are you folks doin'? Trying to get something for nothing out of a couple of city slickers?"

Nothing was said, but he heard the other huff and puff, so he spoke more slowly. "I guess they forgot all about your party. I'm the manager here and have my orders—plenty of them, and there's nothing about the ranch hands and me going to any party tomorrow."

That was enough to stop the woman, who was now worried about how her actions had been viewed by the famous couple. Sweetly she told him they were probably too busy to call her. The ranch manager laughed, then said they should read the papers to see what was going on, then hung up without further thought.

At the other end of the county, women were broiling and scolding each other about how much they had wanted to share their work with Maddie and introduce her to their families. A little bit of jealousy and a lot of envy was now forgotten, but one or two were shocked enough to realize they could no longer rule their far-flung families and conduct affairs as usual. There was a new girl in town, and when she wanted them to call, they would answer and make time to see her—regardless of how many Indians she entertained.

The ranch did not sit out in the open, and there was no main artery passing near it, yet photographers arrived from time-to-time and tried to figure out what was going on then. The manager always drove up and shooed them away, but not before they got off a couple of shots of him *'acting like a macho cowboy'*.

☯Chapter Thirty-Three

"In the studio, I do try to have a thought in my head, so that it's not like a blank stare."
                          ~ Cindy Crawford, 1966-

"We have to get this out—then get going on what we want to do next year—if it's ever gonna' happen." Slim was sitting on a stool in the kitchen looking at the newspaper while working on a list. He looked as if he was about to laugh, but holding it in.

"I guess you could say we needed it—then regained our senses. Now what to do with it? Should we rent out space and let others do whatever they want with it?"

"No! I can see right now that they would run it into the ground in a couple of years, and never do anything worthwhile...Why don't we deed it to someone who can maintain this place, as well as the south side of the corral? We can give away the cattle today, but I think it would be hard on our hired hands to give away work they've done well for over a year. We need to think a bit about how to get rid of that thing, too."

Slim pointed at the huge work of art in the dining room that neither wanted now, but originally could not wait to own. They both wanted to get it out of sight for the rest of their lives.

"You would think a piece of art done for art's sake would last, but this thing is huge—and ugly, and no one else will ever buy it. In fact, I think it's why we want to get out of here. Why did we buy it?" Slim did not exactly look puzzled, but his lips quivered, and his eyes clouded with tears, as if stifling a sneeze or a laugh.

"Go ahead and laugh! It cost me a lot. I was so sure it was going to be the perfect piece for this house, but I haven't been able to find a place that suits it. It disrupts our sleep if we put it too near the bed, and it isn't pretty enough for the family room. So, what do you think—maybe we can put it outside?"

Slim sneezed, then said, "I guess we can use it to scare off everything that flies out of the sky nearby, so it won't bother our garden again—ever. What do you think it is anyway?"

Maddie had not been looking at Slim, so she had to turn to see if he was serious or not. Sensing his mood, rather than having visual proof, she suggested he wasn't being serious and it would do no harm to set it out by the barn.

He didn't like that idea, so he laughed. "What makes you think the horses wouldn't shy if they spotted that monstrosity near the corral?"

"It's got a kind of gothic appeal, if you look at it from the inside out—not from a distance, but up close. Within its reach you feel some kind of power that's eerie and unreal. I wonder what it is."

"Well, Maddie, that's what I've been saying. You feel something unreal or out-of-this-world, maybe mean and hateful, when you stand near it. I want it gone now. I'll get the guys to carry it out and put it in a stall or wherever until someone comes by and buys it."

Shaking her head mournfully, Maddie said, "No, that wouldn't be right. If it's demon-possessed or created with vengeance and too ugly for us to tame, then we can't inflict it on someone else."

"Maybe we can get an exorcist to cleanse it, so it will work miracles and people will flock here from miles around?" Slim looked merry but didn't talk as if it was a joke.

"You better stop talking like that or I might just drive down to Mexico and bring back someone who will know what to do to get rid of that—whatever it is we feel every time we sit near it for a spell."

"Aha, a spell! We sit there and expect it to entrance us."

"Isn't that why we buy art? Don't we want it to take us to another place or introduce us to another state of being?"

Slim scratched his chin, then decided to keep writing on his list.

"You're not going to just let it sit there. Are you? Let's get it out of here now!"

Slim jumped off the stool and moved to grab the wall phone just as his cell phone rang. While talking he started out smiling, then laughing and talking louder. The ranch hands wanted to take the day off and go to the local rodeo, without having much to do when they came home. He said, "Sure, but first you have to come over to the house and move something for my wife."

The men showed up within five minutes and looked around the kitchen, then at Maddie. She could never keep a secret from them. With sudden insight the men decided the monster in the house had to go outside—and it was about time, but why did they have to risk a hernia right when they wanted to go to the rodeo?

They mumbled, but didn't grumble, as each took a bit of the weight and moved it step-by-step out of the dining room, across the kitchen, across the patio and over to the barn. Once inside the barn, they could not move it one more step. It seemed to be cemented to the floor and not about to be moved further into the barn.

Maddie relented then and said they had done a great job and needed to stop and get a drink, then be on their way. The men decided to go to the rodeo before she could find something else that needed to be moved.

"You know, Maddie, that thing isn't going to be easy to sell. Why don't we have a raffle of some kind and give it away? Say it's for charity. You have lots of folks who could use the money. Why not call one of them up right now and get it started? The sooner we see it out of here the better everyone is gonna' feel."

"I guess, but you know, if I give away a piece of art to one, everyone will want a donation of art, and I love everything else."

"Then don't announce it. Just get on the phone and call up the nuns and tell them they can have it for free, if they advertise it as a prize. You and me can ship it anywhere they like—let them know that." Slim looked like he was having a good time and couldn't wait to get moving on his project again.

"Yes, that sounds like a great idea! I just call up the nunnery and tell them I have a big, old ugly piece of pottery someone once called a statue, and now it's become a huge lump of clay that gives off strange vibes to everyone around it, and they say, 'Hey, Maddie, that sounds just perfect. Ship it to Pennsylvania immediately.'" Maddie did not look as if she thought it would be well received, but Slim urged her to make the call anyway.

"Hey, how is everyone? Yes, I know! I meant to stop by when we were out your way, but I couldn't fit it in. You know how it is with Slim!" At that Slim raised his eyebrow and winked, as if he knew exactly how he was.

Continuing with a rush, Maddie said, "In fact, Slim got a brainstorm this morning about a sculpture we had commissioned by a local artist. It isn't exactly what we thought it would be. In fact, it's too big for our house, and not suitable for the garage." Maddie giggled, then looked seriously at the phone when she heard the other yell for the Mother Superior to decide what they could do with this great gift.

Embarrassed to be greeted effusively by the Mother Superior, as if she had called about a generous donation that would help the nunnery get back in the black and out of red ink, Maddie waited until her friend ended her sentence before saying, "I have this problem. It's huge— and so ugly that I can't stand to look at it—and Slim thinks it's haunted."

With that Slim almost fell off his stool. He started wringing his hands as if in agony over what she was saying. He wasn't laughing—and he wasn't surprised. He knew his wife. She could not lie. That is why he loved her more than any woman alive. She never lied, but she could be pretty conservative with the truth at times—if it served her purposes when helping others come up with their best effort. He knew all about that!

"Sure, it's a big piece of clay. It weighs a ton and has some kind of thing about it that when you sit near it for an hour—even less, if you're tired—it feels like it's telling you stuff. Stuff you don't want to know. So, I figured you all could pray over it and chase away the blues catcher who lives inside it now, and someone would buy it for quite a price. What do you think?"

After a minute or so, Slim heard Maddie say, "Yes, it could be raffled off and the proceeds could go to the farm. You bet! Wish I would have thought of that!"

Slim smiled at the way these women made fast and loose with the truth, but always got what they wanted when it wasn't something they could get by lying. He watched Maddie make up a list of what all they had to do to ship it there, then situate it by their arbor close enough to the road so it could be seen by people driving by. It was not a long list, but she promised she and Slim would pay for a concrete pad and anything else they needed to make sure it did not sink into the ground.

Slim looked up from his paper, because Maddie was laughing hilariously, yet not making a sound. He thought maybe he was losing his mind but remembered that things like this happened all the time now. Why? He didn't want to think about it.

When her conversation was over, Maddie walked outside and Slim ambled after her. They stopped long enough to pet the dog and chase the prairie dogs off the lawn that popped up whenever they thought the dog wanted to play. The house was enchanted, or so their friends said, but they knew their ranch hands were responsible for how it looked and how many people dropped by just to pick up tips on how to use manure and such for better lawns and flowers.

The day was far from over, but Maddie and Slim walked into the barn as if they had finished all their work and had nothing else to do. Each wanted to see the old, ugly thing one more time, but neither realized it. They talked and walked around it until the dog started barking.

"Who's coming? Did you call the people in town about the stuff we need for the next party? Maybe that's who's here?" Slim slid his hand away from hers and walked to the front of the barn where he stopped. He appeared stunned by whatever he saw. Finally, he called, "Hey, Maddie, your friends are here. Look, the Maya have arrived."

Unsure what he meant since they often contacted *The Ascended Maya* at night and through their dreams, she did not think they would suddenly arrive during the day—at least not today, but she had to be ready. Stepping quickly, she noticed a group of Mayan shamans smiling at the way the light played upon the huge statue they were getting rid of forever.

The Maya were swift to say the clay was alive, but the sculptor had not asked permission to harvest so many souls so fast. Thus, it was a problem! It had to be reconstructed and changed in major ways, so these souls could go their own way today.

Slim wasn't interested in hearing about taking the monstrosity apart, but Maddie was. She completely forgot she just promised to ship it to her friends as a gift and said, "Can you do that? Can you change the shape, remove clay, and put it back together and have a happy piece of art?"

The elder shaman was not as positive as his wife that it would be easy. He was there to make certain nothing escaped, and no one was hurt. He motioned for his son to move the statue out to the yard surrounding the barn. His son managed to do this without help.

"How do they do that? I can't figure it out," mumbled Slim.

"Oh, we have ways to make energy systems behave and create a stable place, so we can move our work, build pyramids, or rise into the atmosphere at times. You have to be initiated into it, but you, Slim, are going to find out what we do some time soon."

Stunned, Slim had to admit he would love that, so he remained nearby and did whatever he was told the rest of the day. Maddie was pivotal. She was critical of the art about to appear, because she had promised the convent in Pennsylvania it would be shipped there this year.

When the group dissembled and moved away from the finished sculpture later that day, everyone was silent. It was a blessed time. Prayers offered were of greatness and the ability to solve all problems without any difficulty at all. This was their Buddha, as Slim was heard to say, and the shamans were not upset in any way that he called it that. In fact, they agreed with him.

The low energy of the morning rose during the day, and every problem was resolved without anyone getting hurt. It was so amazing that when the cowboys came home after ten that night, they spotted a warm glow coming from the barn and worried there was a fire inside. It turned out to be the big brother of all statues smiling down on them, surrounded by candles in jars every few feet around the base and spilling into the yard outside the barn. It was like an altar, and all the hands felt very, very small.

When the sun came up and everyone was back in harness with only two hands still feeling a bit drunk, they met in front of the barn to see what was going on. They could hear humming, drumming, and all sorts of sounds that didn't belong in a barn. Stepping up to the door to slide it back, expecting to see a huge ugly piece of clay, it was no longer what they thought they saw yesterday. They could not imagine how it could possibly be the same piece of art, so they said to each other, "Good thing we got that piece of crap out of the house yesterday. This one is a whole lot better—and looks like somebody we know."

The folks humming, strumming, and drumming were not the same who did the work with love, but they changed the place and increased its prestige, and many more were now headed this way from all parts of the United States. It was definitely not going to be a good day for the hired hands. They would be asked to park cars, limousines, walk dogs—even cats from now on. Although tips paid more than farming, they still wanted to get their place back to what it was. That happened the day a huge semi came up the drive, and others arrived to move the statue out. They all gladly saw it on its way to Pennsylvania and some Catholic nuns waiting for it there.

☯Chapter Thirty-Four

"Recently I heard a 'wise guy' story that I had a party at my home for 25 men. It's an interesting story, but I don't know 25 men I'd want to invite to a party."
~ Joan Crawford, 1908-1977

The years had mellowed this reporter's instinct to reach out and explore every nook and cranny of the world, discovering what others preferred to keep under wraps, but Maddie still enjoyed talking to complete strangers as if they were going to star in one of her stories, thus get to the heart of what they thought about and what they did with it. She was always amazed by how many women thought they did very little, whereas men doing far less bragged about themselves. Successful women believed themselves to be gifted, and such men swore they earned everything they ever had and deserved more.

The trial-and-error method used by some men to get elected was not sought out by women Maddie encountered years ago and urged to run for public office. She was a part of each race for Congress, even local School Boards, but not at all interested in what they did with their power—until now. Suddenly asked to run for Congress, she was unwilling to contemplate such a fate. Her mind was made up. Slim agreed then, but later began to notice others were probably right, Maddie had what it takes to change the universe, so it had to be easier to change the United States.

"No, I don't want to run the country, and I don't want to give up what I love to have power. You don't get to do what you want when you run. You end up with all kinds of problems from others who expect you to handle them immediately, because they gave you money and helped your campaign. I want to own my mind and my time. I want to write and do what I like—not what others say needs to be done."

"Look, Maddie, you could run the country and still have time left over. You're a powerhouse of energy! I'm not always able to keep up with you even now, so why not try to straighten out the country and return to your own work after that?"

"No, Slim, that would be terrible for me, and not best for the country. I need to be able to cheer on everyone serving out there now. Help them by placing a few well-chosen words here and there. You, however, could run. You don't need any introduction. Everyone assumes you can lead, because you do it so well in the movies. Why don't you run, instead of me?"

Slim slammed the counter and said, "I'm an actor! I'm not someone who really thinks things out. I just act like I'm told. Why, you write my lines! You're the one who says when to move and when to stop. You know the rules of the game better than I could ever figure them out before the play is over. You're the brain. I'm just a puppet."

Firmly and with precision, Maddie said, "You're an actor! You do what you are told to do! You love to be in the center of the action and can rage effectively without ever worrying a bit about it later. You're a born politician of this age. We don't want people who think, and we don't admire those who have a lot of power and can put us all down, PLUS, we want our President to look good—stand tall, be presidential, with a smile that wins over everyone again and again. You may stutter and putter and do nothing, but you can win.

"I, on the other hand, am a thinker and worrier. I complain out loud when I should keep my mouth shut. I would be eaten alive if I tried to run. Everyone would say I was going to run the country into the ground, because of my liberal leanings. I would be run down for wanting to institute social programs to help women and children at the expense of rich ranchers having to pay for their own livestock, acres, and such.

"I would be hated by millionaires everywhere, because my proposals are such that they wouldn't be able to lord it over others as much. I would level the playing field and try to recreate the nation as it once was—or so they would fear and create whatever stories they had to in order to make sure I and women like me never run this country."

Slim remained silent as he looked at Maddie in a different light than he had ever seen her before. He watched the light in her eyes grow and intensify and wondered if she was an angel now or living her own life? She looked great! He wanted to follow her to the ends of the world, but he could not get her to capitulate and run for Congress. It was not going to happen, and he knew it.

Several hours passed before Slim totally relaxed. He was sitting on the back step looking at Maddie lounging on the patio settee. She was not surprised that he was still talking about politics, but he was. He could not forget the many things she had said over the past few hours that made more sense to him now than anything he had ever heard before. He wondered why.

Did you ever *really* listen when you were not directly involved? Maybe he was a lot dumber than he thought? What would happen if the President of the United States kept to a budget and didn't spend a single dime more than was allowed? Would it change anything or make it better than it was now?

As he thought, Maddie channeled: "As far as how much time and effort is wasted marketing a President and creating a viable campaign, they need to start over again. The old days had a lot of problems when a few old guys with stinky cigars sat around a bar and decided who would run, but they did better than we're doing now. We got Harry Truman that way, even FDR—and have you noticed how many Republicans use *their* names as if they were of the same party? Well, in a way FDR was as rich as any Republican, and just as dumb, but he wasn't like any Republican we know when it came to keeping his wife hidden away.

"We all know that a good Republican wife does not stand out! End of sentence—for life. She has to be seen and not heard. She must never laugh at her husband's foibles, and certainly must nod whenever he lies. I guess that has to be the hardest thing of all—to listen to lies and act like you believe them, too. That would really gall me too much! So, you have to run as a Democrat. I would never make a good Republican wife."

As Maddie stopped to laugh, Slim did not. He watched and noticed how much she knew, seemingly instantaneous, about politics, yet it was not her domain nor what she chose to write about this life. She was never into the particular politics of individuals. She was all about improving the nation by educating the population and not restricting public education to kids. She wanted more people to adopt religious principles of some kind, rather than follow those who told them what to do—regardless of where they might live. She wanted people to behave in ethical ways, but not be afraid to experiment with stretching the cloth of the nation a bit further now.

"You want to bring back the age of invention. Don't you Maddie? You want to see new styles, maybe a total re-creation of society into one that looks and acts and works different from the way we live now. You even want to forget that the industrial age ever existed. Right?"

Startled by his analysis, yet unable to disagree, Maddie said nothing. Instead, she rocked back and forth on the settee, then suddenly stood up and began to pace the patio. Each time she reached one side, she stopped to look at a flower, smell it, then turn and walk to the other side. She did this over and over again and never said a word for almost ten minutes, which seemed like hours to Slim.

"You're stopping and smelling the flowers—and that's just great, but what does it have to do with running the country?" Slim smiled, but thought he had possibly insulted his wife, because she was not looking at him with love.

"You think flowers don't need to be here? That they're a waste of time and energy? That we don't really need the arts—which flowers represent. Flowers are the power and energy of this society! Once we forget the flowers, we also forget how they influence us in times of rage and hate. Then we've lost everything we set out to explore—and more. Our country isn't a state where we can lock our doors and explore only our individual lives more. We're being controlled by those who say we have no brain. They would drain our energies and resources, if we didn't have someone censoring our lives now. That is the way conservatives live. They drain others, then waste that money on things that benefit only themselves."

Maddie stopped then and laughed. "You see! Do you understand why I could never run for high office? I would get mad and lash out at the fat cats, and they're the ones who run the country and pay for elections everywhere now. In fact, I think they have rigged the elections. What do you have to say about that?"

Startled by the sudden change in the way she was discussing the world as it stood today, Slim said nothing until she forced him with a glare to speak, even then he spoke reluctantly. "I guess you're buying into the theory that Republicans finally decided to update voting equipment in borderline states and have the technology to cancel out votes they don't like? I guess that's what the kids are doing with lots of stuff on the internet, so it stands to reason that if you can break into the Central Intelligence Agency, you can slant any election. And I guess I would have to worry about that if I wasn't being supported by the inner circle."

Maddie had been about to leave the patio but stopped to look over her shoulder at her husband sitting in a brown muse. She spoke, as if making a final offer, "You can't run! We're too honest, and you're too strong to ever be able to run the country. You would never make it, and I don't intend to stand up and get shot down. Let them all rot! We have each other, and I don't want to talk about it again."

While flinging out her final words, Maddie turned to look at the barn where a car was circling the driveway and heading back toward the corral. "Oh, no, look who's coming to slum with us, maybe get invited to dinner? Did you invite him, or is he just working up courage to ask you to run?"

Slim looked where she pointed, then ambled toward the approaching car. He casually indicated she could do whatever she liked, but he would be polite. Maddie was not about to insult their guest then, so she smiled and waved at the car and walked toward the barn.

"Hey, Slim! Ever seen a prettier day? I was out at my ranch in Texas—thinking about selling off a herd of beef and thought about you. Said to the boys, 'let's get some real barbecue over in Arizona' and here we are. The boys are still in town, but they'll be around by the time we get something on the table."

Shocked at this Easterner's approach to Western hospitality, and his own inability to squash the intruder's pushiness, Slim did not extend his hand. Instead he waited with hands on hips for what would happen next.

"I guess you folks have enough beef, but knowing you all wouldn't be expecting company today, I stopped at a ranch along the way that was raising up a cloud of smoke and bought some barbecue for us all to chew. It's not that good, but it's beef, and that's all that counts!"

His drawl strained as far as the next sentence, but Slim wasn't listening—again. The intruder opened the trunk of his Lincoln Navigator and pulled out a large box wrapped in aluminum foil. Slim was suddenly hungry, and surprised that it was a welcome gift—in a way. Obviously, the truth remains that any man can be reached through food or sex, and Slim was no better than other men when it came to base needs.

When Maddie emerged from the back pasture where she had been riding a pretty young mare, she stopped in confusion to see the back yard of her home seemingly covered with men. How did they get there, and what were they doing?

As she moved closer, the smell of horses, straw, and manure faded, and she realized a party was going on with no women present. She decided to give them a warning that she was about to join them—so they could clean up their language and put on their party manners. Clearing her throat loudly, she waited long enough to catch someone's eye.

"Hey Madeline! Where y'all been? We've been eating for hours and still have half a beef left. You want some beans, or are you on a diet?" The old man laughed as if he had told a funny story, so she laughed and joined them, taking the plate he filled with enough meat for ten men.

"I guess you're still running for Congress, Madeline. Ain't ya?" He kept looking at her plate, not her chest, because he knew he would get into trouble if he did. Eventually, he had to take a little peek, and Maddie was eying him when he did.

To ease his embarrassment for doing what almost every man did in the first second or ten, she said, "Run for Congress? Do I look crazy? No, don't answer that. Running for Congress is what guys who have no jobs do so they can become millionaires and tell us hard-working women what we need to do to survive."

Slim appeared at her elbow and smiled as he ushered her through the crowd. Mumbling as they passed that she had to be hungry and not that happy to see such a crowd. He was nice and polite, but he wasn't happy, either.

"Slim, before you go back to your little soiree, will you please tell me what this is supposed to be? Are you running for office, or is this fat cat using you to run for office again?"

The look that passed over Slim's face was fleeting, but not fast enough to fool Maddie. She saw that he was unhappy, maybe even angry, and was trying to keep his face straight and his mouth shut. She decided it was time to change the subject and get back to what was going on now.

With a lisp, she said, "What's the matter with my wittle brother now? Is he upset that he can't run the country again, or is he afraid he'll have to run somewhere else to keep ahead of all the lies he put out about his life, his wife, and his work for God?"

Slim gave her elbow a little squeeze to indicate he was not going to answer, so she left it up to him to end the party, celebrate a victory, or whatever they were doing now. She took her plate in the house and put her favorite Beethoven CD on and started the laundry.

❦Chapter Thirty-Five

"He that is kind is free, though he is a slave; he that is evil is a slave, though he be a king."
~ *Saint Augustine, 354-430*

The women were running the party and getting nothing done, or so some said, but the women Maddie interviewed were doing great, holding down full-time jobs while running for office on the side. They did not intend to give up their day-jobs and become political pawns, as men still did.

The day arrived when one of her friends was noticed by the media as a woman with many connections—even blessed by an order of nuns who had a convent in Eastern Pennsylvania. Their farm became a hit with television crews who had nothing to do and wanted to interview women instead of the usual bloated politicos. The media now frequently traveled to visit the community of nuns whose conventional work they were unfamiliar with, thus they often made gaffs and created quite a few laughs, but no one made fun of the nuns—not even once.

The original criteria established by the group was meant to hide their support until it was no longer feasible to remain impartial was now a thing of the past. Maddie came forward again and wrote boldly about women in the news and interviewed them. Her copy was readily accepted as is and not overwritten by hacks. She was delighted, yet she wasn't sure if she had done enough with her own life.

"Why do you always stand at the side and cheer everyone else on—never go for the gold yourself?" As he spoke, Slim sipped coffee without cream and only a touch of home-raised honey. Maddie looked up, but said nothing, so he tried again, "You know, you've helped twenty-five women—that I know of, and probably a whole lot more, urging them to rise in the world, but not you! They're not going to remember how much work you did to get them ready—and elected. You practically gave up marrying me to keep some of these women happy enough to run the country—"

"That's enough, Slim. I don't think we ever get what we deserve—and I thank God for that every day!" Maddie laughed, then moved to leave the room.

"No, you're not gonna' run away again. I have a bone to pick with you about this latest lady. She hasn't said a word about you, or any of the others who helped her. In fact, she acts like she did it all herself." Slim pointed at the newspaper laying on the kitchen counter.

"You know, Slim, some people never thank anyone. They really do believe they do it all by themselves. You and I, and a handful of others, are aware we aren't who we look like or even what we think we might be, but know we are spiritual beings here for a limited time in this sphere, and that when we're done, we're gone but never forgotten."

"Well, Honey, I guess you're right. We've had a blessed life with so many friends that we can't invite them in and talk to all of them in one night. To see some of them, we have to fly—and we drive long hours to visit others, but we're always welcome. How many politicians can say that—and be believed? Don't think many can, so I guess you're right. This is the life! We have enough."

Maddie stopped to look at Slim as if she was about to argue, but instead smiled, then sighed. "Why is it when you're right you don't always feel right?"

Surprised at this turn in their conversation, Slim said, "What do you mean? Are you now sorry you didn't run for office? You can still do it, you know. You might not be able to run for President, but you could be appointed by one of your friends to be Press Secretary or one of those interesting positions where you know everything they're covering up—on a regular basis. Better than being in the CIA."

Smiling broadly, Maddie said, "What would you know about the CIA anyway?"

Not smiling now, but still looking mischievous, Slim winked and said, "I've been a CIA agent so many times in my career that people think I'm a spy. I get tagged as one wherever I go, and even real secret agents think I'm one—at times. It gets hairy, but those guys are not as scary as they might appear—except for the lunatics, and unfortunately they're everywhere."

Sighing, Maddie said, "Yes the lunatics and fanatics are always in the news. They keep us thinking we're doing okay when they're the only ones who know what is going on. They get too upset to be perceived as being anything but naïve or crazy, but they do know a lot. Not always great, but ideas planted now become the next generation's work—and generally what they put first."

Slim said nothing, but stood up and folded *The Times*, putting it where they kept the news sections of the daily paper. Even now, Maddie still referred back to articles or events using her old lo-tech system to verify and update work.

"I guess we're gonna' have to move soon. This room is getting too crowded with the past to create a new estate for you and me. What do you think, Maddie, ready to move?"

As if never having given it a thought until this moment, Maddie stopped and looked into the other room, then abruptly walked toward him as if she had an interesting thought she had to share with him. Her mind was not open enough to be easily read, but Slim could still interpret her mood and started laughing as he walked toward her with his arms open wide. They hugged and kissed, then decided it was time to split.

☯Chapter Thirty-Six

"My mind withdrew its thoughts from experience, extracting itself from the contradictory throng of sensuous images that it might find out what that light was wherein it was bathed...And thus, with the flash of one hurried glance, it attained to the vision of That Which Is."
~ Saint Augustine, 354-430

All were sorry to see the moving van depart, but not as sorry as when they discovered they were to be the subject of a movie about life in the U.S. It is never easy to write about people you like and wish to help, but next to impossible when you cannot respect how some rape and pillage the country in the name of God and government. The creative crew put together an enviable list of actors to cover the cast, and enough extras to populate tables in bars and places where you would never expect a famous face to appear. It was to be the greatest epic made about today. Created in such a way that no one knew exactly what would happen when it played.

The work was great and the story up-to-date, but many thought they were not ready to show the world how to live, let alone how to recreate a perfect place. After all, they too had made a mess of their opportunities and had not helped anyone other than car dealers, tailors, and plastic surgeons become rich men—So what could they say about the waste in government seen everywhere now?

The texture of the movie was such that no one proclaimed it was going well—or was off-track, because it was right on budget. The subject of spending money as most do now and how they should spend it in the future was not a documentary as much as a story about greed and family envy.

This was a tale of one great man who created a wave of animosity by saying he knew what to do to create a better life for all. It was such a grand idea that everyone hated him for saying it and set out to prove he was no better than they. This filled the opening frame, then they added layers of hatred and defiance until everyone said he was an ignorant man seeking money from all. It was like that Michael Moore thing, but much bigger! Why?

The main character was from the landed gentry and displayed no humility. How could he defy his destiny and ask friends to contribute to the benefit of those who lost everything, in order to have what they had now? He was an Indian lover and an ignorant giver who would end up dead.

It was said over and over until they plotted to make the Indians give up their casinos that make money like the mob in Las Vegas and Atlantic City. Preferring to see gangsters running the country, as only they can, then let men and women of Earth run their own towns. It was not a Mexican standoff, because Mexicans are Indians, too, but it was interesting to see how many watching the movie ended up rooting for the Indians rather than the cowboys.

The reversal of fortunes caught everyone by surprise and made for great conversations. Who could call it a morality tale when the white settlers were not seen as great people—just human beings who wanted something for nothing and willing to take off and leave behind whatever they had accumulated.

As the movie took off, everyone could easily see generations had been blocked from talking about how the country had actually been founded and sensed it had to turn around and be discussed now. Who was George Washington? No one knew, so he was the first one vindicated and given a good name, because he refused to be put in a corner and shoved around by others even now.

The next personality pulled out from under cover through desperate measures, meant to make him appear less than he was, turned out to be Thomas Jefferson and the man who would be his son, if allowed even now. This discussion replaced what others tried to say was wrong with the USA even today.

Everyone was interrelated, if they dated back to the beginning of time, so who could say a Jew was pure blood and they were not? Who could say they had a relative on the Mayflower and not shudder at what they had to do to recover from the winter and years after they landed here? It was clear the country was a great place to live, but history had not kept pace with its estate.

The course of the film brought up a lot of interesting ideas—even a few facts, but mostly it was about what makes us laugh and what makes us lapse. It was a great idea no one wanted to fund, so everyone involved in making the movie bought a share and resolved to pay for it as long as they could afford it.

The would-be town was outraged after Slim and Maddie left, and the movie debut was announced. They were less upset when it was finally viewed, because they came off looking like great men and women locked into behaving like idiots based on preexisting teachings from people who did not know what life would be like today. The town fathers decided they would become a haven for writers and throw a party every Fourth of July to celebrate some aspect of national pride and how it related to them.

The real work was actually done in the mind of one woman and one man during their partnership over time. It was not the creation of many men and women, just made to appear that way so the word would get out everywhere. How did they get this assignment?

They never knew. They once thought it was due to a plot hatched years back, then again maybe it was due to Maddie following her inner guidance and writing a book about women who could change the way the USA is run today? She was not sure, but she believed too much had been said in her head about others to actually be her work, then realized that made no sense. If she said it in her mind, then it must be what she was taught; but who taught her to think about others? Was it her mother? Was it the way her father ranted and raved about strangers and others he did not like? Who made her aware of what was '*out there*' and how people think now?

The Press said the work was a combined effort of many working together to make the movie, and it was impressive how they brought forth so many great points without lecturing or saying the audience was responsible for whatever. It was not a lecture or sermon, rather a text on how to live well now. If you followed the storyline and bought that it was about men and women who once lived and could still be living now, you could see how Thomas Jefferson changed the work set in place more easily than others. You could also imagine that if George Washington was alive, he would probably thrive, because he had the knack.

If Jefferson, Washington, and Franklin, as well as other forefathers were still in the ether somewhere, why didn't they speak now? That was what everyone ended up being upset about. Not the premise that we of today had made a mess of the USA, or that we were not living as we said we might, but that someone could actually be alive and living now and able to make decisions based on what they set out to do in the old days. That was way too much for The Right, but those left behind loved it anyway.

The movie was the biggest bonanza no one had ever foreseen. Audiences went to count the major stars, to see if they could stop the frames fading as they counted how many were on the screen simultaneously. It was an amazing piece of history, never to be repeated!

The effect of such a blockbuster movie was a lot of bluster from those who thought they ran the country. Political pensions were given a once over—again, and then again, until some were ready to cut politicians off and give them the same as everyone else, but it never got that rough. Politicians began to sing in a different key and admit that perhaps ours was not as ideal a society as it could be now.

They suggested life could be better, if we were willing to pay huge taxes. They swore they would do what Ben Franklin set out to do—only better than he did anything back then. Their hubris was not overlooked by those dedicated to counting actors in every movie scene, as well as how many hid behind others.

The way the country is run today is not the same as it was. Everything changed! The U.S. was not as into the

Right Path as it had pretended to be, so a lot of that support was lost while they tried to do something new to gain support from the Left—or lose them again. It was a mess, but it ended up all right. People could once again make a good living and create a life where they worshipped and talked as they like, but the poor were now considered to be a liability that would not go away in a day. The only way they could change children was to educate and force them to work for a living, and that was not that hard to do.

Once the crowds began to analyze why they made the movie, the thrill was over and gone. An endless parade of reporters sought to interview the duo who made the film and pulled it together, but no one could find them. Searching high and low, they found only a few who knew where they were headed now. It was as if Maddie and Slim once gone were not remembered well, and no one knew where they were going or when they would be back.

Help they received throughout the years was nothing compared to what happened when they entered the realm of *The Ascended Maya* once again. They worked out a way to communicate with a few who could relate what they received in deep meditative states, and other such places, but they never came back. It wasn't that they didn't like where they grew up, worked, and lived within, but they now have a lot more interesting things to do.

"No eulogy is due to him who simply does his duty and nothing more." ~ *Saint Augustine, 354-430*

☯Warm Up Notes

When a reporter starts writing a novel, magazine article, or investigative report requiring more than research, compilation, or verification, she trains for it, warming up like an athlete might. She does warm-up exercises meant to stretch seldom-used muscles before the fight or flight. So, bear with me, or skip ahead, since such notes are not meant to be taken literally. Are they?

After deciding to write a new kind of novel based on what I learned from interviewing women across the U.S., I quickly discovered most were filled with self-doubt and disappointments that led them to drop out of every race before they neared the top of whatever goal they sought—nor could I write about only one woman and what she wanted. It is necessary to create some kind of narrative that would inspire women, rather than stir up envy or jealousy enough to wish my heroes in hell rather than follow their lead. How to begin—where to start?

Let's start with me…What I want is to be a total human being living a simple life and happy full-time.

My mind went blank then and I awoke in a fuzzy state—not my usual one. Once again *You* (what I call the one who lives within me) took over.

So why not let *You* write whatever and say whatever? Would *You* disgrace me? Would *You* deny my ideas and object to everything I write—as if all lies?

The only way to find out is to let my hands run across the keys and not stop *You* from doing whatever. Admittedly, this is quite a state to be in—even for me, but why not run with it? Go ahead and write now whatever you like and compare it to what I found later.

If you don't state immediately and frequently what you want, everyone else gets their message across and becomes your boss. To do this work, set guidelines and ask for help clearing the atmosphere. You may not feel it, but you have much to do and lots of time left on your clock to do it, too.

Get to work on what you have to do for you. We believe you, and we see you in need of others to help and give advice at times, but we doubt you need guidance now.

That was interesting—in a way.

You think God created man, woman, and others as part of an experiment designed to help you all learn from each other what works and what doesn't while on Earth. However, this is where you get a bit foggy. You think everyone has a part to play and must figure it out on their own—alone.

Is that what you meant when you said: "I don't need Spiritual Guides or life plans?"

Not really. You need help, but not the usual. Some you know well are so lost they need Spiritual Guides to help them sort out this life. However, they rely on outside advice on everything they came here to do—instead of moving inward and reading their own minds or listening to their inner wisdom.

What if you were a Guide? You know what I mean— the kind of Guide who helps whenever we make our intentions known?

You want someone to follow your direction, but why would we bother with anyone unwilling to work hard? Why listen to people repeating the same old prayers over and over, boring us—and angels, too? Why would we care about those who are brutes?

That seems like a lot of questions for a Guide who claims to be my inner life. I can figure out the answers if I decide to write about such a life, but instead I put into action books that explain arcane and romantic notions that folks here on Earth are not yet ready to easily understand. How can I get through to them now?

There is so much information in the air and going around this planet that you can't concentrate on one thing without shutting down and entering sleep mode. Fortunately for me, you are ready to begin the work that comes next!

Wait, someone close by is shooting a gun— unaware you are doing your thing. Why would anyone shoot a gun?

It's just the guy who comes and goes while I'm having my office remodeled. I've known him for years. Wonderful man, but such problems!

I haven't been able to get through to him that he is in charge of his life. He says it's the government, Viet Nam, and relatives who did him wrong. He is so hung up with Viet Nam he doesn't want to relate and state what the government should be doing in Kuwait and other Arab states to avoid another all-out war, even though it could end the world he knew back when.

If I sound like I'm out of another time, remember you aren't up-to-date, either! You are far removed from what others did to harm you and your world. You missed the chance to make a difference! The world changed, and you cannot commit to it now. So why not try a new strategy? Begin by working inside your mind to protect your country.

In time, can you be a mental giant or patriot? Would you be seen by the Far Right as an atheist, communist—or whatever they call everyone else now—anyone who doesn't do what they do or say what they say all day? You are not far wrong right now, just to the left-of-center.

As we see it, you can begin writing about life, but describe yourself as an award-winning author or authority in order to urge others to begin building another, better world.

That is a big order—I'm no star! I'm fairly well-off, because I work hard and have gained some attention, but I'm not a Woman of Destiny—and I don't want to be. I want peace, harmony, lively conversation from time-to-time with honest friends. I'd also like to live as well as many who pretend to be able to afford how they live now in Florida. That would be nice, but what is the price?

You cannot have a non-existent life and write about real life. You have to work at what you are doing before you can enjoy the good life and live as you would if a prince or princess, or whatever people think they want now.

I think my jaundiced view of life on the West Coast of Florida is causing you to change, too. Maybe we haven't advanced far enough to write about this life? I doubt I know enough to lead or greet folks and ask them to take over from me, but maybe we can find a way. Maybe write about those who want to be great or ascend to the next plane?

You have to do that! You have to imagine you can translate arcane material and build a world you, too, want to succeed. Each human is a world unto itself and can collaborate to build a better one, but only the wise can make a world last longer than their lives.

Watching the sun fade and set on those who were once leaders we thought did good work, what did they forget? Not what they did, but what they did not do that their fathers and mothers taught them was necessary.

They forgot the most important lesson about raising children. Think on it! Eventually we will meet in your reality to decide what you will write about and how it will change your life.

A week later I felt the urge to walk out and never come back to this world. I had had it! I wasn't sad. I was mad! I wasn't happy about working hard to help others no longer interested in maintaining our country. I wanted out of it. I said it out loud and was told it isn't proper to ask to leave a party before it's over.

When it came time to investigate what was going on around the world, I discovered too many unwilling to play by the old rules, yet no idea what to do without them. So, I decided to open my mind and walk through time. I can do at least that much to help the world—or so I thought then.

As I worked up a flight of pivotal belief systems that could agree with whatever political system I might encounter, I kept finding that only one could work. It wasn't the one we practiced in New York, but one others claim we use daily—and supposedly foreigners want to emulate in their homelands.

Unfortunately, democracy isn't what the USA is all about today. We pretend it's best for us and others—meanwhile forcing aliens to work as slaves, never worrying if it's right or not. If you want to grow—at least know what you can do with your work and the work you trained to do—before you settle down to work it out for yourself. No one wants to build huge institutions to take care of you, nor do they want the government to provide jobs of merit for anyone no longer in their prime.

You may not want to read it, but this book is coming out anyway. In fact, I doubt it will ever be read, because it's not about making money, rather solving mysteries that are probably better off not talked about.

Why bother to write? Why think about life? Why not walk away and leave this work to those who tell others what to do—yet never do it?

Sitting here in my chair, writing as if this is what I want out of life, I feel a wave of anxiety leave my mind. I'm not quite so uptight. Why?

I think I'll give away everything I own. Attack the smug and unafraid alone. Chastise those who are sure this is it and '*Ain't I great!*' Yes, indeed, that is what I should do.

If I write a novel that is not read, what did I do? Nothing for you, but I got whatever said off my chest and into the marketplace to make a few dollars. Is that okay? You bet! It's taking the only commodity a writer has this life and selling it on today's market, like economists might say is our right.

As I sway a bit, feeling like this isn't something I will file—merely an exercise to get words flowing from my mind to paper—I see things changing. How does a writer write about reality anyway?

As I sit drifting in and out of my mind into deepest space and time, I feel like I already wrote this book. I did it all before in a different world. Can that be right? Can you write in this physical time and space, repeating things you did in another space and time? Think about it a bit…How else could I write about something that never existed?

Lots of people propose to wipe out everyone and anyone who misbehaves and doesn't respect America, because we really aren't doing much to increase tolerance here at home. We are victims of our inability to ask questions and demand truthful answers of those we elect to run the political parties and our country. We let whomever has the most money run the most ads and take over now.

Everyone knows this isn't working out as we thought it might, because we aren't as happy as we once were—and no one else thinks we are very bright. Yes, we might have built an empire and done a few things right—and nothing wrong for a time, but then we decided we were Number One! All the old ways are gone now, and we are what we said we hated about the British, Germans, Russians, and so on. We are now negative aspects of games they started, and we wanted to end way back when with World War II.

Thinking about what I will say when this book is done, I get excited. I think of the injustice of asking some to work hard while most do nothing more than count money and steal whatever they can without getting caught. This frustrates me so much I want to stop writing and stop thinking about arguments that will never persuade men who want to run everything and everyone to change their ways before it's too late.

And so, I begin another book and let *You* run with it now…See you at the end.

Spring, 2005
Ruth Lee, Scribe

Study Group Questions
A Timeless Life ~ *Maddie's Story*

If you are fortunate enough to know others of like mind who enjoy discussing books you have all read, you may want to offer opinions on some of the topics suggested here...

1. Did your first impressions of Maddie hold up as you read the book, or did you change your mind over time about who she is or was?

2. What do you think would happen if you could go back in time and change something about your past?

3. Do you think you can cross-over from one entity or life to another as Maddie did several times?

4. Have you ever received an award or honor that turned out to be a mixed blessing? If so, how did you handle it, and how did it affect your personal or professional life?

5. Do you enjoy reading about celebrities? If so, what appeals to you most, their professional or private lives?

6. Are you paying attention to how many women of a certain age are considering some type of communal living where they can share expenses or increase opportunities for self-fulfillment?

7. Have you ever considered isolating yourself from the rest of the world as a nun might? If not, what do you think causes others to seek such a life?

8. Maddie frequently comments on the negative attitudes or behaviors of women toward other women. Do you agree or disagree with her?

9. Have you ever been seriously deceived by another whom you trusted? How do you react to dishonesty?

10. Have you ever organized or participated in a protest of any kind, including marches and sit-ins?

11. Maddie shares a few dreams. Do you agree with her interpretations or do you believe dreams have no meaning?

12. If you experience dream time as Maddie does, how do you explain it to your mind and possibly others? If you disagree that it can happen, explain what you think Maddie experienced.

13. Do you believe in angels? Can you relate a time when you believe you had an encounter with an angelic being?

14. What are your thoughts on levitation? If it is possible, how does it operate—at least in theory?

15. Have you ever worked with a shaman from an indigenous tribe? If not, would you consider doing so?

16. Is this your first encounter with Jorge? Would you be as quick to follow his lead as Maddie seemed to be?

17. What do you think the Mayan women meant when they honored Maddie with the title: *The Woman Who Knows*?

18. Having read a book, how do you explain it to others? What, if anything, is difficult for you to explain about *Maddie's Story*?

19. What twist or turn in the story line surprised you most? Were you satisfied with how the story ended?

20. When you meet with others to discuss subjects that touch upon spirituality, do you initially feel uncomfortable? Do you worry about what others might think of you, if you say what you think?

21. Write out a few lines that sum up Maddie's next move and how she will eventually end this life.

It is either wonderful to join in with others and talk about esoteric subjects, as well as personal lives and opinions, or you are not yet comfortable discussing your mind's output. *Remember:* You are always happiest when you remain true to you.

In the first Book of Wisdom, **We Are Here**, the Teachers of the Higher Planes offer this advice:

"Some go to the mountains—others to the shore—and some to the countryside, but the best place to be is within your heart and soul. It is the only place to seek meditation. When you meditate, the work of life is clear, and you can make changes if it is not to your liking. But if the life you live is unclear, and you cannot calm down enough to see it, your life is one of chaos and war—never knowing peace. That is what you need to see—then you can seek."

We Are Here ~ *Teachers of the Higher Planes*
Available on Amazon and www.LeeWayPublishing.com

About the Author

Ruth Lee (*The Scribe*) began *Writing in Spirit* shortly after leaving a long, successful career with two of America's largest corporations. Stunning everyone then, she walked away and never returned to such work in order to pursue a life of contemplation, service to others, writing, art, and traveling the world.

During the years following her departure from corporate life, she came out of the proverbial closet and admitted to being exceptionally-gifted spiritually, as well as psychic. No one is more amazed by her unusual abilities to help others live more perfect lives than she is.

Scribing *The Teachers of the Higher Planes'* six **Books of Wisdom** earned Ruth Lee a place among the highest level of esoteric writers published today. It took years to publish the materials scribed prior to writing books that teach in *'novel'* ways, including **Within the Veil ~ *An Adventure in Time***, **Angel of The Maya**, and **Writing in Spirit ~ *Jeanne's Story***, but the wait is worth it to the growing legion of fans of Mandy and her friends.

For more information on Ruth Lee, Scribe,
As well as her other publications, visit:
www.LeeWayPublishing.com

www.ingramcontent.com/pod-product-compliance
Lightning Source LLC
Chambersburg PA
CBHW071509260626
47170CB00002B/310